VA

READ ALL THE BOOKS
BY KATE O'HEARN

THE PEGASUS SERIES:
The Flame of Olympus
Olympus at War
The New Olympians
Origins of Olympus
Rise of the Titans
The End of Olympus

THE VALKYRIE SERIES:
Valkyrie
The Runaway

VALKYRIE

BY KATE O'HEARN

ALADDIN

New York London Toronto Sydney New Delhi

ALADDIN

An imprint of Simon & Schuster Children's Publishing Division
1230 Avenue of the Americas, New York, New York 10020
This Aladdin paperback edition December 2016
Text copyright © 2013 by Kate O'Hearn
Cover illustration copyright © 2016 by Anna Steinbauer
Originally published in 2013 in Great Britain by Hodder Children's Books
Also available in an Aladdin hardcover edition.
All rights reserved, including the right of reproduction in whole or in part in any form.
ALADDIN and related logo are registered trademarks of Simon & Schuster, Inc.
For information about special discounts for bulk purchases, please contact
Simon & Schuster Special Sales at 1-866-506-1949 or business@simonandschuster.com.
The Simon & Schuster Speakers Bureau can bring authors to your live event.
For more information or to book an event, contact the Simon & Schuster Speakers
Bureau at 1-866-248-3049 or visit our website at www.simonspeakers.com.
Cover designed by Karin Paprocki
Interior designed by Mike Rosamilia
The text of this book was set in Goudy Old Style.
Manufactured in the United States of America 1116 OFF
2 4 6 8 10 9 7 5 3 1
The Library of Congress has cataloged the hardcover edition as follows:
O'Hearn, Kate.
Valkyrie / by Kate O'Hearn.—First Aladdin hardcover edition.
pages cm.—(Valkyrie ; [1])
Summary: "Freya is a Valkyrie, a reaper of souls. But she hates what she must do.
She doesn't like humans and the pain they inflict on each other, and she never
wants to visit another battlefield. But when a soldier begs her to help his family back
in the human realm, she agrees and discovers a world of friends. Now she'll have
to find a way to keep her promise to the soldier and prevent the wrath of Odin
from destroying the world."—Provided by publisher.
[1. Valkyries (Norse mythology)—Fiction. 2. Mythology, Norse—Fiction.] I. Title.
PZ7.O4137Val 2016
[Fic]—dc23
2015015708
ISBN 978-1-4814-4737-9 (hc)
ISBN 978-1-4814-4738-6 (pbk)
ISBN 978-1-4814-4739-3 (eBook)

DEDICATION

I would like to send a special message to anyone out there who is being bullied, either in school or online.

Please tell someone—your parents, your guardians, or teachers—tell ANYONE! You don't have to suffer alone. . . . We do care.

And I promise you, it does end. I was viciously bullied at a couple of American schools and now I write books that travel all around the world—and I travel with them! In truth, I do often wonder where my tormentors are these days, and what became of them, compared to me. Me, Kate (Cathy) O'Hearn, that odd girl they called Foxy and Loser because I was an awkward Canadian teen that didn't dress like them, had a funny accent, and had traveled just a little too much to be cool.

So believe me, if it can get better for me, it will definitely get better for you.

Always remember:

I wrote this book for YOU!

VALHALLA

IF ON SOME COLD WINTER'S NIGHT YOU GAZE UP
into the darkened sky and see the glow of the northern
lights, consider this: those shimmering colors are not an illusion. They are the glow of the Rainbow Bridge called Bifröst.
Across that magnificent bridge, far from the World of Man,
you will find Asgard, Land of the Norse Gods and Home of
Valhalla.

Also known as Odin's Great Heavenly Hall for the
Heroic Dead, Valhalla sits in the very center of Asgard. Rest-
ing deep within the ethereal plane, it is only accessible from
Earth by crossing Bifröst.

Enormous in size, with a thousand spires rising high into
the clouds, Valhalla has over five hundred entrances. Each

door is wide enough to allow eight hundred slain warriors to pass through, marching side by side.

In ancient times the Vikings fought valiantly to earn a seat in Valhalla. It was all they wanted. But to get there they had to be selected by an elite group of winged Battle-Maidens, known as the Valkyries.

In the middle of the battlefield, the Valkyries would swoop down from the skies, riding their winged Reaping Mares and howling their haunting cries. They came to Earth, or Midgard, as they called it, to choose from among the dead and dying only the bravest warriors to deliver to Odin in Valhalla.

Arriving at Valhalla, these chosen warriors would spend their nights sitting with Odin, feasting and drinking. They would dance with the Valkyries and listen to their enchanting songs.

A warrior's days in Valhalla were spent on the training grounds, as they picked up their weapons and gloried once again in endless battle.

This was their heaven and their paradise. Today's soldiers have forgotten Valhalla and the song of the Valkyries.

But the Valkyries haven't forgotten humans. . . .

1

THE FIRST RAYS OF DAWN SWEPT OVER THE DISTANT horizon and drove away the long night. But Freya did not welcome the rising sun. It was her mortal enemy, bringing only misery. She tilted her wings and flew headlong into the fading darkness, hoping to follow the night, praying day would not find her.

She had been flying all night, soaring high above Asgard, dreading the upcoming First Day Ceremony.

Orus, her raven companion, flew at her side and tried his best to keep up. But his wings were much smaller than hers, and despite his best efforts, he lagged behind. After the long night he was too tired even to beg her to turn back. All he could do was try to stay with her and help guide her through First Day.

"Freya!" a voice called.

Freya looked back and saw her older sister Maya soaring confidently behind them. Her own raven was flying closely at her side.

"Freya, stop!" Maya called. "Please land. We must speak."

Orus forced more speed and caught up with Freya. "*Stop!*" he gasped. "*I can't fly much longer, and your sister is calling.*"

Freya looked over at her companion and saw how exhausted he was. She hadn't been fair, forcing him to fly all night. Pulling in her wings, she descended and gracefully touched down in a field of golden grain. As she folded and settled her midnight-black wings onto her back, Orus landed on her shoulder. "*Don't lose your temper with your sister,*" he panted softly.

"Thank Odin I found you!" Maya cried as she also landed and charged toward Freya. "Mother's in a state. Everyone is searching for you. Where have you been all night?"

Freya used her sleeve to wipe away the beads of sweat from her brow. Now that she had stopped, she felt exhausted from the long flight. The muscles in her wings warned of the stiffness to come. "I needed some fresh air."

"I can see that," Maya cried. "But why didn't you tell anyone you were going? You could have at least told me!"

Freya dropped her head. "I saw you dancing with some of the warriors. I didn't want to disturb you."

"You know I would much rather spend time with you than dance." Maya softened her tone. "Especially on the eve of your First Day."

"I don't want to do this."

Her sister's pale brows knitted together in a frown. "Do what?"

"This! Today!" Freya snapped. "My First Day Ceremony and then going to the battlefield."

"What do you mean? You've been to the battlefields thousands of times. You've spent all of your life there. The only difference is that today you will reap your first warrior."

Freya sighed heavily. "That's what I hate. The warriors and all of the killing and wounding. Thor and Odin may appreciate them, but I don't."

"*Freya, stop,*" Orus warned.

But she couldn't. "Humans are nothing but filthy, blood-thirsty monsters. I don't want to touch them or be part of bringing more of them here. Asgard would be much better off without Valhalla and its dead warriors."

"How can you say that?" Maya cried. "Valhalla is a won-drous place and a home to all the valiant warriors who have fallen in battle since the dawn of time! Those fighters have earned their place here. It's a great honor that we are the ones chosen to escort them. You should celebrate everything they've achieved."

"All they've achieved is becoming good killers!" Freya

replied. "And what does that make us when we reap them? We're even better killers!"

"We do not kill!" her sister said indignantly. "We reap; that's very different. We bring an end to their suffering and escort them home to Valhalla."

"But I don't want to do it," Freya responded as she turned away from her sister. "I don't want to touch a human or even talk to them. All they ever want to do is fight and kill."

Maya started to preen the black feathers on Freya's folded wings. "Freya, listen to me. Those are the old warriors from the early days when it was glorious to fight and die in battle. You haven't spent enough time at Valhalla to get to know the modern soldiers. You just go there, do what you must, and leave. If you took some time to actually speak with them, you'd see they are different."

"A warrior is a warrior," Freya insisted as she turned and pushed her sister's hands away. "They're human, and I don't like them."

"How can you be so judgmental? Trust me. Most modern soldiers don't stay in Asgard. They ascend to be with their families. You'll see today when you reap your first. Just talk to them. I think you'll be surprised."

"But what if I don't want to?"

"Freya, listen to me. Reaping is what we do. You have no choice—it is your duty to Odin."

Freya looked at her sister and sighed. Maya was beautiful.

All four of her sisters were, but Maya was exceptional. She was tall and lean with long flaxen hair. The skin on her sculpted face was unblemished, and she had the palest pearl-gray eyes in all of Asgard. Her wings were fine-boned with elegant white feathers lying neatly over each other. She was everything a Valkyrie should be, which was why most of the reaped warriors fell instantly in love with her.

Compared to Maya, Freya, the youngest of the five sisters, felt like a plow horse. She wasn't as tall, beautiful, or graceful. Her wings were large and stocky. Their raven-black feathers always looked as if they could use a good grooming. Instead of pearl-gray eyes, Freya's were dark blue. And although she was the fastest flier in Asgard, it was always Maya who attracted attention.

But for all their differences, Freya adored her older sister. Many times she had watched Maya with envy as she confidently approached the battlefields. Without a trace of hesitation, Maya reaped the warriors she was assigned and escorted them back to Valhalla.

"Don't you ever question what we do?"

Maya shook her head. "We do as we are intended to do. As Odin tells us to."

"And if we don't want to do it?"

Maya put her hands on her hips and tilted her head to the side. "Sometimes I wonder if you're even my sister. How can you not want to be a Valkyrie? We are most respected in

Asgard. Odin favors us above all others. It is an honor to do what we do. We escort the best warriors home."

Sitting on her shoulder, Orus whispered into her ear, "*Stop arguing. Maya cannot understand. Don't condemn her for that.*"

Freya looked into the dark eyes of the raven on her shoulder. Orus was right. No one in Asgard could understand how she felt. At times *she* didn't even understand it. She hated humans, and nothing could change that.

"I'm sorry," she said finally. "I guess I'm nervous for today."

Maya nodded and combed her fine fingers through Freya's wild, unkempt hair. "Of course you are. C'mon, let's get you ready for the ceremony—before Odin sends out a Dark Searcher to find us."

Freya and Orus followed Maya and her raven back to Valhalla. Beneath them the Great Heavenly Hall was being prepared for her First Day Ceremony. This was to be the final ceremony for some time, as there were no Valkyries younger than Freya. Everyone in Asgard wanted this ceremony to be the best ever—everyone except Freya.

In the fields surrounding Valhalla, the reaped warriors who had chosen to remain in Asgard did what they were always doing. Fight. Thor, son of Odin and greatest warrior of them all, was among them, taking on hundreds at a time. Some called this training; Thor just called it fun.

Looking down, Freya could see his bloodred cape billowing in the wind and wild reddish-blond hair blazing as he used his sword against the other Valhalla warriors. He could have used his hammer, Mjölnir, but that wasn't fair. One swing of the enchanted weapon would literally blow all of the warriors away.

The clanging sounds of sword upon sword rose up in the air as the fighters spent all day battling each other. Then when night fell, they would enter Valhalla together and drink, sing, and tell stories of their great victories, before preparing for the next day's battle.

To Freya it all seemed so pointless. There were so many other things to see and do. Why these warriors should choose to fight, day in, day out, was something she couldn't comprehend.

Freya and Maya veered away from Valhalla and flew over the beautiful buildings that made up the main city of Asgard and back to their home. It was a magnificent mansion standing alone on a hill, surrounded by gardens that turned into dense forests.

The Valkyries always had the best housing, and as Freya's mother, Eir, was senior Valkyrie, she had the biggest, most opulent home—second in size and beauty only to Odin's palace.

Landing on the main balcony, they found their mother pacing the large, richly decorated living area. Shields and weapons from battles throughout the ages adorned the walls, and the floor was lined with sheepskin rugs.

Eir was dressed in her shining silver armor. The feathers on her wings were groomed and bejeweled, and her ceremonial dagger hung at her waist. Her winged helmet sat on a chair.

"Freya!" Her ice-blue eyes blazed, and her white wings were half-open in fury. "Where have you been? Do you realize the time? You will be late for your own First Day Ceremony! Odin will be in a rage."

"Mother, it's all right," Maya said calmly. "Freya and Orus went out for a quick flight and lost track of time. Odin need never know. If you tell him we're on our way, we'll be there shortly."

"It will take an age to get her prepared," her mother ranted. "Just look at the state of her. She's filthy!" She snatched up a comb and tried to drag it through Freya's tangled blond hair. "It will take all day just to get this mess cleared. Not to mention your feathers. Just look at the state of them! I'm amazed you can even fly—"

"Mother, please," Freya begged. She caught the comb as her mother pulled it through a large tangle. "I can do this. Just give me some time."

"For the life of me, I just don't understand how my own daughter could do this to me on this day of all days. Of all my children, you have given me the most trouble. Your sisters were dressed and ready to leave at sunup. They've already gone to Valhalla to join the honor guard. Don't you realize how important this is? You are my youngest child and the last Valkyrie. Today, finally, you will join us in the reaping. It is a great honor."

Freya opened her mouth to protest, but her sister cut in. "Of course Freya understands the importance. We all do. Just give us a moment to prepare, and we'll meet you at the entrance to Valhalla."

Her mother remained unconvinced, but nodded as she reached for her winged helmet. "Just don't keep Odin waiting long. You know how impatient he can be." Without a backward glance, she crossed to the balcony, opened her wings, and leaped off.

"Remember to bow when you approach Odin," Orus warned. Well preened, he sat on Freya's shoulder as they prepared to leave for Valhalla.

Freya nodded her head nervously. "I'll remember."

Maya put the finishing touches to Freya's gold-and-white gown as she flitted around her. "And try not to yawn when he gives his speech."

"I'll try. But why does he always have to talk for so long?"

Orus leaned closer to her ear. *"To hear himself speak!"* The raven cackled at his insult to the leader of Asgard.

"Don't let Odin hear you say that," Maya warned, swatting

at him. "Orus, you should show more respect—like my Grul." Maya reached up and stroked the raven at her shoulder.

"*Don't try to educate Orus, Maya,*" Grul teased. "*He's too thick to learn anything.*"

"*Who are you calling thick?*" Orus challenged, cawing loudly and flapping his wings.

"*You,*" Grul answered.

As the two ravens cawed at each other, Maya held up her hand. "Enough! When will you two finally get along?"

"*Never!*" the ravens said as one.

Freya reached up and stroked Orus's smooth black chest. "Calm down. He's just trying to upset you before the ceremony."

"*He's doing a fine job of it,*" Orus muttered. "*One of these days, Freya, I'm going to show that Grul just how clever I really am. . . .*"

Ignoring the bickering birds, Maya finished fastening a plain gold chain at her sister's neck. "Oh, and try to look interested when Odin tells the story of Frigha."

"Oh no, not again," Freya moaned. "Why does he keep telling us the same old story every time there is a First Day Ceremony? Surely, by now, we all know it."

"He tells it as a warning to all of us," Maya said. "So no one forgets what he did to the one Valkyrie who defied him and ran away from her duties in Asgard."

"But we all know the story. There's no need to keep repeating it!"

"I know, but just show him some respect and try not to look too bored."

"I'll try." Freya inhaled deeply. "So how do I look?"

Maya took a step back and surveyed her work. "You look beautiful. Not even Mother could find fault. Your face is clean, hair combed and braided, and your feathers are sparkling."

Freya grinned and opened her dark wings. Her sister had applied fragrant oils to the feathers, and now the black feathers glowed with rainbow iridescence.

Freya looked to Orus. "Well, what do you think?"

"*You'll do,*" the raven said casually. He gave her a playful nip on the ear with his polished long beak. "*Just as long as they don't look too closely at your fingernails.*" He cawed in laughter and flew off her shoulder toward the balcony. "*Now hurry up, before they start the ceremony without us!*"

Valhalla had been decorated for the ceremony with the most beautiful flowers that grew in Asgard. The high walls had been scrubbed; the spires that rose high into the air flew the colorful flags of the Valkyries. The numerous weapons adorning the many doors had been cleaned and polished, and all the grounds surrounding the hall had been groomed. There wasn't a thing out of place.

Outside the great hall the warriors stopped fighting and gathered together along either side of the entrance to greet Freya. As she approached, they all bowed their heads.

"See, they're not so bad," Maya whispered as she smiled at them.

Freya wasn't convinced. "Just you wait. The moment we're inside, they'll go back to slaughtering each other in the name of amusement."

Maya sighed. "That is the afterlife they have chosen for themselves. Why must you condemn them for that?"

"Because it's foolish."

"It's their choice!" Maya insisted.

The girls' mother appeared at the entrance. "You're late," she chastised. "Everyone is waiting."

"I'm sorry, Mother," Maya said. "But doesn't Freya look beautiful?"

Their mother was much like Maya—tall, elegant, and Odin's favorite Valkyrie. "Yes, she does," she admitted, embracing Freya warmly. "I am proud to welcome you into the sisterhood of the Valkyries. Come, my youngest daughter. Come and take your rightful place among us."

Freya stood directly behind her mother, while Maya took her position behind Freya. As they approached the wide doors of Valhalla, Maya donned her winged helmet and then placed a reassuring hand on her sister's shoulder. "I'm right behind you, Freya. Always."

Grateful for Maya's calm presence, Freya reached up and gave Orus a stroke on the chest. "Well, this is it."

"*Good luck,*" the raven whispered. "*You'll do fine.*"

Her mother led them into Valhalla. Its high arched ceiling rose far above her head, and the shields of countless centuries adorned it. Seemingly endless rows of seated Asgardians lay before her. Freya felt everyone's head turn and focus on her. Lining the long aisle leading up to Odin were all the other Valkyries. They were dressed in their battle armor and wearing their winged helmets, and their wings were open in salute as they raised their swords high in the air.

Freya knew them all by name, but there was none among them that she could call friend. She was the youngest and the last in the long line of Valkyries. But this wasn't all that made her different. For reasons no one understood, Freya was the first Valkyrie born with jet-black feathers, as opposed to the white or gray wings of the other Valkyries. Her mother had always said that her father was a powerful warrior with dark hair and piercing black eyes. Maybe she'd gotten her dark feathers from him.

Freya had been told that he was one of the warriors at Valhalla. But her mother had never pointed him out. When she was younger, she would walk among the fighters, hoping to find him. But as time passed and she saw how brutal the warriors could be, she lost interest in meeting him.

The blaring of horns pulled Freya from her thoughts. Everyone in the huge hall rose and stood at attention. As Freya followed her mother down the long aisle, she walked past her three sisters at the front. Their swords held high, their armor shining, and their extended wings glistening as they all smiled proudly at her.

Finally, Odin appeared with his family on a tall dais at the front of the hall and took a position to receive her. Following close at his heels were Odin's two pet wolves, Geri and Freki. At Odin's command they sat and panted softly.

Freya's mother bowed before the leader of Asgard, stepped to the left, and knelt down. Freya followed suit and knelt before Odin. Her sister bowed and then knelt on Freya's right.

"Rise!" commanded Odin.

Freya rose and stood before the imposing leader. She felt awed in his presence. Odin in his battle armor was a terrifying sight. His wild red hair spilled out from under his large horned helmet, and his red beard grew long and thick, down to his waist. His left eye socket was covered with a gold patch. It was rumored that he had sacrificed his eye in pursuit of wisdom, but Freya didn't know if this was true or not. In his bare arms he carried his famous spear, Gungnir.

Freya had never been this close to Odin before, and the sight of him petrified her. All the wild stories told about his strength and battle prowess now seemed possible as she stood before him.

Standing behind Odin was his wife, Frigg. She too was dressed in her golden battle armor, and in her hands was the new silver breastplate that would be given to Freya. Her long blond hair was neatly styled in two bejeweled braids that almost reached down to her fur-lined boots. It was said she was the most beautiful woman in Asgard. Up close, Freya could see it was true. The only one who could ever rival her beauty was Freya's own sister Maya.

Beside Frigg was Thor. He was the spitting image of his father, Odin, except for the color of his hair. Thor's hair was long and reddish blond; only his beard showed a distinct hint of his father's red. Thor stood, stone-faced and unmoving, as his blue eyes bored into her. He had changed from the well-used battle armor she'd seen him wearing earlier into his formal armor with a clear red cape. He was clutching his hammer in one hand and holding a newly crafted winged helmet in the other.

It was said that Thor didn't have a lot of time for the Valkyries, and by the dark expression on his face, Freya could see that this was true. What caused the enmity remained a mystery. But for as long as she had lived, Freya had done her best to avoid him and his sharp tongue.

Standing back against the wall behind the dais was Loki, the trickster and unrelated blood brother to Odin. Unlike the other men of Asgard, he wasn't strongly built. He wore leather armor, not metal, and was often seen with a staff. Loki had long, dark brown hair and sparkling, mischievous eyes. Freya hadn't had a lot of direct experience with Loki, but she knew the stories of the trouble he caused. Yet for all that, Odin not only tolerated Loki's presence in Asgard; he welcomed it.

When he felt her eyes on him, Loki gave her a big grin, bowed elegantly, and winked at her. Freya's face went instantly red and she looked away. But not before she caught him laughing at her discomfort.

Odin cleared his throat loudly to ensure he had everyone's attention. "Welcome to this final First Day Ceremony." He dropped his eyes, and they landed directly on Freya.

"Freya, today you are the last to join your sisters in the reaping. This is a somber occasion indeed, filled with reverence for a time-honored duty assigned only to the Valkyries. It falls upon you to bring only the best of the slain to me, here at Valhalla. They have earned their place among the glorious dead and share in the celebration of battle. . . ."

Freya stood before Odin, trying her best to stay focused and listen to his long speech, but as the moments passed, it was becoming harder. Her eyes drifted around the great hall, and she saw how everyone else was hanging on his every word. Looking at the masses of people, Freya had never felt more alone.

Why was she so different? Why couldn't she feel the same way everyone else in Asgard did? What was wrong with her?

A sharp nip at her ear brought her out of her reverie. She stole a quick look at Orus on her shoulder. *"Freya, stop daydreaming!"* he warned softly. *"Prepare to swear your oath."*

With a quick nod Freya turned her attention back to Odin. She hadn't been aware of his speech and suddenly realized he was now deep into telling the story of Frigha, the runaway Valkyrie.

"It gave me no joy to blind and de-wing her, but her defiance of my command was too great," he was saying. "Finally she was banished from her home in Asgard. To this day she wanders the Earth alone, lost in her shame and betrayal. . . ."

On and on Odin droned, giving warning to all Valkyries that once they swore the oath, they were bound to their duties and forbidden to leave Asgard without permission. Then with that permission, they were only permitted to visit battlefields to reap the valiant dead. Freya wondered if he ever stopped talking long enough to actually breathe.

Finally he offered her his large hand. "Come forward, Freya," he commanded.

"Go on," Orus ordered into her ear. *"This is it!"*

Freya nervously took hold of Odin's outstretched hand and stepped up onto the dais. "Kneel, child."

Freya opened her wings wide enough to allow her to kneel before the leader of Asgard. Odin placed a hand on the top of her head. "Freya, do you swear to carry out your duties to the best of your abilities?"

"*Say 'I swear,'*" Orus whispered softly into her ear.

"I swear," Freya repeated somberly.

"Do you swear allegiance to the sisterhood of the Valkyries and promise to fulfill your obligations as one of the favored?"

"I swear."

"Do you swear your allegiance to me to do my bidding according to the laws of the Valkyries—bringing only the best of the best warriors to my Great Heavenly Hall, Valhalla, and leaving the others to Azrael and his Angels of Death?"

Freya hesitated. This was the one order she knew was going to be hardest to follow. Who were they to decide who was worthy or not? How could she be expected to judge someone? It was all so unfair.

"*Say 'I swear'!*" Orus whispered. "*Freya, swear it!*"

Freya could hear the sharp intake of breath from the others behind her as she hesitated.

"Answer me," Odin commanded. "Do you swear?"

It went against everything Freya believed, but with the pressure of her mother beside her and all of Asgard gathered behind her, Freya finally nodded. "I swear."

She could hear her mother release her held breath.

Odin inhaled deeply before continuing. "Do you understand your position as Valkyrie? That you possess the power to keep the Angels of Death at bay and with a word can command them away from the battlefield."

"I understand," Freya said.

"Then it is by my order that I command you to arise, Valkyrie. Rise and receive your armor and sword."

Freya climbed to her feet as Odin took her hand. He drew her back to his wife, Frigg.

Frigg raised the new silver armor. "By this breastplate, I give you the power of wisdom in choosing the best for Valhalla. May it guide you and protect you always. I welcome you, young Valkyrie."

"*Lift your arms and open your wings,*" Orus softly instructed.

Freya felt as if she were in a dream as she lifted her arms and opened her wings fully. Frigg approached and placed the silver breastplate into position on her chest. The heavy armor fell down past her waist. She had never been measured for it, yet somehow it fit the lines of her body perfectly. The leather straps were then fed around her body and under the wings at her back to be fastened at her right side.

With her breastplate in position, Frigg kissed Freya lightly on the forehead and took several steps back.

Next Thor came forward. He put his hammer down as he lifted the silver winged helmet high above Freya's head.

"With this helmet, I grant you speed and stealth. No human eyes will rest upon you as long as you wear it. Only the dead and dying may see you as you truly are. Take this helmet, Valkyrie, and protect it. With it lies your power of secrecy." He paused, and his blue eyes threatened. "But be warned. Never allow a living human to wear it. To do so will cause your helmet great suffering, and its cries will be heard in all Asgard."

Thor took a step closer and put the silver winged helmet on Freya's head. When it was in place, Freya felt everything change. She became dizzy and light-headed. The world around her drained of color, as though she were gazing through a dense fog. Maya always said it was harder to see with her helmet on. Freya now understood what she meant. Though the helmet made her invisible and a part of the ethereal realm, it had a cost. That cost was her clear, color-filled vision.

She felt herself starting to fall. Thor's strong arms held her up.

"Steady . . . ," he said. "It takes a moment to adjust."

Freya recovered but still felt very strange, almost as if she weighed nothing. Distracted by the strange sensations coursing through her body, Freya was unaware of the silver gauntlets being drawn up her arms or the heavily jeweled dagger being placed at her waist.

When she was fully dressed in the armor of the Valkyrie, Odin came forward again. In his hand he carried a newly forged sword. Her sword.

Freya had seen Odin perform this part of the ceremony

many times, and had watched Maya going through it. But now that it was her turn, her fear returned.

Odin lowered the sword until the tip was resting halfway down her gown, just above her knees. He reached forward and pierced the fine fabric with the sharp tip. Then as Freya stood perfectly still, he used the sword to cut away the lower length of the gown all the way around her body.

When he finished, the jagged edge of fabric rested against her thighs as the lower half of her beautiful gown lay in ruins on the floor. Looking down at herself, she knew this signaled the end of the life she had known. It meant she was no longer a child, or a girl or even a young woman. She was now . . .

Valkyrie.

2

THE REST OF THE CEREMONY PROCEEDED IN A KIND OF blur. Freya was given gifts and her first taste of mead—the strong drink of Valhalla. It was what all the fallen warriors drank, and most nights it left them unconscious on the floor of the great hall.

Freya couldn't see what all the fuss was about. Mead was bitter and left an awful taste in her mouth that no amount of water could wash away. She much preferred the fruit juices that she usually drank.

When the formal celebration ended, Freya waited outside Valhalla to prepare to join her sisters on her first reap. Everyone else retired to their homes or back to the battlefield to join in the fighting of the slain warriors. Freya watched them taking up their arms and cheering as they entered the battle. She sighed heavily. Would she ever understand it all?

Lost in thought, Freya didn't hear her mother approach until the clopping of horse's hooves was almost upon her. She turned to see her mother standing with a stunning, winged chestnut mare.

Each Valkyrie had a horse to ride to the battlefields. These special Reaping Mares were used to transport the valiant dead over the Rainbow Bridge to Asgard and Valhalla. This was the only part of the First Day Ceremony that Freya had been excited about. She loved the Reaping Mares and spent a lot of time in the stables, brushing their rich manes and grooming their feathers.

"Freya," her mother started as she handed over the leather reins to the mare, "this is Sylt. She is to be your Reaping Mare."

Freya's heart thudded with excitement as she approached the tall mare. "She's beautiful. Is she really mine?"

Her mother nodded. "I chose her especially for you. Look at the feathers under her wings."

Freya stroked the smooth neck of the mare and approached one of the heavy, chestnut wings folded neatly on her back. Lifting it, she was shocked to find black feathers instead of brown.

"Black?"

Her mother smiled. "Sylt is as unique to Asgard as you are,

my child. Treat her well, and she will serve you for all time."

"Sylt," Freya repeated. "Hello, Sylt. We are going to be the best of friends."

The mare's rich brown eyes followed Freya as the Valkyrie moved back to her head. As Freya stroked her muzzle, Sylt nickered softly.

"Thank you, Mother. She's beautiful."

"*Hey, what about me?*" Orus complained as he flapped his wings and nipped her ear.

Freya couldn't help but smile. "Orus, are you jealous?"

"*Of that great big thing?*" he blustered. "*Of course not! But I didn't spend all morning trying to look nice for your ceremony, just to be ignored because of this beast.*"

Freya reached up and pulled Orus off her shoulder. She gave the raven a hug that nearly squeezed the life out of him, before kissing the top of his feathered head. "Orus, you know you will always be my first love. All I was saying is that Sylt is beautiful. And she is, isn't she?"

"*She's just a horse, Freya,*" he said indignantly as he wiggled free of her grip. Getting back to her shoulder, he ruffled his feathers into place again. "*There are hundreds of them in the stables.*"

"Yes, there are. But Sylt is unique. And now she's all ours."

"*Oh, joy,*" the raven complained.

Freya's eldest sister, Gwyn, approached. She was putting her sword back into its sheath and adjusting her gauntlets.

"Honestly, Freya, why you put up with that ill-tempered bird is beyond me. You should have chosen a better companion, like my own bird, Gondul." Gwyn raised her arm in the air, and a black raven soared down and landed neatly on it. It crawled up to her shoulder and settled there.

"See what I mean? Gondul loves me and would never nip my ear or speak rudely."

"*Yeah*," Orus agreed. "*That's because Gondul doesn't have the sense to come in from the rain! He's hardly companion material, if you ask me.*"

"I didn't ask you!" Gwyn huffed at Orus before focusing on Freya. "Are you ready for your first reaping?"

The smile dropped from Freya's face as she was reminded of the horse's purpose and her dark mission.

Maya came up behind her, dressed in her silver armor and helmet. She had a big grin on her face. "Of course she's ready. She's been looking forward to this for ages."

Freya put on a strained smile as Maya put her arm around her and whispered, "It won't be so bad. I promise. Just stay with me and do what I do. It won't be a big reaping today, just a few soldiers."

"*One* is too many," Freya muttered softly.

Maya looked at her and shook her head. "Just talk to your soldier. Let him show you they aren't all bad. Now, mount up—it's time to go."

* * *

As it was Freya's first mission, she took a position directly behind her mother, who was on her massive pearl-gray Reaping Mare. Freya was riding Sylt as they made their way to Bifröst, the Rainbow Bridge, which linked Asgard to Earth. Even with their wings, the Valkyrie and Reaping Mares could not leave any other way. The bridge was the only route into or out of Asgard.

Maya rode behind Freya, and her three other sisters followed further back. As they approached Bifröst, the bridge's Watchman stepped forward and held up his heavy sword. He was massive and immensely powerful, with a head of bushy blond hair and a mustache that went down to his stomach. It was said that Heimdall's senses were so keen, he could hear grass grow and could see across all of Asgard both day and night. And if Heimdall didn't want you to cross the bridge, there was almost nothing you could do to get past him.

"Greetings, Valkyries. State your purpose," he said formally.

"Greetings, Heimdall," her mother responded with equal formality as she bowed her head to the Watchman. "We come in the service of Odin. It is Freya's First Day, and we journey to the reaping."

"Be welcome and journey well," Heimdall said as he bowed and swept his sword wide to invite them onto the bridge.

As Freya directed Sylt past Heimdall, he winked at her. "Good luck, child."

Freya really liked Heimdall. Often when she was feeling

particularly lost or restless, she would fly to Bifröst, and Heimdall would let her go halfway across the bridge to peer down into the other realms. He wasn't big on conversation, but that was another thing she liked about him. Sometimes they would walk out together and he would stand silently beside her. She often felt that Heimdall was as lonely as she was and understood how she felt.

Bifröst was the longest bridge in Asgard and was aptly named the Rainbow Bridge. It shimmered and glistened with the many colors of the rainbow. The brightest colors were the flaming reds and oranges. From a distance their brilliance gave the bridge the illusion of being on fire.

Once across, Freya's mother commanded her mare to fly. Almost immediately her mother started to howl with a sound unique to their kind. It preceded their arrival on the battlefields.

Freya joined in the howling as she, her mother, and her sisters soared high in the sky over a rocky, golden desert. A tall mountain range loomed in the distance, and the sun was starting to descend behind it, casting long shadows on the ground. As Freya gazed down, she saw very little growing on the dry, dusty earth.

A shiver started down her back at the sight of smoke rising in the air. The howling of her sisters grew louder and more intense, letting her know they had arrived at the appointed place.

Down below, three trucks in a long military convoy had been blown off the road and knocked to the side. The vehicle at the end was burning brightly, while the two in front smoldered and threatened to explode. Men were pouring out of the still-functioning trucks and running back to help the soldiers in the flipped transports.

Near the damaged vehicles, others arrived from the sky. These were the Angels of Death, who would take the dying soldiers not chosen by the Valkyries. They landed on the ground and folded their white wings to wait for the selection to finish.

The Reaping Mares landed together several yards from the burning trucks. Freya climbed off Sylt and handed the reins to her eldest sister. As long as one of the Valkyries touched the reins while wearing their helmet, the mares remained as invisible as the Valkyries.

"Are you ready?" Maya asked, coming up to her.

"*She is*," Orus answered from Freya's shoulder. "*Aren't you?*" he asked, turning to Freya.

Freya felt like there was a fist in her throat. She couldn't swallow and could barely breathe. She nodded.

"Ours is the last vehicle over there, the one on fire. There are two soldiers inside that we are to reap. Most of the others within it are destined to survive, so be extra careful not to touch them. But there are three others who will die and are to be taken by *them*." Maya indicated the Angels of Death.

As Freya looked at the closest angel, he bowed his head to her. Freya returned the bow.

"You'll know who your warrior is when we enter," Maya finished.

"I understand." Somehow Freya already knew who she was meant to reap. She could feel him calling to her. There was something about him—something good and very brave. He had lived a decent life, and though he lay dying, he felt no fear. She'd been to battlefields before, but she'd never felt this. Freya couldn't deny his call.

"Remember," Maya said. "As long as you wear your armor, the flames can't harm you, even if the truck explodes. We'll just go in and reap the soldiers."

Freya took a deep breath.

"You'll be fine," Orus said at her shoulder. *"I'm right here with you."*

"Thanks, Orus," Freya said as she followed her sister.

The sound of shouting and crying filled the air, and the acrid smell of burning stung Freya's nostrils. Several men in camouflage fatigues rushed past her, brushing against her wings. If they felt her there, they gave no indication. They ran into the back of the truck and started to pull out survivors.

"Freya, come," Maya called. "Ignore them. We have work to do. The longer we delay, the more our warriors will suffer."

Close behind her sister, Freya climbed into the back of

the overturned truck. She crawled past the men struggling to get at survivors, being careful not to touch anyone as she headed toward the front of the vehicle.

The flames hadn't reached the inside yet, but the smoke had. It was thick and choking. As the seconds ticked, the heat was increasing. The sight of the wounded soldiers around her made Freya all the more resentful toward humans. How could they do this to each other?

To her right she saw a young woman dressed the same as the men. There was blood on her face and hair, and her arm was obviously broken, but Freya could see that she would live.

"Over here," Maya called.

Up ahead, Freya saw two men lying near each other. Maya was before one of them. He was covered in blood and appeared near death. But as Maya knelt down beside him, he opened his eyes.

"Do not fear me, brave warrior," Maya said gently. "I am here to bring you home."

As she had done thousands of times before, Maya leaned forward and stroked the cheek of the soldier with her bare hand. "Come with me now. Leave this world of suffering behind you."

The soldier actually thanked Maya as she touched him. He closed his eyes and died. Freya could see his spirit rise from his broken body, looking just the same as he had in life.

He grinned and took Maya's outstretched hand. Together they moved toward the opening of the truck.

"Have you come for me? Am I going to die?"

Freya looked down into the face of the soldier who had spoken. He was the one she was meant to reap. His dark skin was covered in beads of sweat. She could feel his pain. A crimson stain was spreading on his camouflage shirt.

"Yes," Freya said. "I am here to end your suffering."

"You can't." The soldier's voice rose in desperation. "I can't die."

Freya had heard warriors beg many times before. They would try anything to stop their death. They would plead, try to bargain, or even fight. But in the end the Valkyries always succeeded.

"Please don't be afraid," Freya said gently. "You will suffer no more."

"I'm not frightened for myself," the soldier said. "But my family . . ." He gasped as he tried to catch his breath. "Who will look after them? My wife . . . my girls?"

For the first time, Freya noticed the soldier was clutching something in his hand. It was his cell phone. She had seen other soldiers with them before but had never seen one up close. With fading strength, he lifted it to show to Freya.

"Here," he managed to pant. "I can't leave them."

Freya crept closer and gazed at a photograph displayed on the cell phone. It was the image of a dark-skinned girl, not much younger than her, holding a baby. The girl's face was beaming with joy.

"That's my Tamika and her new baby sister, Uniik," the soldier said proudly, with a sudden surge of strength. "I've never even held her. I was supposed to go on leave next week. . . ." The soldier started to cough and shiver but managed to recover himself as he focused on Freya.

"Please, I have to see my baby. I need to know they'll be all right."

He coughed again and struggled to breathe, as though his chest were filled with water. "I'm begging you," he gasped. "My wife says they're in trouble. I have to go back. . . ."

Freya was almost too shocked to speak. This soldier was fighting to live. Not for himself but for his family. He was nothing like the warriors at Valhalla. As he lay dying, his only thoughts were for his family.

"I am so sorry," Freya said softly. "There is nothing I can do. I must bring you back with me. It is your destiny. Your time on Earth has ended."

"What's your name?" the soldier rasped. "I'm Tyrone. Tyrone Johnson."

"I—"

"*Freya, no!*" Orus warned. "*You can't give him your name while he lives. You must wait until he's dead!*"

Freya looked at Orus, already knowing that. "I can't tell you," she said to the soldier.

"Please, spare me. If not for me, then for my family."

"Tyrone," Freya said softly. "I'm sorry, but it's time for you to go. I'm sure your family will be fine."

"How can you be sure?" He coughed, fighting to get each word out. "Does being the Angel of Death give you insight into the living?"

"I'm not an Angel of Death," Freya said. "I'm a Valkyrie, chooser of the slain. I am here to take you to Valhalla. You have earned your place among the valiant dead."

His eyes were fading with each passing moment. "It's not valiant to die in a land-mine explosion," he said, coughing.

"But your heart is valiant. I can see that. You must be rewarded."

"I don't need rewards," he struggled to say. "I need to protect my family. Please—" He started coughing again and fought to catch his breath. Death was very near.

From the back of the truck came Maya's urgent voice. "Sister, hurry! You must take him. Mother is waiting. Just touch him with your bare skin and bring him home."

Freya looked back at the soldier. "I am sorry. I cannot leave you here. It is your time. Odin commands me to bring you."

Tyrone coughed harder, and blood pooled at the corners of his mouth.

"You are suffering," she continued. "Let me end it for you."

As Freya reached to touch the soldier's cheek, his gloved hands caught hold of hers. He placed his cell phone in her hand and closed her fingers around it. "Take this. . . . They're in danger. . . . I can't die until they're safe. . . ."

He started to choke, but then he stopped abruptly and his eyes closed. Freya finally understood. Whether she reaped him or not would not change the final outcome.

"*Do it now,*" Orus said softly. "*You must take him.*"

Still clutching his phone, Freya did as she was born to do. She reached out her hand and gently stroked his warm cheek. "Come with me, Tyrone Johnson. Let me end your suffering. . . ."

3

WITH HIS BODY LEFT BEHIND IN THE BURNING TRUCK, Tyrone took Freya's hand and followed her to Sylt. He paused briefly to gaze back at the friends he was leaving behind. But then he did as Freya instructed and climbed up onto the Reaping Mare.

Back in Asgard, Freya started the second part of her Valkyrie duties. As Tyrone's reaper, it was her job to take him around Valhalla and familiarize him with his new life. Together they explored the immense building—from the uppermost lookout spires, right down to the armories in the lowest levels. She gathered together fresh clothing for him and helped him locate his private quarters on the same level as other soldiers from his unit. Despite having lived near Valhalla all her life, Freya explored it with wonder. No matter how many warriors the Valkyries delivered here, Valhalla always seemed to have room for more.

At sunset Freya escorted Tyrone into the large dining hall where the warriors gathered for the nightly feast. They were dressed in clothes that crossed the ages and came from every part of Midgard. Samurai warriors sat with knights of the Crusades and recently reaped American soldiers. Native Americans shared food and drink with Gurkhas. Chinese and Russian warriors drank with a group of German soldiers. In Valhalla it didn't matter where they came from or who they had fought for. These warriors were now brothers and sisters in arms.

Odin sat at the front of the hall with his wolves, welcoming the new arrivals and sharing in the festivities. Thor and his brother Balder were sitting at the back, drinking and singing loudly with a group of warrior friends while the Valkyries darted around the great hall, serving drinks and entertaining the warriors. Ancient tunes were played, and later Freya and her sisters would sing.

When Freya served mead to Tyrone, he choked and spat out the bitter drink. "That's disgusting!" he cried.

"I know." Freya laughed. "Here, try mine. It's fruit juice."

Tyrone accepted the tankard of juice and took a long draft. "Thanks, that's much better." He gazed around the great hall. "So, what do we do now?"

"You eat your fill and then you dance with the Valkyries."

"And?"

"And?" Freya repeated.

"What else? You can't mean that all we do is eat, drink, and dance. There has to be something more."

Freya frowned. "I don't understand. You're a warrior; you should love this. You will celebrate all night here in Valhalla, and in the morning you will join the others outside on the battlefield to fight."

It was Tyrone's turn to frown. "Who are we fighting?"

"Each other," Freya said. "You spend the night here with everyone, and in the morning you take up arms against them."

"What kind of asylum is this?" Tyrone rose to his feet and kicked back his chair. "I didn't become a soldier because I wanted to fight. I joined the service to protect my family and country. I'm not going to fight these people. Not without a very good reason—especially if I've spent the night eating and drinking with them. It's barbaric!"

"But this is Valhalla; you must want it. Everyone who comes here does."

"Well, I don't!" Tyrone insisted.

Freya caught sight of Maya. Her soldier was laughing and trying to follow her up onstage to sing with her sisters. He looked so happy and content. What was she doing wrong with Tyrone? If her mother found out that her first reaped warrior was unhappy, Freya was sure to be punished.

She quickly shook her head. "But—but you're a warrior.

How can you not be happy among your own kind?"

Tyrone started to walk away. "If you expect me to find eternal peace in this madhouse while my family needs me back home, you're out of your mind."

Freya caught his arm. "Wait, please. Just give it a day or two. You don't have to fight if you don't want to. Let me show you Asgard and all the wonderful things you can be part of. I'm sure you'll love it here."

Towering above her, Tyrone was an imposing sight, but his eyes were soft and gentle. His shoulders slumped and he sighed. "All right, you win. Convince me."

They left the noise and celebrations and walked the quiet, cobbled streets of Asgard. Freya introduced Tyrone to some Light Elves on their way home for the night. Then they paused beneath a street torch to watch a bunch of faeries flying after swarming lightning bugs. When the tiny faeries caught them, they tied thin ropes around the flashing bugs and dragged them away.

Tyrone watched the roundup in complete shock. "If I hadn't just seen that for myself, I wouldn't have believed it. What do they do with the fireflies?"

Freya shrugged. "I'm not too sure. I don't pay much attention to faeries. They're nasty little thieves that steal anything shiny or sparkly. But I think they use the fireflies in their magic."

Further along the road they bumped into a group of dwarfs who were too busy arguing over some building plans to pay attention to where they were going.

"Dwarfs are the best craftsmen in all the realms," Freya explained. "They designed most of our buildings, work gold into amazing objects and jewelry, and they even made Thor's hammer, Mjölnir."

Tyrone actually smiled as he watched the dwarfs walking away without missing a beat in their argument. "That's some hammer. Thor let me try to lift it. But I couldn't even make it move!"

"I know," Freya said. "Very few have the strength to lift it, and only Thor can wield it. I've never tried."

"That's because you're too scared of him," Orus teased from her shoulder.

"I am not!" Freya insisted.

"You are!"

"Am not!"

"Enough fighting!" Tyrone said. "Geez, it doesn't matter where I go. Kids are kids, and you two are no different."

"We don't fight," Freya said. "We debate. And I'm a lot older than you."

"And I'm even older than Freya," Orus cawed.

"Doesn't matter. You're still just kids to me," Tyrone said.

As the sun started to break on the horizon, they crossed an old stone bridge over a wide, swiftly moving river. They stopped and gazed down into the rushing water beneath them.

"Tamika and I used to walk along the shores of Lake Michigan on stormy days and watch the waves pounding in. We would charge at them and try not to get hit by the water. It used to terrify her mother. She was convinced we'd be washed away." His voice became distant. "I guess we'll never do it again."

"I'm sorry," Freya said.

His dark brown eyes misted. "So am I. Tamika would sure love it here. She'd go nuts if she saw those faeries." He paused and then smiled. "And you with those wings of yours. I'm sure you two would get along like a house on fire."

Freya watched him for a moment. Maya was right. Modern humans were nothing like the warriors of old. He was so much nicer than she'd expected. "You don't have faeries in Midgard, do you?"

"*Earth*," Orus corrected. "*Remember, humans call it Earth.*"

"Yes, Earth," Tyrone said. "And no, we don't have these amazing buildings, faeries, elves, women with wings, or even talking ravens."

"Does it make you want to stay?" Freya asked hopefully.

Before the soldier could answer, they heard howling above them. They looked up to see three large, black-winged beings swooping over them. They touched down at an open area on the far side of the bridge and started to walk across it.

The creatures were dressed in long, flowing, hooded

cloaks that covered their heads and obscured their faces. Black leather armor could be seen beneath their dark cloaks. Their large black wings were folded on their backs. Two short swords were crossed over their wide chests.

As the creatures drew near, Freya and Tyrone could see that each was dragging a shackled, protesting Light Elf.

"What are they?" Tyrone cried as the creatures stormed past them without a sideward glance.

"Dark Searchers," Freya whispered, hoping the Searchers wouldn't notice them. "They serve Odin. If someone breaks the law and then flees, he sends the Searchers after them. No one gets away from a Dark Searcher once they're after you. I hate them. I'm supposed to be brave, but they scare me."

"You'd be crazy not to be scared of them!" Tyrone said. "They're terrifying."

Another howl followed from above as the Valkyrie Hrist landed before the group of Dark Searchers. She was just a bit older than Freya's mother and was known for her raging temper. She looked as if she were ready to explode at any moment.

Freya took a step back and drew Tyrone with her. "Be careful. This can't be good."

"Stop!" Hrist called, advancing on the largest Dark Searcher. "You have no right to take them. Odin made a mistake—these elves have done nothing wrong! Tring is a dear friend of mine. Whatever he's accused of, he didn't do!"

One of the Light Elves tried to step forward. "Hrist, no, don't risk yourself for us. It is a simple misunderstanding—"

The large Dark Searcher shook him into silence.

"Stop that. You're hurting him!" the Valkyrie cried as she charged forward.

The Dark Searcher stepped into her charge and shoved Hrist away, knocking her to the ground.

"Hey," Tyrone cried.

"No!" Freya caught him by the arm. "You can't get involved. Dark Searchers are deadly. They won't hesitate to kill you if you interfere with their duties."

"I thought I was already dead."

"On Earth you are. Here you have a body, and it can be killed. You will rise again at dawn, but it will hurt! You must never challenge a Dark Searcher."

Hrist wasn't going to be put off. She rose and charged at the Searchers again. "I told you to release them!"

The largest Searcher handed his prisoner over to his partner. He loomed menacingly above Hrist and drew his two black swords. As the early-morning sun glinted off the black blades, he advanced on the Valkyrie.

Hrist drew her own weapon. "I'm not afraid of you, Searcher, and I never have been. And despite what you think, you're not always right. Now let the elves go before I'm forced to take them from you!"

The Dark Searcher didn't speak a single word. Instead

he let his blades speak for him. As fast as lightning, the two swords flashed at Hrist.

But Hrist didn't stand down. Moving just as quickly, her single blade kept up with her attacker's two.

"We've got to stop them!" Tyrone cried.

"We can't," Freya said, catching him by the arm. "Dark Searchers are monsters. You can't reason with them. Once they have a prisoner, there's no stopping them. Only Odin can call them off."

"But two blades against one isn't fair!" He pulled free of Freya's grip and started forward.

As Freya ran to stop Tyrone, one of the Dark Searchers sensed their approach. He turned sharply and growled at Freya. She couldn't see his face because of his helmet, but she felt the hate of his stare.

The message was clear. Stay back or die.

There was something about the creature that stopped Tyrone in his tracks. He stood with Freya, watching the fight between the Dark Searcher and Valkyrie intensify.

"Stop!" a voice commanded.

Thor marched up the bridge, his face filled with fury at having been disturbed from the feast. He raised his mighty hammer in the air and drew lightning from the sky. He directed it at the Dark Searchers and the Valkyrie, knocking them all down to the ground with a single, crackling boom. "I said stop!"

The son of Odin charged forward and stood among the fighters on the ground. They were stirring slowly as they recovered from the blast. The feathers on Hrist's wings were singed black and were smoldering from the lightning burn.

"When I say stop, I mean *stop*!" Thor shouted. He roughly hauled the largest Dark Searcher to his feet. "All of you will come with me now. Odin will hear of this."

Hrist started to protest, but Thor raised his hammer again and silenced her with the threat. "I don't care who started it or what this is about. Hrist, you know better than to interfere with the Searchers' duty." He turned his fierce blue eyes on the Dark Searchers. "And I am tired of your unending feud with the Valkyries. I am warning you all now, I will not tolerate fighting in the streets of Asgard—do you understand me!"

Freya stood frozen as she watched Thor's anger growing. As though feeling her eyes on him, he focused his full attention on her.

"Freya, it's late. Get your warrior back to Valhalla. He has a long day of training and fighting ahead of him."

Without another word Thor commanded the Searchers, Light Elves, and Hrist back in the direction of the Great Heavenly Hall to face Odin.

Freya looked up into Tyrone's shocked face. "Come. We'd better get back to Valhalla before he loses his temper completely."

* * *

Over the next few days Freya showed Tyrone around Asgard, from the bustling city to the rolling hills outside it and deep into the Asgard forests. They saw dragons, stags the size of buses, and boars that could talk. They met friendly mountain giants and creatures Tyrone couldn't have imagined. But as the time passed, the soldier wanted none of it.

"I'm sorry. I just can't do it," he said as the sun set on the fourth day. "You've shown me so much, but I know I'll never find peace here. My family needs me. How could I rest knowing they're in danger? To stay would be torture, not paradise."

"Are you sure you can't find happiness here? We have much to offer."

They were walking together to the Gates of Ascension. Through these, soldiers could leave Asgard to go to the afterlife and join those who were taken by the Angels of Death. On Earth it was called heaven.

Standing before the gates, Tyrone took Freya's hands. "You've been so kind to me. Showing me around and offering me something that most men could only dream of. But I can't stay. I have to find a way back to my family."

"When you pass through those gates, you won't be allowed back on Earth. Your time there is done."

"But my family . . ."

Freya dropped her head. "I'm so sorry, Tyrone, but you can't help them now."

"If I can't go back, will you go for me?" he asked desperately. "Please, I'm begging you. Go to Chicago and find my family. Do whatever you must, but get them away from the danger."

"I can't," Freya insisted. "You know my duties are here. It's forbidden."

"Just think about it," Tyrone pressed. "How can I ever find peace if I don't know what's happening to them?"

Seeing the desperation in his eyes, Freya didn't have the heart to say no. "I will try. I promise. If I can find a way to go, I'll do all I can to protect your family."

She regretted the words the moment they left her mouth. Had she really just made a promise she knew she couldn't possibly keep?

"*What?*" Orus cried hysterically. "*Tell me you didn't just say that!*"

Tears of relief filled Tyrone's eyes. "How can I ever thank you?"

"There is no need," Freya said guiltily. "Just find your peace."

Freya had never been through the Gates of Ascension. As a Valkyrie, she was not permitted. But watching Tyrone Johnson's radiant face as he passed through and saw what lay on the other side, suddenly she envied him.

She also realized how much she would miss him. He was the first human she'd ever spent time with, and she'd discovered he was nothing like she'd imagined. He was gentle and kind.

"I told you they were nice," Maya said softly, coming up to her right after Tyrone ascended. "The soldiers of today are nothing like the warriors of old. Most of them don't stay. We aren't needed like we used to be. There are actually too many Valkyries now, even though wars on Earth continue."

Freya sighed. "I feel bad for his family. They'll never know how much he loved them." She pulled Tyrone's cell phone from her pocket. "Here, look at his children."

"Freya, no!" Maya cried in alarm. "You can't have that here!"

"It's all right. Tyrone gave it to me."

Fear filled Maya's eyes. "Get rid of it right now. Throw it off Bifröst. You know it's forbidden. If Odin finds that you've brought something back from a reap, he'll have your wings!"

"I know we aren't allowed to take things, but Tyrone gave this to me. I didn't steal it."

"It doesn't matter how you got it. We can't have anything from Midgard here."

"Why?" Freya asked.

Maya shook her head. "I don't know. All I do know is that as long as it's here, you are in danger. Please, let's fly to Bifröst right now and throw it off together."

Freya hid the cell phone in her pocket and shook her

head. "No. Tyrone gave it to me. It's all I have left from him. I'm keeping it."

"Orus, talk to her," Maya said to the raven. "Tell her what will happen if she's caught with it."

"I've tried," Orus said. "But she won't listen to me."

"It was a gift," Freya insisted. "I'm not throwing it away."

Maya threw up her arms in frustration, and her wings fluttered in annoyance. "You are going to be the death of me!" As she stormed off, she turned back to Freya. "Just keep it hidden."

Freya watched her sister go. Once again she was overcome with a feeling of emptiness. When Tyrone had been with her, the feeling had stopped. Now it was back and even stronger.

"What's wrong with me, Orus? Why am I so unhappy? Why can't I be satisfied like everyone else is here?"

The raven pressed closer to Freya's neck. "You're lonely. You've never had friends your own age. You are the youngest in all Asgard. Even Maya is much older than you."

"Then I'm doomed," Freya said. "There will be no more Valkyries after me. I am cursed to be alone forever."

"That's not true. You have me."

Freya smiled sadly at the raven. "You know what I mean. There will never be anyone here my age."

"You could give a soldier your name before he dies. Then when you reap him, he will have to stay with you forever."

Freya shook her head. She knew the rules. If she had told Tyrone Johnson her name before he had died, he would have belonged to her and would not have been allowed to ascend. That wasn't the way she wanted to find friendship.

"I'll never give my name away. It's not fair, especially if soldiers wish to ascend. I would only give it to someone who really wanted to stay with me. But that will never happen. . . ."

She pulled the phone from her pocket and stared wistfully at the photograph of Tyrone's daughters. "Do you think Tamika is like her father? Would we be friends if we met?"

"What are you saying?" Orus said cautiously. *"You're not really considering going to help Tyrone's family, are you?"*

"She is saying exactly that. She wants to go to Chicago to meet her soldier's daughter."

Freya jumped at the voice behind her. She turned and saw Loki—Odin's trickster blood brother. "And I don't blame you. Earth is a very exciting place. There are lots of things to see and do and millions of people your age. Having human friends could be just the thing to ease your restlessness."

Orus fluttered his black wings. *"Go away, Loki. This is a private conversation."*

"Is it?" Loki said, concentrating on Freya. "I'm sorry if I'm intruding, but I just thought that you might like to know some of the wonders I've seen on Earth."

The raven cawed a warning. *"Move away from him, Freya.*

He's just telling you this to cause mischief. He wants to see you get into trouble with Odin."

Loki placed his hand on his chest, and his face was all innocence. "You wound me, bird! All I want is to help Freya." He turned his attention back to her. "I saw how troubled you looked at the First Day Ceremony and how you grieve over your soldier's ascension. I just wanted to let you know that you can find happiness on Earth."

Orus cawed again. *"You know Earth is forbidden to the Valkyries except on reaping missions."* The raven nipped Freya's ear. *"Don't listen to him. He's trying to get you in trouble. Loki is jealous that your mother is in Odin's favor. He'll do anything to discredit her. If you disobey the rules, that's just what will happen!"*

"I never realized ravens could be such liars." Loki's dark eyes threatened Orus for a moment. Finally he turned his gaze back to Freya. "Forget him. I just wanted to help you find what you're looking for, and a trip to Midgard could be just what you need."

Freya looked from Orus back to Loki. "What is Midgard like? I mean the parts that aren't battlefields. Is it beautiful like Asgard?"

"Even more beautiful," Loki said. "I have seen things there you wouldn't believe—animals beyond description, and so many different and friendly people. It is a wonderland."

"Don't listen to him, Freya," Orus warned. *"Loki isn't your*

friend. He won't help you. He'll just lead you into trouble and laugh when Odin punishes you."

"Are you going to listen to this dumb bird?" Loki said teasingly. "Or do you want my help? I can get you past Heimdall and across Bifröst. Then you can decide for yourself if I'm lying or not."

Freya looked away from Loki's inviting eyes. He was a troublemaker, plain and simple. But what if he really did want to help? She had promised Tyrone she would protect his family. It would mean breaking the rules and sneaking across Bifröst. If she were to try, Loki might be the only one who could help.

"*Freya, no!*" Orus shouted into her ear. "*I know that look. He's trying to lead you astray. Don't listen—fly away!*"

Finally Freya shook her head. "Thank you for the offer, Loki, but I can't. I took the oath to obey Odin, and I'm sworn to my duty here."

Loki bowed and his eyes flashed. "Of course. But do find me if you ever change your mind. I would hate to see you remain so sad and lonely when help is just a realm away."

"*Thank Odin!*" the raven cawed loudly as they watched Loki walking away. "*You must stay away from him, Freya. He would lead you into harm and smile as he does it.*"

It was several days before there was another reaping. With so many Valkyries available, they took it in turns to go. Freya remained in Asgard and volunteered to work in the stables grooming the Reaping Mares. By the time she'd finished, her own mare, Sylt, had a gleaming coat and her wings were perfectly preened.

When the Valkyries returned, for the first time ever, Freya took an interest in the warriors they brought back. She counted the soldiers who arrived and saw several women among the men. She tracked their movements throughout Asgard and watched all but one pass through the Gates of Ascension. The single remaining warrior happily joined the others in Valhalla, drinking and fighting.

Maya had been right. The soldiers of this age had an entirely different attitude from the warriors of the past. Seeing this difference only added to her sense of confusion. Had humans changed so much? There was only one way to find out. She would have to go see for herself.

4

"NO!" ORUS SCREAMED INTO HER EAR. "YOU CAN'T GO."

"I must," Freya said. "It's all I've thought about since Tyrone ascended. He begged me to help his family. How can I refuse?"

"Because if Odin finds out, he'll tear off our wings and rip out your eyes, and we'll be banished!"

"You don't have to come with me," Freya said as she packed a small bag to take with her. "I won't be long. I just need enough time to check on his family. Then I'll come right back. No one will even notice I've gone."

"Freya, listen to me," Orus begged. *"That troublemaker Loki has filled your head with lies about Midgard. It's not beautiful like here. All Earth has is death, war, and hatred. You have seen the battlefields for yourself. They are truly ugly. Stay here with me."*

"Yes, it is ugly," Freya agreed as she pulled on her new breastplate, drew the straps under her wings, and secured the buckles at her side. Then she attached the jeweled dagger at her waist and put her sword in its scabbard. This she clipped to her hip guard. "But I need to see Earth for myself. The *real* Earth, not just the battlefields."

"That is all Earth is," Orus cried. *"One big battlefield."*

"Then I will know and this will be over." She placed the gauntlets on her arms.

The raven shook his head. *"Remember the story of Frigha. We will be banished."*

"I told you, you don't have to come." Freya finally reached for her winged helmet.

"I'm not leaving you. We have been together far too long. Even if it means I will be blinded, de-winged, and banished with you."

Freya smiled at her raven. "Oh, Orus, it won't be that bad. You'll see. We'll be back before we're missed."

They waited until darkness fell. Freya leaped off the balcony of her home and glided silently over the small stand of trees and bushes where she had arranged to meet Loki. She circled overhead several times to see if it was some kind of trick. She wasn't completely fooled by his smooth charms.

Not far ahead stood Bifröst. The bridge shimmered and glowed in all the glorious colors of the rainbow. Bifröst always looked the most magnificent at night as its brilliance reached high into the dark sky. Her mother once told her that on Earth, the glow of the bridge could sometimes be seen at night and was called the northern lights.

When Freya first went to Loki to ask for help getting past Heimdall and across Bifröst, he told her to travel in her helmet and full battle armor. She thought she stood a better chance of getting across the bridge dressed normally or even in a dark cloak, but he insisted that she would need the invisibility her helmet offered and the protection of her armor. Freya began to fear that Earth really was one big battlefield, if she needed the protection of her armor.

"Can you see anything?" Freya called to Orus.

"YES!" the raven cawed. "*I can see this is a terrible idea. Let's go back now before it's too late.*"

"You can go home if you want to, Orus, but I'm going to do this. I need to see what Earth is really like, and I promised Tyrone. I won't break my promise."

"*Foolish child,*" Orus said. "*If you insist on this insane course, I'm coming with you. Who else will keep you safe?*"

Freya smiled over at her raven. Despite what her sisters and mother said, Orus was the best companion she could ask for.

They landed a short distance from the spot where they were to meet Loki. As Orus settled on her shoulder, Freya started to look around. Every nerve in her body was alive,

KATE O'HEARN

and every sound of the night added to the sense of mystery and adventure.

Suddenly she heard heavy footsteps coming her way. She considered hiding, but it was too late. She groaned when she saw who it was.

"Freya? What are you doing here?" Thor asked. "And dressed in your armor? Are you going somewhere?"

"Thor, good evening," Freya said lightly, bowing her head. "No, I'm not going anywhere. I'm just practicing moving in my armor. All my life I've gone to the battlefields dressed normally. It's taking time to get used to my helmet and flying with the extra weight of my breastplate and sword. I like to go out flying at night so I don't disturb anyone."

Thor nodded, but his blond brows knitted together. "Shouldn't you be at Valhalla serving mead and entertaining the warriors? They look forward to hearing you and your sisters sing, and I wouldn't want them disappointed."

"Yes, yes, of course. I was going to go there later. But I wanted to take a quick flight first, if that's all right with you."

"I'm heading there now. Come with me. You can train another time."

"But I'm not dressed for Valhalla. I should change first."

"No need. Come, let's not keep them waiting." Thor took her arm, and his grip let her know the discussion was over.

Along the way to Valhalla, Freya listened to Thor

rambling on about his conversation with Heimdall. "So I told him if any of those frost giants try to get across Bifröst again, he's to tell me. We can't have them coming and going as they please. We have rules, and they must be obeyed."

"Of course," Freya agreed. Her eyes kept darting around, searching for Loki. She hoped he would understand why she wasn't at the meeting place. No sooner had her thoughts gone to Loki than he appeared on the path before them.

"Thor, Freya," Loki said casually. "What a surprise to find you both here." His intense eyes settled on Freya, and he pointed his finger at her sword. "Are you expecting trouble, Freya? That's not your normal evening wear."

"I asked the same thing," Thor said. "No, she's just in training, getting used to her new armor."

Loki nodded. "Very wise. You never know when all that training will come in handy."

"True," Thor agreed. "But duties must come first. We're heading to Valhalla. Come, join us."

"No, Thor," Freya said quickly, trying to hide her panic that Loki might say too much. "I'm sure Loki has other things to do."

"Nonsense!" Loki laughed. "There is nothing I love more than going to Valhalla for a good tankard of mead and to listen to the Valkyries sing."

Freya was soon walking with Thor on one side of her

and Loki on the other. She had never felt more trapped. When they finally reached the Great Heavenly Hall, she was ready to jump out of her skin.

The pressure only eased when Thor was called away by Balder. Left alone with Loki, Freya turned quickly to him. "I'm sorry. I tried to get away, but Thor insisted I join him."

"I thought you might have changed your mind. I waited for you, but you never came."

"I was there, but then Thor came. He said the warriors wanted to hear me sing tonight."

"Then you shouldn't deny them. I will meet you back there after you finish your duties here." He paused and then looked at her. "Don't disappoint me again." Loki turned and strode away.

"*I don't like or trust him,*" Orus cawed.

"Neither do I, but he's the only one who can get us across Bifröst. We have no choice."

Freya felt very uncomfortable in her armor as she joined the other Valkyries serving mead. The stares and comments she received from her sisters were almost as bad.

After everyone was served, Freya followed Maya and her sisters up onto the stage. The musicians started to play a tune, and before long, the five sisters were singing a haunting song that stilled all the warriors in Valhalla. Even Thor put down his tankard to listen.

The evening dragged as Freya tried to find the right

moment to slip away from Valhalla. Finally the warriors began to drift away to their quarters to sleep.

When her duties finished, Freya ran out of the entrance doors and launched into the sky. It was still dark out, but dawn wasn't far off. Flapping her wings hard, she flew back to the meeting place.

When she landed, Orus settled on her shoulder. *"There's still time to change your mind."*

"I'm not changing my mind. I promised Tyrone." Freya looked around and started to call softly, "Loki?"

"Hush . . . ," a voice from the bushes scolded. "Do you want everyone in Asgard to hear you?"

Freya thought she had powerful senses. But she and Orus had walked right past Loki's hiding place with no idea he was there. It was said that stealth was one of his many special talents, and it was true.

"Are you finally ready to go? Maybe you want to sing another song or two?" He stepped free of the bushes and approached her.

"I told you! That wasn't my choice," Freya said. "Thor found me here waiting for you. I couldn't exactly say no to him."

"True," Loki surrendered. "Now, I have a sleeping powder that will stun Heimdall for no more than a moment. You must use that time to fly past him. Don't look back and don't hesitate. Just fly as fast as you can across the bridge."

"It won't hurt him?"

Loki looked shocked. "Are you mad? Thor couldn't hurt that thick-skulled rock with his hammer! Trust me; I have used this powder many times to get across Bifröst. He won't feel a thing and will have no memory of anything. But you must be quick. The effects don't last long."

"What do I do?" Freya asked.

Orus whispered into her ear, *"Forget this crazy idea and go home!"*

Swatting the raven, Freya concentrated on Loki. "How will I know when to fly?"

"Get into the air and soar above us. Watch for my signal. The moment I drop my arm, you soar past Heimdall and straight onto the bridge. Is that clear?"

Freya nodded as knots tied her stomach. "How can I ever thank you?"

"You don't have to," Loki said. "Just go and find happiness. That's all that matters."

On her shoulder, Orus made a gagging sound. *"Oh, I think I'm going to be sick!"*

"Orus, stop!" Freya said. She looked sheepishly at Loki. "I'm sorry. He still thinks this is some kind of trick."

Loki looked innocently at the bird. "Once again, you wound me. I want only the best for young Freya."

Orus cawed in anger. *"What you want is a higher position with Odin by removing Freya's mother from his favor. Freya may* be blind to your tricks, Loki, but I am not. You will not succeed. I will protect her."

Loki threw up his arms and turned to leave. "Fine. Let's forget it. Go back to reaping warriors and singing at Valhalla. I don't care."

"Loki, no, please don't go!" Freya ran to catch up with him. "Orus doesn't trust you, but I do. Please, help me get across Bifröst."

Loki paused and turned. "I do this for you, Freya, not Orus. If you still wish to go to Earth, I will help you." He gave Orus a threatening glare.

"Yes," Freya said. "I want to go."

"All right, I can be forgiving. Take to the sky and keep your eyes on me. The moment I drop my arm, you fly as fast as your wings will carry you."

Freya nodded. Before Orus could say more, she opened her wings and jumped up into the sky. Gaining height, she flew in a tight circle, never taking her eyes off Loki.

On the ground, Loki trotted over to the entrance to the Rainbow Bridge. Heimdall was at his usual position on guard. Freya often wondered what kind of life it was for the poor, lonely Watchman. He rarely slept and never left his post. But like the others of Asgard, he served only Odin.

Heimdall's posture changed when Loki approached. No one in Asgard trusted Loki—very few people even liked him—and everyone always raised their guard when he was near. It was only Odin's generosity that allowed him to remain.

From her position in the sky, Freya could see that one of Loki's hands was behind his back.

As the Watchman stood before him, Loki brought his hand forward and blew a powder up into his face. Heimdall staggered back and collapsed to the ground. Loki dropped his arm, giving the signal to move.

"This is it, Orus!" Freya called as she tilted her wings, changed direction, and flew with all her might toward the entrance to Bifröst. Freya clutched the raven in her hands as she gained more speed.

In a flash she was passing over Heimdall and flying into the bright colors of the Rainbow Bridge. She did not slow as she reached the halfway point. Nor did she look back to see if Heimdall had noticed and was chasing after her. All she wanted, all she needed, was to get to Earth.

5

BIFRÖST WAS A LIVING BRIDGE. ANYONE WHO USED IT TO reach the other realms knew they could not control where it would release them when they arrived. In this case, when Freya flew free of the rainbow colors, she discovered that she was soaring high above Europe. It was night.

As part of her training, Freya had studied the geography and history of all the countries of Midgard, including their ever-changing borders. She was trained in warfare and knew details of every battle fought since the dawn of time. While growing up, she had attended many of the battlefields to watch the Valkyries work.

Setting a course, she headed toward the United States. It had been a long time since she had been to this country. Soon she and Orus were soaring over a vast ocean.

"*Are we there yet?*" Orus panted. "*My wings are about to fall off.*"

They had flown all night and into the day to reach the American coastline. Like him, Freya was growing fatigued. But unlike him, her larger wingspan meant she could go longer and further than he could. She opened her arms. "Here, let me carry you for a while."

Orus gratefully flew into Freya's embrace. "I wish Bifröst had taken us closer," she said. "We've lost time getting here."

"*Sometimes I think that bridge knows where we want to go and does its best to send us as far away from our destination as possible.*"

Freya hugged the cynical raven. "Has anyone ever told you you've got a dark streak?"

"*You,*" Orus said. "*All the time.*"

The landscape beneath them soon changed. Autumn-colored fields and trees with their falling leaves of blazing reds and oranges made way for incredibly tall buildings and heavily congested roads as Chicago loomed ahead.

Freya pulled in her wings and landed on one of the tallest buildings. Two white metal antennae rose high above her, and the rooftop was cluttered with equipment and strangely shaped structures. But it offered the perfect place to hide while she got her bearings.

"Let's take a break for a moment while I try to figure out where we're going."

She released Orus and removed her helmet. Instantly the sights, sounds, and colors of Chicago hit her. She looked down at the busy streets teeming with people. Car horns blared, police sirens squealed, and all around were the sounds of life.

The sensations were like nothing she'd ever experienced before. She could sense laughter, joy, sorrow, fear, hatred, and love. Every emotion merged together in a great wave of feelings rising up to her.

She peered over the side of the rooftop in excitement. "Orus, look. Isn't it amazing? You can see all those people down there. They're not fighting or killing each other! Loki was right. Earth can be beautiful."

Orus cawed. *"You think this is beautiful? It's filthy. The air is choked with poison, and there are too many people. I can't hear myself think with all this noise. Let's go back to Asgard before we are missed."*

"You can go back if you want, but I'm not going anywhere. Not until we've seen Tyrone's family."

Orus huffed in surrender. *"How are we supposed to find them in all of this? It's not like you can go down there and ask directions."*

"Tyrone said he lived north of the city in a place called Lincolnwood. Number forty-five, Orchard Street. We can fly north and try to find it."

"That's your suggestion?" Orus complained. *"Just fly north?"*

"Do you have a better idea?"

The raven ruffled his feathers. *"Well, no, not exactly."*

Suddenly a door behind her opened and two men emerged onto the roof before Freya could pull on her helmet. Their eyes flew open when they saw her.

"What are you doing up here?" a tall, dark-skinned man with graying hair demanded as he looked her up and down.

"Yeah, kid," said the other. "How'd you get up here? The door was locked, and the roof is off-limits to the public."

There was something very aggressive about him. He was pale and much shorter and heavier than the first man. He had a thick beard and a shaved head. His bare arms were covered in tattoos. "I flew here," Freya answered.

"Sure you did, kid," the tattooed man said. "And I'm the Easter Bunny. Now get off this roof before I throw you off."

Freya's Valkyrie senses were acute, and she could see beyond his exterior appearance to what lay beneath. This was a dangerous man. Locked deep inside were dark secrets about things he had done. In him she recognized all the things she despised about the human race.

Freya spread her wings, drew her sword, and advanced on him. "Are you threatening me?"

Their mouths hung open at the sight of her wings. Freya sensed that the taller man was not unkind. He fell instantly to his knees. "Please forgive me," he begged. "We meant no disrespect."

It was the shorter, tattooed man who she approached. "I don't like people who threaten me. And I especially do not like men who hurt others for their own pleasure. You cannot hide what you are from me, human. I see right into your heart."

"What are you?" he demanded.

"Joe, get down on your knees," the taller man warned, reaching for him. "Can't you see she's an angel? Show some respect."

"That thing ain't no angel," Joe insisted. "Angels ain't got black wings, and they don't carry no swords or wear no armor. This is some kind of demon straight from the gates of hell." He focused on Freya. "And that's just where I'm sending it."

Freya could feel his violent intentions long before he lunged at her.

"I am *not* a demon!" she fired back as she stepped forward to meet his charge.

Freya couldn't touch him with her bare hands. One touch would reap him, and there could be no explaining *that* to Odin. Instead she moved faster than his eye could follow and struck him in the jaw with the pommel of her sword.

He collapsed to the ground in an unconscious heap.

"You," she said, pointing her sword at the taller man. "Get up. Tell me your name."

He slowly rose until he stood above her, but he kept his eyes cast down to the ground. "Curtis," he mumbled. "Curtis Banks."

Freya could feel the fear coming from him. She put her sword back in its sheath. "Do not fear me, Curtis Banks; I am not here to hurt you. I just need your help."

Curtis's dark eyes rose to hers. "How could I possibly help you? I'm just a simple man."

"A man who knows this area, I hope," Freya said.

"I—I've lived in Chicago all my life."

"Can you tell me how to find a place called Lincoln-wood?"

"Lincolnwood?" he repeated. "That's not far from here." He walked up to the edge of the building and pointed north. "It's in that direction, just about ten miles away—you can almost see it from here. If you follow the Chicago River down below us, it passes right beside it. There's a bus you can catch that will take you right there."

"I will find it, thank you," Freya said.

"Who are you?" Curtis asked timidly. "What's in Lincolnwood?"

"I cannot tell you who I am," Freya answered. "But I'm here to save a family who is in danger. I promised their father I would protect them. They're in Lincolnwood."

"What kind of danger are they in?"

"I don't know. All I know is they are in trouble and there is no one to help them now that Tyrone is dead—"

"*Freya, stop! Don't say any more,*" Orus warned her. "*You are already risking too much by speaking with him.*"

"Why?" Freya turned to the raven.

"He may tell others you are here. He could endanger you."

"He won't. I can trust him. His heart is true."

The raven sighed. *"You are too trusting. First Loki and now this man. It will lead to no good."*

"And you worry too much."

She focused on Curtis again. His eyes were locked on the raven. "Can you talk to him?"

Freya nodded. "He told me not to trust you. But I can feel what is in your heart. I know you won't betray us."

The fear was leaving Curtis's face, to be replaced by awe. "Are you really an angel?"

"I'm not an angel; I'm a Valkyrie."

"A what?"

Freya frowned. "A Valkyrie. Don't you know what that is?"

Curtis shook his head.

"We're the Battle-Maidens of Odin."

"Who?"

"You don't know Odin?" Freya cried in shock.

"I'm sorry, no."

"But everyone knows Odin!"

"I'm sorry, *I* don't."

Freya was almost too stunned to speak. Finally she looked at Orus. "How can this be?"

"This is a different age," the raven said. *"Perhaps they have forgotten us."*

Still in shock, she focused on Curtis. "Our time here grows short; we must go." As she turned to leave, Curtis called after her.

"Valkyrie, wait. Let me take you to Lincolnwood in my van. Chicago is a dangerous place. If people saw you, they might try to hurt you. Besides, if there's a family in danger, I want to help. My wife is a lawyer and my nephew's a cop. I'm sure they'd want to help too."

She was stunned by his sudden concern. Freya gazed down on the unconscious man and back to Curtis. She couldn't understand how there could be such kindness in some people and yet such darkness in others. "Thank you, but I prefer to fly. I will be fine."

She walked over to her helmet. "You are a good man, Curtis Banks. If I need your help, I will return. But if you don't see me again, please be careful. That man with you is very bad. He holds many secrets and has done many terrible things. You would do well to stay away from him."

Curtis looked at the man lying on the ground. "He's only been working for me a couple of weeks. I own the company that cleans the windows for most of the big high-rises around here. My instincts told me not to hire him, but I needed the workers—though I can't say I've warmed to him. I came up here to check on his work, but after today I'm going to cut him loose."

"Be careful when you do. He's very dangerous," Freya

finished. "Now I must ask you not to tell him what we've discussed or where I'm going."

Curtis nodded. "It's none of his business." He reached forward to shake her hand. "It has been a great honor to meet you, Valkyrie. I wish we had more time together. I have so many questions. . . ."

Freya held up her hands and stepped back. "My touch is death to you. But I have enjoyed meeting you too." She reached for her helmet and drew it on. The world around her lost its color again.

"Well, I'll be . . . ," Curtis said. "Valkyrie, are you still here?"

"I am," Freya said. "But I must go. Live well, Curtis Banks."

His laughter followed her as she walked to the edge of the building. She climbed up onto the short wall and looked to Orus. "You ready to go?"

"Finally," Orus cawed. *"I was ready the moment we landed here."*

Freya leaped off the top of the building. She let herself fall more than halfway to the ground before opening her wings and gliding smoothly through the city streets.

"Orus, come on!" she cried, laughing as she expertly dodged around tall trucks and buses. She was playing among the traffic and having the time of her life.

"Freya, fly higher!" Orus cried from above. *"Please, you're going to get hurt!"*

Surrendering to the panic-stricken raven, Freya flapped her wings and rose higher in the sky. "I'm just having a little fun."

"Well, don't. Are you trying to scare me to death?"

"You worry too much," she teased as she settled on her course and followed the winding river north.

It didn't take them long to reach Lincolnwood. They had left the city behind and now soared above a less congested area. Tall buildings were replaced with houses and short, squat buildings.

Not far ahead she could hear the sound of children's loud, excited shouts as they poured out of a building surrounded by parkland. Large, yellow buses filled a parking area, and as she flew above them, Freya watched children climb onto them.

Her heart pounded with excitement at the sight of kids her own age. These were the first she'd ever seen in her life. Until now, her only experiences with humans had been with the warriors on the battlefields or those who made it to Valhalla. Occasionally there were some very young fighters. But war had changed them. They were as brutal as the adults.

"Look at them!" she called excitedly to Orus. "Can't you feel their joy? Their love of life?"

Orus flew closer. *"All I feel is trouble brewing. We are on a mission to check on Tyrone's family, that's all. You can't go down there to meet them. One look at you, and they'll run away screaming. You are a Valkyrie—a reaper of souls. You don't belong in*

Midgard. Especially near human children. You are a child of war. That must be your playground. Not here and not now."

Freya was about to protest when the sound of frightened shouts reached her ears. She could feel genuine fear behind them, like hot breath on her face. Following the shouting, she changed direction in the sky.

"*Freya—no!*" Orus called, flying after her.

Her keen eyes caught sight of a boy running as if his life depended on it. He was passing through backyards and climbing over fences, trying to get away from the others chasing him. She could almost hear his heart pounding ferociously in his chest as he tried to flee. But like deadly predators, his pursuers seemed to anticipate his every move. They split into two groups, each taking a different direction.

From her vantage point in the sky, Freya could see the boy was heading into a trap.

"*Freya, leave them to their business,*" Orus said. "*Come, we must find Tyrone's family. And then return to Asgard.*"

Orus tried to draw her away, but she wouldn't go. "No, I want to see."

"*Why? They're just playing. They won't hurt him.*"

Freya flew closer and flapped her wings to hover over the pursuers. These boys weren't playing. This was deadly serious. Within seconds the trap snapped shut on the frightened boy. He was cornered as his tormentors charged at him from two directions behind a house.

The boy kicked the first attacker and knocked him to the ground. But the others quickly pounced. He was punched repeatedly in the stomach and face until he collapsed to the ground and curled into a tight ball.

"Orus, look what they're doing to him!"

"That's their way. We can't get involved."

Freya looked over at the raven. "Maya is always saying that humans aren't bad, but look down there. Six against one just isn't fair! We've got to help him."

Tilting her wings, Freya started to descend.

"Freya, stop. . . ."

Ignoring the raven's pleas, Freya landed in the yard behind the group of boys. With her helmet still in place, she was invisible. Stepping closer, she was careful not to let a single feather graze against any of their exposed skin.

"C'mon, put up a fight!" cried the largest of the boys as he kicked his prey.

Their victim lay on the ground in a tight ball. "Leave me alone!"

"Aw, is he crying?" called the bully. He pulled back his foot and gave the boy another brutal kick in the back. Then he looked at the others. "Pick him up. Let's show him what we think of people who bug me!"

Several gang members rushed forward and dragged the boy to his feet. They pinned back his arms and laughed as they held him. Blood was running from his nose, and a large, angry bruise was already forming on his cheek and eye.

Freya's temper flared. The sight of the boy's blood and fear excited the attackers even more. She could feel their heated anticipation at the beating about to come.

"No more!" Freya roared. Charging at the boys, she lifted her booted foot and kicked the bullies aside.

Their terrified screams filled the air as Freya continued to kick them across the yard. They huddled together like frightened sheep as they desperately searched for her. Finding nothing, they fled in terror, leaving their leader to face her alone.

His eyes were filled with hatred as he scanned the yard. He was much bigger than the others and stood almost a head taller than Freya. Just like the man on the roof, Freya sensed rage and violence.

He was backed up to the fence, holding his victim as a shield against her. "Whatever you are, show yourself!" he demanded. "Do it now or I swear I'll break his neck!"

Freya's senses told her the threat was real. The bully was just a boy himself, but he enjoyed violence.

"If you do that," she warned in her softest, most menacing voice, "you will know terrors beyond imagining. Release him now, or I will show you the true meaning of 'terror.'"

The bully's voice faltered as his eyes searched madly for her. "You're—you're just a dumb girl. I—I'm not scared of you, even if I can't see you." He shoved his victim aside and held up his fists to fight. "C'mon, then. You wanna fight, let's fight!"

"You cannot win against me, human," Freya warned darkly, stepping closer. "This is your last warning. Leave here now or you will regret it."

When he refused, Freya struck. With one swift kick, she sent him flying several feet across the yard. He hit the ground hard, and the wind was driven from his lungs. As he coughed and tried to regain his breath, Freya charged over and placed her booted foot on the bully's arm. She applied enough pressure to let him know she meant business. "If I ever hear of you attacking anyone again, not even the Midgard Serpent will be able to save you from me!"

She applied more pressure.

"Freya, stop," Orus warned in her ear. *"You'll break his arm. Leave him."*

Freya hesitated but then lifted her foot. "Get out of here!"

The bully climbed to his feet and turned quickly to attack her with a vicious punch. But when his fist impacted Freya's breastplate, she heard the bones in his wrist snap. The bully howled in pain and pulled his hand to his chest.

"This ain't over," he roared furiously as he started to leave. "You hear me? Whatever you are, I swear, you're gonna pay for this!"

"Just go!" Freya cried as she gave him a final kick in the backside.

Furious, he kept looking back, trying to catch a glimpse of her. Even after he disappeared from view, Freya could still feel him lingering in the area, waiting for her to appear. Finally he gave up and moved away.

Alone in the yard, Freya returned to the boy. He was still on the ground looking around. She could feel his disbelief that his attackers had gone.

"Can we please leave now?" Orus asked. *"You saved the boy. Let's go."*

"In a minute," Freya said. She knelt beside the boy, just out of his reach. "Are you all right?"

His blond hair was tousled, and a deep cut split his head. The beating had been brutal. He turned toward her and scooted back to escape. "Where are you? Why can't I see you?"

Freya rose and looked around. She closed her eyes and listened to her senses. No one was in the house behind them, and the bullies had all gone. They were completely alone.

Kneeling again, she removed her helmet and became visible. "Don't be afraid. I promise I won't hurt you."

The boy looked up at her in disbelief. His blue eyes were wide with shock, and his mouth hung open. Finally he uttered, "How'd you do that?" Suddenly his eyes landed on her folded wings. "Wait—you—you've got wings. Are they for real?"

Freya nodded.

"Whoa," he said, forgetting his pain and injuries. He

leaned closer, staring intently. "Nah, you're kidding me. They're not real."

"I told you they are." Freya looked over her shoulder and opened her left wing and fluttered it up and down. "See? Real feathers, real wing."

"Cool!" He rose a little higher and smiled, but winced as it pulled his swollen lip. "Are you my guardian angel?"

Freya sighed and sat back on her heels. "Why does everyone always assume I'm an angel?"

"Because you look like a guardian angel," he said. "You're wearing armor, carrying a sword, and you just kicked the butt of the meanest bully in school. Oh, and, hello—*You've got wings!* What else can you be?"

"Well, I'm not an angel," Freya said.

"Alien?" he suggested hopefully.

"I don't even know what that is," Freya said.

"That's someone from another planet."

Freya frowned. "Is that like another realm? I'm from Asgard."

"Where?"

"Asgard," Freya repeated. "The highest realm? I'm a Valkyrie."

The boy reached into his pocket and pulled out a tissue. He pressed it to his bleeding nose. With a nasal voice he said, "I've never heard of Asgard and I'm not sure I know what a Valkyrie is. But thanks for saving my life. I'm Archie."

"You—you're welcome," Freya stuttered, unable to believe he'd never heard of Asgard.

"What's your name?" Archie asked.

"Don't tell him!" Orus cawed. *"Look, the boy is fine. Can we please go now?"*

"Orus, calm down." Freya pulled the raven from her shoulder and placed him on the ground. "This is Orus."

"You've got a pet raven?"

"I'm no pet!" Orus cawed indignantly. *"Freya, tell him, I'm not your pet!"*

"I wouldn't call him my pet, if I were you," Freya warned. "He might bite your finger off. He's my companion and adviser."

"Not that you ever listen to my advice," Orus complained.

Freya chuckled at the raven and continued. "Orus and I travel together. Now, do you think you're strong enough to stand up?"

Archie inhaled sharply as he leaned forward to stand. His brows furrowed in pain as he made it to his feet. He was taller than her, and looked a bit older. Archie started to sway and had to lean back against the fence.

"Are you all right?"

He nodded. "I don't think anything's broken, but they got me good this time."

"Why were they attacking you?"

"It's a long story."

"That we don't have time to listen to," Orus cawed as he flew back up to Freya's shoulder. *"Freya, we must go!"*

Freya ignored him and asked, "Tell me. Why did they want to hurt you?"

Archie dropped his head. "Because they can and because JP blames me for what happened to his family. His brother and my brother got into trouble together, and now they're both in prison."

"He blames you for the actions of others?"

Archie nodded. "But it's not just me they pick on. There's a whole bunch of us they beat up and steal from. They call us the Geek Squad. We don't fit into any of the groups at school. And because we're a little bit different and get higher grades than them, they always pick on us."

Freya shook her head. "I don't understand. Why don't you fight back? Defend yourself?"

"I can't," Archie said. "There are too many of them, and I don't know how to fight."

"Yes, you do. I saw you kick that boy. You might have done better if you kept at it."

"Yeah, great idea it was too, wasn't it?" Archie said sarcastically. "Look what it got me, a bloody nose and a black eye. I should have just let him hit me a few more times. They'd have gotten bored and left me alone."

"Surely you could learn to fight better. I am sure no one taught them how."

"I told you, there's too many of them."

Freya frowned. "But you just said there are others they pick on. You could unite to protect yourselves."

"I don't really know the others in the Geek Squad. It's not like we're friends or anything like that. The only thing we have in common is JP beating us up."

"This makes no sense," Freya said. "In war, if your army is smaller than your opponent's, you increase your army's size or its skill base. It's a simple principle that has worked for thousands of years."

"This isn't a war," Archie said.

"It sounds like it is. . . ."

Archie sighed. "You'd understand better if you went to my school. Bullies are always picking on the outcasts or weaker students. It's just the way it is."

Freya shook her head. "And my sister wonders why I hate humans. . . ."

"You hate us?"

"Not all humans," Freya corrected. "Just most, because of things like this. The stronger should protect the weaker, not abuse them."

"Maybe in a perfect world," Archie said. "But in case you hadn't noticed, this world isn't perfect."

Freya paused and stared at him. There was something about Archie that intrigued her. Granted, he wasn't unattractive, but she'd seen better-looking and stronger warriors at Valhalla. However, he was the first boy her age she'd ever spoken to, and he was so different from what she'd expected. There was so much more she wanted to learn from him.

Just as she was about to ask another question, her senses warned of the others returning. "The boys who attacked you are coming back."

"C'mon, we've got to get out of here!" Archie said. "They may just beat me up, but there's no telling what they'll do to you."

He surprised her with his sudden concern for her safety. "It's too late to flee. I have an idea. Whatever happens, don't touch my bare skin, hair, or feathers. Put your hands in your pockets and keep them there. I'll do the rest. My helmet will keep us both hidden from their sight."

Freya put her helmet on, then reached her arm around his waist. Her gauntlets and his heavy winter coat kept them from actually touching.

"What happens if I touch you?" Archie whispered.

"If you touch any part of me with your bare skin, you'll die."

"What?" Archie cried.

"Quiet!" Freya ordered. "Here they come!"

Freya held on to Archie as they watched the boys arrive in the yard. They listened as three of the bullies described in detail what had happened.

"I swear, it was right here," one of them claimed. "Look, you can still see the blood from geek boy's nose."

"Where is he?" a new boy demanded. "Or did the invisible creature take him away?" He started to laugh and make scary, cartoony sounds.

"I don't know," said the other from the attack. "Maybe it did."

"Ah, you're full of it," chimed a new boy. He was standing with his hands on his hips, looking doubtful.

"You don't believe us? Who do you think broke JP's wrist? It sure wasn't Archie. He was too busy bleeding."

"Yeah, it was the invisible creature. She did it," claimed one of the bullies.

The boys searched the yard. When they moved close to where Freya stood, she tensed to fight again.

"I'll tell you one thing," the first one said. "Archie better hope that thing does take him away and keep him away. I ain't ever seen JP so mad. He says he's gonna put him in the ground on Monday."

Freya felt Archie react to the comment. Fear was pouring from him in heavy waves. She realized that by saving him today, she'd made it worse for him.

When the group of boys gave up the search and left the yard, Freya stood with Archie for several minutes.

"Are you all right?"

He said nothing, but nodded.

"Where do you live?"

"Not far," he said softly.

"Take me there."

"*Freya, what are you doing?*" Orus whispered as she walked with Archie to his house. "*It is unfortunate, but you can't save him. That awful boy is going to get him, no matter what you do. You are here to check on Tyrone's family. You don't have time for others.*"

Freya shot him a look but said nothing as they made their way along the tree-lined streets. It was late autumn, and the leaves were falling. There was a crisp smell of winter coming on. It wouldn't be long until it snowed.

They walked in silence, but Freya could still feel the fear coming from Archie. Arriving at a small house, Archie carefully led them up the front steps. Freya looked up at the door.

"Do you have family here who can help you?"

At first Archie was hesitant to answer. Finally he said, "I'll be okay. Thanks again . . ." He paused. "I still don't know your name."

"I can't tell you," Freya said. "It's a rule."

"Well, thank you anyway," he said softly as he approached the front door.

Freya watched him pause before the door and felt something more than fear coming from him. Something much worse—it was resignation. Archie knew he was going to receive a worse beating on Monday. But he wasn't going to do anything about it.

"I could teach you," Freya finally offered.

Archie pulled his key from his pocket and put it in the lock. "Teach me what?"

"How to fight and defend yourself against those boys."

"*What?*" Orus cried. "*Have you lost your mind?*"

"Why would you do that?" Archie asked.

Freya ignored the cawing raven at her shoulder. "I have been around battlefields my whole life, and I've seen brutalities I'll never forget. Those boys today are just the same. I can help you, Archie, if you let me. I would do it in exchange for your assistance."

A spark of life began to glow in Archie's eyes. "What could I do to help you? You're already amazing!"

Freya flushed at the compliment. "I need to find a family. I came here to make sure they're all right. If you show me how to find them, I'll help you with those boys."

For the first time, Archie gave her a wide, genuine smile. It was a beautiful smile that lit his bruised and bloodied face. "Is that what Valkyries do?" he asked. "They help people?"

"Not quite," Freya answered. "But I do want to help them."

"And me?"

Freya looked long and hard at Archie. This was madness. She had run away from Asgard to help one family, and now she was going to take on more? But with all the hope she felt coming from him, how could she say no?

"Yes, Archie, I am here for you, too."

Archie unlocked the front door and held it wide to invite her in. He grinned again. "If you really hate humans so much, you have a weird way of showing it."

Freya laughed and shoved him lightly through the door. "Just shut up and get inside!"

6

WHILE ARCHIE SHOWERED AND CHANGED HIS CLOTHES, Freya looked around the small house. This was the first human home she'd ever been in, and it was nothing like her home in Asgard. It was a fraction of the size, and the furnishings were very different. She discovered things she'd never seen before and was anxious for Archie to explain what they were.

After going through the main living area of the house, Freya and Orus started to explore other rooms. Down a short hall she opened a door and saw a bedroom that seemed very out of place with the rest of the well-cleaned house.

Clothes were thrown all over the floor, and empty bottles covered every surface. The bed was unmade, and the sheets were stained and smelly.

Freya moved on and found another room that was a small wonderland. It was a bedroom, but nothing like she'd ever seen before. The walls were covered in colorful posters, and there were interesting figurines on shelves. She laughed and picked up a small figure that was the spitting image of Thor with his hammer.

She held it up to show the raven. "What do you think Thor would say if he saw this?"

"He'd say, *Freya, what in the name of Odin are you doing there!*"

Freya chuckled and put the figure down. Hanging on the back of the door was a floor-length, burgundy-colored velvet coat, while the closet was filled with strange clothes that had chains and cogs and levers all over them.

"This is my brother's room."

Freya jumped at Archie's quiet arrival behind her. Her wings flew open in alarm and knocked Thor and several other figures off the shelf.

"Brian is really into strange things." As Archie bent down to collect the figurines, Freya noticed he was wearing yellow rubber gloves on his hands and extra layers of clothing. The only skin exposed was his face.

"You said be careful," Archie said. He held up his gloved hands. "I'm being *extra* careful."

Freya was still wearing her gauntlets and held up her hands. "Me too. What is all this?"

Archie handed her a figurine. It was of a woman in a top hat with goggles perched on top of it. She was wearing a long, open coat. Tiny cogs were on the lapels of the coat and in her hands. Under the coat she wore a corset and a long, layered skirt. "It's my brother's collection of figures. He's really into comics and stuff like this. That one's Steampunk."

Nothing Archie had just said made any sense to her, and she handed back the strange figurine. Though she did like what she saw of Steampunk.

"Who else lives here with you?"

"Just my mother, but she's away right now."

"What about your father?"

Archie shrugged. "He left years ago. I've never heard from him."

Freya frowned, sensing there was a lot more he wasn't saying. He carried a deep sadness and loneliness. "So you are alone?"

"It's all right. I'm used to it." Archie hesitated. "While you're here, where are you going to stay?"

"I'm not sure," Freya said. "I don't know how long we'll be here."

"Well, if you need a place to crash, there's plenty of room here. While my mom's gone and Brian's in prison, you can use his room."

At her shoulder, Orus was having a fit. *"Freya, you can't stay here! If Odin finds out, he'll send a Dark Searcher after us!*

We must find Tyrone's family and then return to Asgard before we're missed. It doesn't matter how much you like this boy, you just can't stay!"

"What's he saying?" Archie asked as he watched Orus caw.

Freya smiled. "He says thank you. We'd love to stay here."

"I did not!" the raven raged. *"Freya, stop putting words in my mouth!"*

Archie leaned closer to Orus. "You're welcome."

When an awkward silence filled the room, Freya walked closer to one of the posters on the wall. It showed a squat little girl dressed in the Steampunk style. She had a crooked mouth and jet-black hair with a red stripe. There was an even smaller boy with her. His eyes looked madly demented. Beside them was a brightly colored caterpillar on a leash, wearing multiple military boots.

"That's Gruesome Greta," Archie offered. "She's my brother's all-time favorite character." He crossed the room and reached for a thin book on a shelf. Freya's eyes glowed as she leafed through the colorful pages, filled with lots of little pictures.

"This is wonderful," she said. "I've never seen anything like it."

"It's just a comic book," Archie said. "Don't they have comics where you come from?"

Freya couldn't draw her eyes from the pages. "We have a

few books, but they are all about war. We have nothing like this. May I keep it?"

Archie shrugged. "Sure. My brother has lots of them. I don't think he'd miss that one."

He walked over to the closet. "I bet you can find something to wear in here too. I mean, if you don't mind men's clothes. It might even help hide your wings." Archie pulled the long, heavy velvet coat off the door. "Here, try this on."

Freya removed her sword, dagger, gauntlets, and breastplate. Standing only in her tunic, she pulled in her wings as tight as they would go and pulled on the coat.

It was several sizes too big for her and hung down to the floor. The arms draped down past her hands. But the fullness of the back fit perfectly over her folded wings.

"Here, put these on," Archie said, handing Freya a pair of winter gloves. When she had them on, he rolled up the sleeves on the coat. Then he lifted the collar so that it stood up around her neck. He stood back and considered his work. "Not bad, not bad at all. Turn around."

Freya turned slowly and raised her hands high over her head to lift the bottom hem of the coat. "Well? Can you see my feathers?"

Archie shook his head. "Nope. You just look like you've got a hunched back. No one would ever suspect wings under there."

Freya looked down at herself. "So, do I look Steampunk?"

"A Steampunk angel? Why not!"

Freya laughed. "No, Archie, a Steampunk *Valkyrie*."

Hours later Freya sat in Archie's kitchen as he made a simple meal of salad and macaroni and cheese. She watched him in fascination as he prepared the food with the confidence of one who had done it many times before.

"Where is your mother?"

Archie stopped cooking and sat at the table with her. "It's like this," he started awkwardly. "My mom drinks— a lot. When it's really bad, she disappears, sometimes for weeks. She doesn't call and won't tell me where she's going. But she always comes home. But sometimes that's even worse than when she's gone."

"How can you live like this?" Freya asked. "Don't you have other family?"

Archie shook his head. "I'm doing all right," he said. "I earn money by delivering newspapers in the mornings before school. And my mother gets assistance. I use her bank card to buy food and pay the bills. A social worker visits, but not very often, and she doesn't seem to care that my mom is a drunk."

Freya watched Archie as he rose and got back to work. His words were brave, but his inner feelings betrayed him. He was very lonely.

"I understand, Archie. I have seen the damage that drink can do."

Archie turned to her, inviting her to say more.

"Where I come from, we have a place called Valhalla. Human warriors spend all day fighting, and then drink all night. My father is there, somewhere. But I've never met him. After seeing what drink does to them, I don't think I want to."

"Your father is *human?*" Archie asked in shock.

Freya nodded. "Sort of."

"Wow," he said softly. "Aren't you curious to know who he is?"

"A bit. I'm sure one day I'll know. Right now it's just me, my sisters, and my mother."

Eating human food was something she'd never experienced before. Orus was beside her, picking at his own bowl full of the cheesy macaroni and getting it all over his smooth black feathers.

After her second helping, Freya sighed contentedly. She sat on a chair turned back to front to avoid sitting against her exposed wings.

"Does it hurt having them?" Archie asked as his eyes lingered on her semi-open wings. When she sat, the bottom flight feathers rested on the floor.

Freya shrugged. "Not really. Valkyries are born with wings, so I don't know what it's like not to have them."

"But you can't sleep on your back or sit properly."

"No, I guess not. But I can fly, and that makes up for it.

There's nothing better than flying really high and pulling in your wings tight and diving. Right before you hit the ground, you open your wings and soar."

Archie sighed. "It sounds awesome. I wish I had wings to fly away from here."

"Where would you go?"

"I don't know, just away." Archie pulled open his laptop computer. "So, uh . . ." He paused. "You can't tell me your name. I get that. But I have to call you something."

Freya considered.

"Don't do it, Freya," Orus warned. *"I know you really like him, but you can't give him your name."*

She looked at the raven. "I wasn't going to." Finally she nodded. "I know. You can call me Greta, just like in the comic."

"Greta?" Archie cried. "Are you serious? Did you look at her? She's . . . she's . . ."

"She's what?"

"Well, she's not you. You're beautiful—Gruesome Greta is definitely not."

Freya's cheeks blushed crimson. She had never thought of herself as even remotely pretty. All she was known for in Asgard was being a great flier and a good singer. It was her sisters who held all the beauty in the family. "You really think I'm beautiful?"

"Of course you are," Archie said. "So I won't call you Greta."

"But it is the name I have chosen."

"How about I call you Gee? It's the first letter of the name, but not actually Greta."

"Gee," Freya repeated. "All right, you can call me Gee."

Archie tilted his head to the side. "Okay, Gee, if you are a Valkyrie, let's see what the Internet says about you."

"*V-A-L-K-Y-R-I-E*," Archie spelled as he typed on his keyboard. Freya leaned forward to see what the laptop would do.

"Okay, here we go." Archie started to read aloud. "Norse mythology. A Valkyrie—from Old Norse *valkyrja*, 'chooser of the slain'—is one of a host of winged female figures who decide who dies and wins in battle. . . ." His voice tapered off as he continued to read in stunned silence.

After a few minutes his wide eyes settled on her. "If you're a Valkyrie, that means you're a reaper. You go to battlefields and collect the souls of the dying soldiers."

A mix of doubt and confusion poured from him. Freya nodded. "But we aren't myths and we don't really decide who lives or dies. We just reap the souls of the valiant dead and take them to that place I told you about, Valhalla."

Archie frowned. "Wait, earlier you said your father was human, right? And that he was at Valhalla?" When Freya nodded, he continued. "Does that mean he's dead?"

"Yes. All the humans in Asgard are dead. That's the only way they can go there."

"Wow," Archie said. "That's intense. So you still do that? I mean, like, reap, today in the modern age?"

"Yes, that is why I am here."

Freya explained about her life in Asgard and her First Day Ceremony. Finally she told Archie about her first reap, Tyrone, and how he'd begged her to help his family.

"Can Valkyries do that?" Archie asked. "Can they come here to help people?"

Orus was still on the table and cawed loudly. *"Go on, Freya; tell him how you are breaking the rules to be here and what will happen if Odin finds out."*

"What did he say?" Archie asked, watching the cawing raven.

Freya sighed. "He told me to tell you how I'm breaking the rules by being here. Valkyries aren't allowed in Midgard unless it's to reap warriors' souls. We aren't supposed to get involved with living humans."

"What's Midgard?" Archie asked.

"This is," Freya explained. "There are nine realms altogether. I come from the highest realm, Asgard. Here—Earth—also known as Midgard, is one of the lower middle realms. Then there are seven others."

"And what happens if you are caught out of Asgard?"

"Well . . ." She hesitated, not wanting to go into details. "Let's just say it won't be good."

Archie reached out a rubber-gloved hand and touched

Freya's hand. He leaned closer to her. "Then you've got to go back, right now!"

"*He is intelligent!*" Orus cried in shock. "*Listen to the boy, Freya. We must return to Asgard right now.*"

Freya shook her head. "Not until I've seen Tyrone's family and made sure they are safe." Her deep blue eyes settled on Archie. "And made sure those boys leave you alone."

"Don't worry about me," Archie said. "I'm used to being beaten up. I don't like it, but that's how it is. Let's just find out about that soldier's family, and then we can get you home."

"You will help me?" Freya asked in wonder. "Why would you do that?"

Archie shrugged. "Because that's what friends do."

7

ARCHIE USED HIS LAPTOP TO PULL UP A MAP AND LOCATE
the Johnsons' house.

"It's really not too far from here," he said. "I bet Tamika
goes to my school. I've probably walked past her in the
hall a hundred times." He looked up at Freya. "What do
you want to do first?"

They went back to Brian's bedroom, and Freya pulled
on her full armor. "I'm not sure. I guess just take a look and
see if we can discover what the trouble is, if there is any."

"Are you going to let them see you?"

"No. Not yet. I don't want to scare them. The
moment people see me, they think I'm either an angel
or a demon."

Archie grinned. "Well, can you blame them? Girls with

wings aren't exactly common around here. What else are they supposed to think?"

"I guess," Freya surrendered.

As she secured her sword into place, Archie pulled on his winter coat. "Do you want to wear my brother's coat? It's really cold out."

"I'm fine. We don't feel the cold, and Asgard is much colder than here."

The air was fresh and crisp as they walked through the darkened neighborhood. Most of the homes they passed had their lights on and gave off a warm, welcoming glow. From each home, Freya could feel the emotions of the people inside. She was wearing her helmet, so no one saw her.

"Okay, this is their street," Archie said. They looked down the road and saw that most of the houses were dark. Many front yards had SOLD signs in them, and other houses were boarded up. Two were burned down. The entire area was moving out.

They counted down the numbers until they reached one of the few lit houses, right beside a burned-out hulk.

"Number forty-five, here it is," Archie said.

Freya looked up at the house her soldier had lived in with his family. It was a simple, two-story structure. The house looked like it had seen better days and was in desperate need of repair.

"Tyrone lived here?" Orus said. *"No wonder he went off to war!"*

Freya swatted the bird. "Be nice."

From the street, Freya could hear the sound of a baby crying. "That's Tyrone's daughter, Uniik. He never got to hold her. She was born while he was on the battlefield, and he died before he could come home to see her."

"That's so sad," Archie said.

Freya removed her helmet and came into view. "It is. It was one of Tyrone's biggest regrets."

They stood in silence and listened to the healthy cries of the baby. Finally Freya opened her wings and pulled her helmet back on. "Stay here. I'll get in through the baby's window up there. Then I'll take a look around. I won't be long."

"Be careful," Archie warned.

Freya smiled at her new friend, knowing he wouldn't see it. "I will." She leaped into the air and flapped her wings. It was a short flight up to the window of the baby's room. Freya gripped the sill with one hand and shoved open the window with the other.

With little effort she hauled herself inside. Orus returned to her shoulder when she stood. Keeping her helmet on, Freya walked over to the crib.

Uniik was the first human baby she had ever seen up close. She was beautiful. Her skin was the same color as Tyrone's. She had a head of dark curly hair and a powerful cry, bursting with life. She had kicked off her covers.

"She's cute, but a little loud," Orus complained.

Still wearing her gauntlets, Freya drew the blanket back up and gently stroked the baby's forehead. "Shhhh, little one," she whispered softly. "It will be all right. Your father loved you very much."

Suddenly a light came on in the room as a woman's voice cried, "No, please, you can't take her!"

Startled, Freya's wings flashed open as she turned and saw an old woman in the doorway. Her dark face bore the wrinkles of a long life, and her body was wasted by age and illness. "Take me if you must, but leave my baby girl alone."

It took a moment for Freya to realize that she was still wearing her helmet. "You can see me?"

The old woman moved stiffly and knelt before Freya. "Please," she begged. "She has her whole life ahead of her. If you must take someone, take me. I am old and ready to go."

"This is not good," Orus said. *"If she can see you, she's dying."*

Freya removed her helmet. "I'm not here to take anyone. I knew Uniik's father and promised I would check on her. Please don't be afraid of me."

Freya watched as the old woman stood. Freya could feel the pain coming from her. Pain, and something else; something hovering very near. It was a feeling of impending death.

The old woman squinted up at her. "You're just a child!"

"I'm old enough," Freya said. "I was with Tyrone when he died."

The old woman grasped her chest and staggered back. "My Tyrone? You were the one who took my son?"

Freya reached into her pouch and pulled out Tyrone's cell phone. "Your son gave me this. He showed me his daughters and begged me to protect them. He wanted to hold his new baby and tell his wife how much he loved her." Freya paused for a moment. "But it was his time. I had no choice. He was wounded and dying. All I did was end his suffering."

The old woman looked at the cell phone. Tears rose in her eyes and she shook her head. "Victoria was killed in a hit-and-run accident almost six months ago, not long after Tyrone died. They never caught the driver."

"She's dead?" Freya felt her anger rise as she learned of yet more violence. "Is that all this world is? Violence and war? People hurting each other for no reason?"

"It may seem that way at times," the old woman said. "But there's goodness as well."

"Where?" Freya demanded. "I have been to the battle-fields of war and witnessed the horrors that people do. I came here to help a soldier's family, but all I find is pain and loss. Boys are beating up boys for no reason, and Tyrone's wife has been killed. It is all so ugly."

She crossed the room, balling her hands into fists. "My sister tried to tell me people had changed. That soldiers cared more than they used to and I was wrong to judge them so harshly." She turned quickly on the old woman. "But I am not wrong. All there is here is hatred and fighting! Midgard is by far the ugliest of the realms!"

"*I told you,*" Orus whispered into her ear. "*There is no beauty in Midgard. Asgard is where you'll find it.*"

The old woman reached out for Freya's gloved hands. "Don't judge us all so harshly. Believe me, child, our world does have more. Look at my granddaughter. . . ." The old woman led Freya back to the crib. She stroked the baby's head with a trembling hand. "So filled with life and so innocent. She'll do no harm in this world. And Tamika wants to be a doctor. She'll help people."

She turned pleading eyes to Freya. "All you've seen are the horrors. Stay awhile. Soon you'll learn there is beauty, too."

Freya shook her head. "I wish I could believe that, but I find it impossible. Perhaps there are some individuals who are good. But as a whole . . ."

"As a whole, we must still find a way to live together."

"Yes," Freya agreed. She gazed down on the baby. Uniik had stopped crying and was reaching up to her. Freya let the baby grasp her gloved finger and smiled as she giggled and tried to pull it to her mouth. "What will happen to Uniik and Tamika when you die?"

"You know I'm dying?"

Freya nodded. "You could see me while I was wearing my helmet. Only the dead or dying can. And I can feel your pain. You're unwell."

"Cancer," the old woman sighed. "Just been diagnosed. But I can't afford the treatment, and the doctors can't tell me how long I've got. I know Tamika suspects something, but I've told her it's not serious. I've been using this time to try to figure out how to help my girls. But we don't have any family left."

Freya turned to the window and saw Archie down on the street. He was alone in this world too. This old woman insisted there was goodness, but from the few living people Freya had met so far, she held little hope.

"I'm Alma," the old woman finally said.

"You may call me Greta."

"Greta, I was about to make myself some cocoa. It helps me sleep. Why don't you come down with me? We can talk for a while. Let me tell you about the good of this world."

Freya glanced out the window again. "I have someone with me. It's very cold out and he is shivering. May he come in?"

"Of course," Alma said. "Is he an angel too?"

"No, he's just a boy." Before leaving the room, Freya looked back down on Uniik. The baby had settled back to sleep. "This is the closest I've ever been to a living human baby. I can see traces of her father's face. Tyrone would have been proud."

Alma smiled at the baby. "Just like her grandma is proud."

* * *

Settling in the small kitchen, Archie and Freya joined Alma at the table. Archie was still shivering as he grasped his steaming cup of cocoa. Freya and Orus were also enjoying homemade chocolate-chip cookies.

"If someone had ever told me I'd have an angel sitting right here at my kitchen table drinking cocoa with me," Alma said, "I'd have said they were crazy."

Freya and Archie exchanged glances but said nothing. "Tell me what happened to Tyrone's wife," Freya asked.

The old woman sighed and shook her head. "There's nothing to tell. Victoria was walking home from work when a car jumped the curb and hit her. We're sure we know who it was, but the police said there was no evidence. It's been six months and still no justice."

Archie frowned in confusion. "You said you reaped Tyrone a few days ago."

Freya nodded. "I did. But time moves differently between Asgard and here. A day there can be weeks here." She focused on the old woman. "If you know who killed Victoria, there should be no problem."

Tears rimmed the old woman's eyes. "It is not as simple as that. We need proof, but we have none. So those people get away with murder."

"Before I reaped him, Tyrone said his family was in trouble, but he didn't know what it was. Even after I delivered him to Valhalla, it was all he talked about. But his wife was still alive then. I don't understand."

Alma nodded. "Victoria didn't want to worry him, but it was getting bad."

"What is it?" Archie asked. "Maybe we can help."

"Not even an angel can help us," Alma said sadly. "Developers want this house and will stop at nothing to take it."

"I don't understand," Freya said. "What are developers?"

"John Roberts Developments," Alma said. "They're a company that has been buying up most of the houses on this street and the street behind us. They want to knock everything down so they can build condominiums for Chicago commuters. But me and several others won't sell because they're offering less than the value of our homes. When we refused, they became violent. I think they killed Victoria, and just last week an arsonist burned down our neighbor's house."

"So we've seen," Archie said.

"But if they are using violence," Freya said, "wouldn't it be better to leave?"

"If we let men like that drive us away, we're surrendering to evil. I will fight them. They won't move my grandbabies from their rightful home. It's all the girls have."

"Even if it means you may be hurt?"

The old woman nodded. Fiery determination rose in her eyes. "Even if it means that." She paused, and the determination in her eyes faded. "It's Tamika I worry about. She walks to school. I'm afraid that they might go after her. I've asked for help, but the police won't give it."

"I could walk with her," Archie volunteered. "You don't live too far from me. I could come here right after my paper route."

"Would you do that?" Alma asked. "I would pay you."

Archie shook his head. "I don't want your money. Just to help, if I can."

Freya looked at him in utter disbelief. Archie was being threatened by bullies, and yet he was offering to help a stranger. This offer only confused her further.

"And me," Freya finally added. "I will go to school with you both."

"*What!*" Orus cried. "*Freya, this is getting ridiculous! YOU CANNOT STAY HERE!*"

Freya looked at the raven on the table. "I promised Tyrone, and I intend to keep my promise." She looked up at Archie and Alma. "I am going to stay here until the danger has passed. But I need your help."

"What can we do?" Alma asked. "Tell me. I'll do anything."

Freya rose and opened her large black wings. "Teach me how to look like a human."

8

IT WAS LATE AT NIGHT, AND FREYA WAS STILL AWAKE.
Archie had gone to bed hours before. In Asgard, Freya did
sleep. But here she felt no need. Instead she used the time to
explore Brian's closet.

She pulled on his leather trousers and a belt to keep them
secured. Then she tried his heavy black boots. They were too
big, but when Freya stuffed the ends with tissue, they fit fine.
Finally she tried on some of his black shirts. She cut slits in
the back so they fell around her large, bulky wings.

"*Are you trying to look like a boy?*" Orus complained. He
was seated on the bed, pecking at the shiny buttons on a
discarded shirt.

"No, I'm trying to look human," Freya explained. "And
you really aren't helping."

"*Why should I help you destroy yourself?*" the raven said. "*The moment Odin sees us, he'll have our wings.*"

"He's not going to see us. We won't be here that long."

"*We've already been here too long!*" the bird complained. "*Heimdall is bound to realize what happened. He'll tell Odin or Thor, and then they'll send out a Dark Searcher for us. Have you forgotten what happened on the bridge with the elves?*"

"No, I haven't, but don't you think this is exciting? I'm going to a human school, filled with human kids my own age." She held a frilly black shirt up against herself and admired it in the mirror.

"*There are no humans your age,*" Orus said. "*You are over six hundred of their years old.*"

"All right," she surrendered. "But at least I *look* their age."

"*And act it,*" Orus muttered.

Freya threw the shirt over the raven as she continued her search. She wasn't going to let Orus ruin the excitement she felt at the new adventure. Alma had promised to help her register with the school, so she wouldn't have any problems attending, and Archie had said they'd try to get her in the same classes as him. It was all arranged.

After selecting a range of clothing, Freya and Orus spent the rest of the night settled in front of the television. By the time Archie rose the next morning, he found them huddled together on the sofa, watching a horror movie.

"I thought I'd dreamed you," Archie said breathlessly. "But I didn't. You're really here and you did beat up JP to save me."

"That was me," Freya agreed. She reached for the remote and turned off the television.

"*Hey, I was watching that!*" Orus complained. The raven hopped over to the remote and clicked the television back on again.

Freya stood, yawned, and gave a long stretch that had her wings touching the walls of the room. "If I am going to try to look human, we need to go back to Alma's. She promised to make me some clothes that will help hide my wings. Oh, and I need your help with this." She tossed a box to him. "I found this in your brother's drawer and want to try it."

"Hair dye?" Archie said. "You want to dye your hair crimson red?"

Freya nodded.

"Why? Your hair's beautiful. I know some girls who would kill to have it."

"Every Valkyrie in Asgard has the same long, flaxen hair. Since I'm the only one with black feathers, I want my hair to be different too. Will you help me?"

He shrugged. "Sure. I think you're crazy for wanting to change it, but if that's what you really want, that's what you'll get."

* * *

After they delivered newspapers and had a quick break-fast, Freya settled in a kitchen chair, wearing only her light tunic and a bath towel wrapped around her shoulders and upper wings.

Archie pulled on the heavy kitchen rubber gloves over the latex gloves that came with the hair dye. He was wearing a thick turtleneck and long sleeves that he tucked into the gloves. "You're sure you want me to do this?" He was holding scissors and a comb. "Once I start, I can't stop."

Freya looked up at him. "Are you sure you're completely covered and won't touch my skin?"

Archie nodded. "The only skin that's showing is my face."

"Then go ahead," Freya said confidently. "Start cutting."

From his place on the back of a chair Orus moaned, *"Your mother is going to kill you! Then she'll kill me for not stop-ping you!"*

"What did he say?" Archie asked.

"He wished you luck."

"Thanks, Orus," Archie said as he stroked the raven.

Orus huffed at Freya. *"I never realized you were such a liar."*

Several hours later Freya stood before the bathroom mir-ror. Her hair had been cut much shorter and was falling in flowing waves, and it was now bright crimson.

"Well?" Archie asked nervously.

"It's magic!" Freya said, still hardly recognizing herself in the mirror. "I wish my sister could see this."

"*I don't,*" Orus complained. "*She's going to be just as furious as your mother.*"

They arranged to go to Alma's for lunch to meet Tamika and set up times to escort her to school. Pulling on the long velvet coat over the leather trousers and black frilly shirt, Freya looked down at herself. "You sure I look human enough in this?"

Archie nodded. "You're setting a fashion trend with your hair and that coat. Soon all the girls at school will dress the same, right down to the raven on their shoulders."

Walking down the quiet street toward the Johnsons' house in full daylight, they could see just how empty and abandoned most of the homes were. The two that had been burned to the ground had also been vandalized and covered in graffiti.

"They're doing a good job of clearing the street," Archie said.

Freya nodded. "But they won't get Tyrone's house. Not as long as I am here."

"*Which won't be long,*" Orus reminded her. "*I hope you can help them quickly.*"

This time Freya told Archie what the raven had said. "I agree with him. I don't want you getting into trouble with

Odin. I've read that he's got a big temper and gives out harsh punishments," Archie said.

"He does," Freya agreed. "But he's not as bad as Thor. When Thor is angry, he can rattle mountains!"

Archie's eyes went wide. "You know the real Thor? Does he actually carry a huge hammer?"

Freya nodded. "It's called Mjölnir. He's very protective of it. Loki's taken it from him a couple of times, but Thor always gets it back."

"Loki's real too!" Archie exclaimed. "Is he really as bad as they say he is?"

"*Yes!*" Orus cawed.

"He can be," Freya admitted. "But he helped us get here, so he's not all bad."

Archie chuckled. "Wow, that's so cool. I'd love to see Asgard and meet Thor. You know that Gruesome Greta comic? Well, there are lots about Thor and his hammer. Do you think you could take me there when this is over?"

Freya shook her head. "Valhalla is only for warriors who die valiantly in battle. You're alive, so you can't go."

"That sucks," Archie said.

Freya looked at him and smiled. "Yes, it does."

When they arrived at the house, Archie knocked on the front door. A pretty, young, dark-skinned girl answered. She was shorter than Freya, with her hair styled in long cornrows with multicolored beads at the ends. Freya saw traces of

Tyrone in her face—and she had the same cleft in her chin as her father. It was Tamika.

"What do you want?" Tamika demanded. Her eyes lingered on Freya and then moved to Orus.

Archie spoke first. "Hi, Tamika. We're friends of your grandmother. She invited us for lunch."

Tamika's eyes were still on Orus. "I don't like birds. He stays outside."

The raven cawed in protest.

"Orus goes where I go," Freya said firmly. Tamika was nothing like she'd expected—not the same smiling girl she'd seen in the photographs. "If he is not welcome, I will not stay."

"Fine. Go, then. I didn't invite you."

Freya turned to leave. But before she reached the porch steps, Archie caught her sleeve. "Gee, calm down. Remember why you're here. I'm sure Tamika didn't mean it."

"Yes, I did!" Tamika replied. "Birds are filthy, and blackbirds are evil. They don't belong indoors."

Freya turned around in a fury. "Orus is not filthy! And he's a raven, not a blackbird, and he's not evil. If he's not welcome here, neither am I."

"Good!" Orus cawed. "Now that that's settled, we can go back to Asgard!"

"Of course he's welcome!" Alma called as she arrived on the porch. "You are all welcome here." Her eyes went wide when she saw the changes in Freya. "Why, my sweet angel, what on earth have you done to yourself?"

Freya looked down, still furious at Tamika's comments. "I have made a few changes before I go to school."

"But last night you said you wanted to blend in. This is not blending. And your beautiful long blond hair, what have you done to it?"

"Archie cut it for me," Freya said. "I like it."

"It looks stupid," Tamika remarked unkindly.

Freya took a threatening step forward. "What are you saying?"

"*Freya, don't,*" Orus cawed. "*She is just a grieving child. Think of her dead parents and leave her be.*"

"Tamika!" Alma cried. "Your mama raised you better than that! You apologize to our guests right now."

"I will not!" Tamika shouted. "And I don't need anyone to take me to school!" She turned and ran from the door. She stomped up the stairs, and they heard her slam her bedroom door.

Freya had felt the mixed emotions pour from the girl. There was grief at the loss of both her parents mixed with deep-seated anger and fear. Her world had been shattered, and she still hadn't dealt with all the changes.

"Angel, I am so sorry," Alma said as she invited them in. "Please forgive her. She's hurting."

Freya and Archie entered the house and were greeted

by the welcoming aroma of homemade soup and baking bread.

"I understand. She's angry at the loss of her parents," Freya said. "And she's frightened about the developers taking her home."

"Maybe I should speak to her. Can I go up?" Archie asked.

"Perhaps I should go," Freya volunteered.

"No!" Archie cried.

Freya frowned. "Why not? You know I'd never hurt her."

"It's not that," Archie said quickly. "You are still getting used to things here on Earth. What if she says something that you misunderstand, Greta, or she sees your wings? I don't think she could handle that yet. Just let me go, Gee."

Freya huffed indignantly. "I wouldn't tell her what I am."

Alma stepped forward. "Let Archie go. It will give me time to take your measurements. Look at you; you can't go around dressed as a boy. You need some better clothes."

"I like these," Freya insisted.

"But, child, you can't wear the same clothes all the time. You'll need more. Let me make you some skirts and maybe something to help hide your wings."

"My wings are fine," Freya shot back angrily.

Fear rose on the old woman's face. "I'm sorry; I didn't mean to be rude."

Archie elbowed her in the side. "Gee, calm down. Be nice."

Freya inhaled deeply and let it out slowly. This wasn't

going as she had planned. "No, I'm sorry, Alma. I just didn't expect Tamika to be so angry. Her father told me about her, and I was looking forward to meeting her."

"She's in pain," the old woman said. "Give her time to get to know you. You'll see, she's a sweet child with a kind heart."

Freya nodded and looked to Archie. "Go talk to her."

Freya followed Alma into her sewing room. There were several dress forms with clothing in the process of being finished. An old sewing machine was set up in the corner, and there were racks of fabric against one wall.

Alma closed and locked the door. "Take off your coat."

Freya did as she was told and removed the heavy velvet coat. She stretched out her wings and settled them comfortably on her back.

"The first thing I've got to make for you is a slipcover to go over those wings. Even with the coat, when you walk, you can see the feathers right between your legs. That's why I suggested you wear skirts."

"*She's right,*" Orus cawed from his place on the back of the sewing chair. "*I can see your wings from here.*"

Freya frowned. "I won't bind my wings. They must remain free."

"I'm not talking about binding them," Alma corrected as she reached for a tape measure, "just covering them up a bit better."

When Alma came near, Freya held up her hands. "Wait.

You mustn't touch me with your bare hands."

"That's right," Alma said, shaking her head. "Of course, you told me last night." She crossed to her cutting table and retrieved a pair of rubber kitchen gloves. "I brought these in here earlier. Will they be all right?"

Freya nodded. "Just be aware of your face and any exposed skin. I should hate for there to be an accident."

"*And it would be impossible to explain to Odin,*" Orus added.

The old woman pulled on the gloves. "Fine, then. Let's get started."

After they finished, they moved into the kitchen. Freya watched Alma feed Uniik. She was enchanted by the baby and wanted desperately to hold her.

"She is so full of life."

The old woman's eyes were sparkling with pride. "Just like her papa. I wish he could have seen how beautiful she is."

"He wanted that too. As he lay dying, his thoughts were only of his girls, as he called them."

Alma's eyes fogged and she sniffed. "I just hope I live long enough to see the girls safe. I know I couldn't rest if anything happened to them."

"Nothing's going to happen, Grandma." Tamika entered the kitchen, followed by Archie. "They're not going to take our home away from us."

She lifted her sister from her grandmother's arms and

started to burp the baby. Tamika's face brightened as Uniik giggled in her arms.

Alma's eyes lingered on Freya before replying to Tamika. "Of course, child, but you know your old grandma won't live forever."

"Sure you will," Tamika said. She looked at Freya while gently bouncing the baby in her arms. "I'm sorry about earlier. Take off your coat—you can stay."

Freya rose and stepped closer. With her gloved hand she stroked the baby's head. "Thank you, but I prefer to keep it on."

"I told Tamika about your problem," Archie said. "She's agreed we can all walk to school together."

"My problem?"

A lot of emotion came from Archie. He was very anxious. Obviously he'd told Tamika something and was frightened to be caught in the lie.

"Yes, Gee," he said cautiously. "I hope you don't mind, but I told her what happened to your family in Denmark and how you are staying at my house to hide from the men who are searching for you?"

"Oh, *that* problem," Freya agreed. Her eyes caught hold of Alma, and the old woman was nodding. "Yes, well, Tamika, I hope you can help me."

"Sure. They won't hear about you from me."

"Thank you."

Alma put her arm around Tamika. "And I'll be going with you to school tomorrow to register Greta. I'll tell them she's my brother's niece and that she's come to spend some time with me and you. There is no need to tell them the real problem."

Archie added, "We'll also need a note from you excusing Greta from PE. With her back problem, she can't do it. And maybe one that explains her skin problem so she needs to wear her coat and gloves all the time."

"Of course," Alma agreed.

"You're going to love our school," Tamika said.

Freya smiled. "I'm sure I will."

9

THAT NIGHT FREYA COULDN'T SETTLE DOWN. IT WAS LONG past midnight, and she still didn't feel the need for sleep. Archie had already gone to bed, and there was nothing left to do.

"*What are you doing?*" Orus asked as she pulled on her armor and gauntlets. Then she attached the sword to her side and walked to the back door.

"I haven't stretched my wings in ages," she said. "Let's go for a short flight."

"*Now? But it's raining out. We'll get soaked. Stay here with me. We can watch movies all night. I'll even let you choose.*"

Freya sighed. "Orus, a little rain never hurt anyone."

"*How do you know? This is Midgard rain, not Asgard. Maybe it has something in it that will damage our feathers.*"

Freya burst out laughing. "Nice try. Now come on. You need exercise too."

Orus ruffled his feathers in disappointment. *"What about your helmet?"*

"Not tonight. I want to see the city with my own eyes, not distorted by the helmet's powers."

Rain was coming down in heavy sheets as they entered the backyard. Opening her wings, Freya took a few long strides and leaped into the air. With one beat of her powerful wings, she climbed higher in the sky.

"Where do you want to go?" Orus called.

Freya caught sight of Chicago's glowing skyline in the distance. "That way," she said, and pointed. "Let's go see the city."

With the rain soon forgotten, they played together in the sky. Freya flew circles around Orus and won every race. By the time they reached the large city, the two were laughing from the sheer delight of flying.

Without her helmet's protection, Freya stayed up high. But her curiosity tugged at her and she couldn't resist the temptation to land on the flat roof of a building. It offered an amazing view of the city.

"Look at all the lights! It's so beautiful here at night, isn't it?" She walked around, wide-eyed, taking in all the sights and staring down at the world below.

But within minutes of her landing, the sound of gunshots

shattered the city's silence. Freya ran to the other side of the roof and peered down. "I think it came from that direction!"

"*Oh no,*" Orus warned. "*I know what you're thinking. Don't get involved!*"

"But someone may be hurt. We've been to enough battlefields. You know what guns can do." Spreading her wings, Freya leaped off the roof and flew in the direction of the noise. "Come on," she called. "Let's just see what it is."

"*I'm going to regret this. I just know it!*" Orus cawed as he chased her.

Freya flew toward the sound of the gunshots—away from the city center and into an area where the buildings looked more run-down. She opened her senses and felt people on the neighboring streets running away from the trouble.

Just ahead she felt heavy waves of terror rising to meet her. As she flew closer, Freya crested a building and gazed down to the street below. A man and a woman were cowering in the doorway of a burned-out building. They were cornered by five men who were threatening them with guns. The men's intentions were as clear as they were bad.

Freya landed on the closest roof and drew her sword.

"*Freya, you can't!*" Orus warned. "*This is their world, not ours. We can't get involved, even if we wanted to.*"

"But they are going to kill them. Look . . ." She pointed with her sword tip as two Angels of Death landed unseen on the street behind them. Their heads and wings were held low, and a great sadness was on their faces at the tragedy about to unfold.

"This is their territory, not ours. They will not be happy if we interfere."

"But it's wrong."

"Yes, it is, but we don't belong here. If you interfere, Odin may find out and you won't be able to help Tyrone's family."

"Orus, how can I help one family, but let another be destroyed when we have the power to save both? Is that what you want? To ignore their plight and let them be killed when you know we could stop it?"

Orus made a sound like a sigh. *"No. Go on, then . . ."*

Freya leaped off the roof and glided down to the street several feet from the attack.

Coming up behind the Angels of Death, she touched the arm of the older one. "I'm sorry, but you've wasted a trip. There will be no death here tonight. You may return to your realm."

The angel's eyes went wide at the sight of her. "Valkyrie?" he said. "This is not a battlefield. You have no jurisdiction here. What will happen must happen. You are forbidden to intervene."

Freya held up her sword. "Yes, well, I've never been very good at following the rules. I declare that these people will live."

Freya charged past the shocked angels toward the group of attackers. "Stop now or face my wrath!"

"What the . . . ," one of the attackers called as he turned and saw Freya storming forward. He wiped rain from his eyes in disbelief.

With her sword held high, Freya shielded the two innocent victims with her body. She turned to face their attackers. "I will give you one warning and one only. Drop your weapons and leave now, or you will feel my sword."

In the dimly lit street with the heavy rain pouring down, Freya was confident they couldn't see her clearly. But even if the attackers couldn't, it was certain that the victims cowering behind her could.

She heard their sharp intakes of breath and felt their fear changing. They were now more frightened for her than for themselves. Freya turned quickly to them. "Say nothing—and, for your lives, don't touch me!"

"Are you suicidal or just plain stupid?" one of the attackers said as he pointed his gun at her.

"Neither," Freya answered calmly. "But I am sick of you humans hurting each other for no other reason than personal gain. These people have done nothing wrong, and yet you intend to kill them to steal their possessions."

"*Us humans?*" the leader called as he laughed and nudged his friends. "And what does that make you, then?"

Freya could clearly feel his thoughts. He was preparing to use his weapon against her. "What does that make me?" she repeated as her temper flared. "Not human!"

Freya's wings flashed open, and she charged the men. Stealing a quick look back at the two people, she cried, "Get down and stay down!"

Loud, sharp sounds of gunfire filled the air as the attackers opened fire on her. Freya heard pinging as the bullets struck her breastplate and fell harmlessly to the ground.

The rules of Asgard said that if she, a Valkyrie, touched a human with her bare skin, or wings, they would be reaped by her and have to go to Valhalla. But she wasn't too sure what would happen if she killed someone with her sword.

Not wanting to risk it, Freya used all her skills and wielded her sword with precision to avoid making her cuts lethal. Instead she sliced guns out of hands and left the attackers on the wet ground, moaning and crying as they clutched their wounds.

When the leader of the group finally went down, Freya placed her black leather boot on his chest and pointed the tip of her sword at his throat.

"Your reign of terror in this neighborhood ends now. If I learn of you or your men attacking anyone ever again, I will not be so generous and spare your lives."

"W-what are you?" the man sputtered as his eyes lingered on her extended wings. "I shot you. I know I did."

"Your weapons are useless against me. Remember my warning. Bring peace to these streets or you will face me again. There will be no second chances."

Freya turned and left the man. She approached the two

victims. "Come," she commanded as she walked further down the street.

Too frightened to disobey, the couple dashed past the men on the ground and followed Freya along the street.

"Thank you, thank you," cried the man. "I don't know who or what you are, but you saved our lives."

They were only young—not very much older than her, by Midgard standards. He was handsome with pale eyes and smooth skin, apart from a spread of stubble around his chin. She was pretty and had an air of gentleness. She reminded Freya of a delicate little fawn in the woods. Freya could also feel that they cared deeply for each other.

In that moment Freya realized she'd never felt more alive. She shared in their pure joy of existence. They all knew something amazing had just happened—even if the couple didn't fully understand that she, a Valkyrie and reaper of souls, had saved lives and not taken them.

The Angels of Death were still on the street and drew near. The older-looking angel spoke in a grave tone. "Azrael will hear of this, Valkyrie. He will not be pleased at your intervention. You have broken the rules. These streets are ours."

"Tell Azrael if you must," Freya said softly. "But I meant no disrespect. I just couldn't let this happen when it's within my power to stop it."

The angel shook his head. "You have changed their

destinies tonight. They were meant to come with us. Tell them they have new lives and to make the best of them. We will be watching. If they do evil in their new lives, or if their future children do harm, the judgment will be on you."

"I understand," Freya said, bowing her head.

The two angels bowed, opened their white wings, and took to the sky.

The man turned quickly and looked behind him. When he returned to Freya, his eyes were wide. "What just happened? Who were you talking to? It felt like someone was standing right behind us."

Freya nodded. "They were Angels of Death, here to take you with them. You are safe now. They have gone."

The young woman cried out, and her shaking hands went to her mouth. The man put his arm around her for comfort. "We—we weren't supposed to be here," he started. "It's our first visit to Chicago and we got lost. Then we ran out of gas and those men attacked us. If you hadn't come . . ."

"They would have killed you," Freya said.

In the distance the sound of sirens filled the air. They were getting closer. "You saved us, and we'll never be able to thank you enough."

"You're welcome."

He was relaxing more in her presence and tilted his head to the side. "What are you?" His wide eyes settled on her wings. "Those are real, aren't they?"

Freya nodded.

"Can you fly with them?"

"There'd be no point to having them if I couldn't."

He chuckled. "I guess not."

At that moment Orus returned to her shoulder. *"Freya, we've got to go."*

Freya nodded. To the couple she said, "I have intervened on your behalf and changed your destinies—even though it broke the rules. The angels wanted me to tell you that from this moment forward, you have new lives. You must take this opportunity to do good work in this world. Teach your children the same. Remember, you should not have survived beyond tonight. If you or your children do harm, I will also be punished for it. Please don't make me regret my actions."

"I swear," the man promised. "We won't disappoint you."

Finally the woman beside him nodded and spoke. "You have our word, Angel. Thank you, thank you for our lives."

The sounds of sirens drew closer. At the far end of the street, police cars with their flashing lights raced forward.

"You'd better go," said the man as he split his attention between Freya and the approaching police cars. "You saved our lives, and we can never repay that debt. But we can try to protect you. We won't tell them what really happened here. Go now, before they see you."

Freya was reluctant to leave. But the police cars with their flashing lights and noisy sirens were not something she wanted to meet.

"Live well and live long," she said as she stepped back. Opening her wings, Freya jumped into the air and started to fly. She landed on a rooftop and peered over the side. The couple was staring up at the spot where she'd vanished.

"*It's time to go,*" Orus said.

Freya put her sword back in its sheath. When she turned to fly again, she was startled to find Loki standing on the roof directly behind her.

"My, my, my, Freya. I didn't think you cared for humans."

Her eyes flashed back to the couple on the street, and then to Loki again. "I don't, not really. But that wasn't a fair fight. How did you find us?"

"You're not that difficult to track. A child could have done it. . . ." Loki's penetrating eyes bored into her. "Or even a Dark Searcher." He walked up to the edge of the building and peered over. Police cars pulled up, and officers were getting out. Some went to the wounded gang on the street and others to the couple. Soon more vehicles arrived.

"Since I risked my life to get you over Bifröst, I wanted to see what you were up to. Finding you playing superhero isn't what I expected."

"Super-what?"

"Never mind," he said casually. "So, when can we expect

you back in Asgard? Or have you taken a liking to Midgard and plan to stay?"

"*We're coming back soon,*" Orus cawed. "*So there is no need for you to tell Odin or Thor.*"

Loki tried to look shocked, but it wasn't working. "As if I would! Do you forget? I was the one that got you over the bridge. It's my neck on the line too. Which is why I am not pleased you are out here risking capture. What about the soldier's family you were so anxious to help. Have you forgotten them?"

Freya couldn't get a sense of him. How was that possible? She couldn't even feel him standing before her! "We're working on that. And actually, if you will excuse us, we've got to get back. I just came out to stretch my wings."

Loki chuckled. "Yes, of course you did. But tell me, do you always stretch your wings in your armor and weapons? I hardly think so." A sly smile came to his lips. "Certainly, you must go before those police down there see you. So fly away, little Valkyrie, fly, fly, fly . . . but don't wait too long to come home. You never know who will find out."

Freya didn't like his tone and took off before he could say more. She flapped her wings and climbed higher into the dark, rainy sky, leaving Loki on the rooftop. His hysterical laughter followed her as she made her way back to Archie's house.

* * *

They arrived back at the house just before sunrise. Freya was too upset to watch early-morning television with Orus. She retired to her room and started to pace.

Saving those people had felt wonderful, as though she had accomplished something with her life. But at the highest point, Loki had been there to ruin it. Why had he followed her to Chicago? What was he planning? Was he going to tell Odin what she'd done? Suddenly, being in Midgard didn't seem like such a good idea. She had made a deal with Loki, but what would it cost her in the end?

She walked over to the window and peered out at the rainy world. As the sky lightened, it was the dawn of her first day at a human school. But what would the day bring if Loki went back to Asgard and told?

Leaning her head against the glass, Freya moaned softly. "What have I done?"

10

JUST BEFORE DAWN MAYA RETURNED FROM DANCING AT
Valhalla and retired to the room she shared with Freya. As
she changed for bed, she noticed Freya wasn't there.

"Have you seen Freya and Orus?" she asked her raven as
she settled him on his perch.

"Not since earlier," Grul said. *"I saw them talking to Loki."*

"Loki? Why would they talk to him?" Maya crossed the
room and felt her sister's bed. "It's cold. She hasn't been here."

*"You know Freya. She's probably gone for another long flight.
Orus is always putting her up to these things and leading her
astray. I'm sure they'll be back soon."*

"I hope so," Maya agreed. "We're on the list for the reaping later today. I don't want her to be late."

Maya started her nightly routine of combing out her

beautiful, long flaxen hair and grooming her wings. She put fragrant oils on her feathers and preened them until they shone. As she climbed into bed, she looked over at her sister's empty place. "Don't be too late, Freya," she muttered softly. "You know how angry Mother gets."

But even as Maya lay her head down, the thought of Freya nagged at her. She hadn't been to bed. Grul had said he'd seen her and Orus speaking with Loki earlier. But why would Freya be talking to Thor's brother?

Maya tried to force herself to sleep. But she couldn't. Freya was a constant worry to her. All her life her youngest sister had been different—somehow lost and unable to find her way. Something was missing in her life, but what that was remained a mystery.

Finally giving up, Maya rose and got dressed.

"*What's happening?*" Grul asked as he was roused on his perch.

"I'm going to find Freya."

"*Why? She's probably just out flying again, like she did on the eve of her First Day Ceremony.*"

"No, this is different." Maya reached for her armor and pulled it on. "Last time, I could feel her and knew where she went. I can't feel anything now. It's like she's not here anymore."

"*Freya wouldn't go anywhere,*" insisted the raven. "*Orus may be incompetent and ill tempered, but he would never let her get into trouble.*"

Maya shook her head. "I know my sister, Grul. Something is very wrong. Freya has always been restless, but it's been worse since she reaped that soldier. She goes off flying alone, and I've heard that she's been seen with Loki. Something is up, and I need to know what it is. I won't be able to sleep until I know she's safe."

Grul made an impatient huffing sound but flew onto Maya's shoulder. "Why are you wearing your armor? You don't need it here."

Maya reached for her winged helmet. "Because I have the strange feeling that Freya isn't here."

"Do you mean, not in this house?"

Maya shook her head as she leaped out the window and spread her wings. "No, I mean in Asgard."

11

UNABLE TO REST, FREYA WANDERED INTO THE LIVING
room and found Orus on the sofa watching television. Par-
tially opening her wings, Freya slumped down beside him
and put her feet up on the coffee table.

They were still there when Archie got up. Sleepy-eyed,
he came into the room, yawning. "Don't you two ever sleep?"

"I don't get tired here," Freya said as she stood up. "But I
do get hungry. How about some breakfast?"

After a quick meal Freya dressed for her first day at school.
As well as a slipcover for her wings, Alma had made her a
lovely, long skirt and had promised to make more. She'd also
given Freya elbow-high, soft, burgundy-colored leather gloves
so she didn't have to wear Archie's winter pair. Then Freya
pulled on one of Brian's altered frilly tops over her breastplate.

"*You're wearing your armor?*" Orus asked. "*What kind of school do you think this is? Or are you expecting another visitor from Asgard?*"

Freya shook her head. "No. Hopefully we've seen the last of Loki. Do you remember what the bullies said? They were going to get Archie today. I want to make sure nothing happens to him."

Orus hopped across the bed and picked at a feather poking out of the duvet. "*You really like him, don't you?*"

Freya paused. "He's all right, for a human."

Orus cawed in laughter. "*What a liar. You really like him! I can see it.*"

"You don't know what you are talking about."

A knock at the door cut off further conversation, and Freya was grateful for the interruption. "Come in."

Archie entered. "Are you ready? I've got the newspapers folded and set to go."

Freya nodded. "All set."

Freya rode on the back of Archie's bike as they delivered the newspapers in record time. When they finished, they headed over to the Johnsons' house. Alma and Tamika were waiting for them on the front porch.

"You look lovely," Alma said as she looked at Freya. "Skirts suit you much better than those leather trousers. So, are you ready for your first day at school?"

Freya nodded. "I'm a bit nervous."

Alma's eyebrows shot up. "*You*, nervous?" she cried. "Sweet child, there's not a thing to be nervous about. Just follow Archie's and Tamika's lead, and you'll do fine."

Getting Freya registered was easier than everyone had expected. With Alma's talent for telling sad tales about the loss of Greta's family in Denmark and her long list of illnesses, she had the office staff looking at Freya with pity.

"All right, Greta," the secretary said. "I think it will be best to keep you with Archie until your Danish paperwork catches up with you and we see where you should be."

When registration finished, they walked Alma to the front door. "Will you be okay getting home, Grandma?" Tamika asked.

"'Course I will. God gave me two good legs, and I'm going to use them."

Freya felt great warmth toward this kind old woman. "Thank you, Alma, for everything."

The old woman's eyes fogged. "No, Angel, thank *you*."

When she was gone, Tamika turned to Archie and Freya. "We have the same lunch hour. Want to meet up?"

Archie nodded. "Let's meet at the old oak tree in the front yard."

Tamika nodded and smiled at Freya. "Good luck with your classes."

When she was gone, Archie caught Freya by the arm. "Well, Gee, this is it. Math is our first class."

Hidden inside her coat, Freya heard Orus moan, *"It would have to be, wouldn't it!"*

By the lunchtime bell, Freya's head was spinning. Each class she entered seemed worse than the one before. Every time she and Archie showed the new teacher the note from the school's office, explaining about her strange dress and seating requirements at the very back of the room, the teacher would give her a look that suggested they would have found it easier to believe she had wings.

Then there was her lack of comprehension of most of the subjects. Archie had tried to prepare her, but it hadn't worked. There were four classes in the morning, and although she had a perfect understanding of geography, she was lost when it came to math, English, and something called humanities.

Walking through the crowded hall, Archie helped Freya find her locker. After showing her how to use the combination lock, he put her books inside and closed the door.

"I don't think I can do this," Freya said. "I've only been here half a day, and already I want to fly home screaming. This is nothing like my education in Asgard."

"Don't worry about it," Archie said. "First days are always the worst."

Freya leaned her forehead against the locker and sighed. "But it's like I know nothing! I have lived over six hundred Earth years, and yet I still don't understand what 'humanities' means. You're already human. Why do you need a class to tell you what it is to be human?"

Archie put a consoling arm around her. "Don't sweat it. Just do what I do and you'll be fine."

"*I doubt that,*" Orus called from under Freya's coat. "*Now will you please take me outside before I suffocate under here?*"

Tamika was already waiting by the old oak tree at the front of the school. Freya was opening her coat and releasing Orus as they met up with her.

"Why did you bring him?" she asked, fearfully eyeing the raven.

"I told you before. I go where he goes, and he goes with me."

"But this is school. You can't bring a bird to school."

"I can and I will," Freya said. "And if anyone tries to stop me—"

"We can sit over there!" Archie called, cutting off Freya and pointing to a private place to eat.

Freya tried to sit, but with her wings, it was impossible—at least in the classroom she'd been able to turn her chair around. Now she leaned against the school wall and ate her packed lunch. She handed pieces of sandwich to Orus and listened as Tamika and Archie spoke about their families.

"You have four sisters, don't you, Gee?" Archie asked.

"Yes, four . . . ," Freya agreed absently. She stood up straight and sensed waves of fear in the air. Looking around, she scanned the direction it came from. "I'll be right back."

"Uh-oh," Orus cawed. *"Freya, what are you doing?"*

"Can't you feel it? Someone is very frightened." She started to jog and then moved into a full run.

"Slow down!" Orus cried, digging his claws into her shoulder. Finally he took off and circled overhead.

"Gee, what's wrong?" Archie said, running to catch up with her. Tamika was close behind him.

"Someone is being threatened. It's the same fear I felt from you the first time we met."

"Gee, slow down," Archie called.

But Freya couldn't. The fear beckoned her. When she rounded the building, she saw the same bullies who'd attacked Archie, pressing a boy to the wall. He was Archie's age with a similarly slight build. His glasses had been knocked to the ground, and tears of fear were streaming down his cheeks.

"Come on, hand it over!" the bully, JP, demanded. His right arm was in a cast from his encounter with Freya's breastplate. But he was still able to command his gang to hurt people. "Search him," he ordered.

Two of JP's friends raced to follow his orders and rifled through the boy's pockets. When they found what they were looking for, they shoved the boy to the ground and handed the money over to JP.

"Gee, stop!" Archie caught her by the arm. "You'll only make it worse for him. They'll just take his money and let him go. He's one of the Geek Squad I told you about. They pick on him because he's Jewish and wears glasses."

Freya looked at Archie in disgust. "What does his religion have to do with anything? Archie, they have no right to attack him or steal his things. It's wrong."

"Yes, it's wrong," Archie said fearfully. "But that's just the way it is."

Freya straightened her back and ruffled her wings under her coat. "Not while I'm here."

Orus landed on her shoulder. *"Listen to Archie. You can't get involved. Leave them be."*

"I can't." Freya looked back to Archie. "What's that boy's name?"

"Leo. Leo Max Michaelson."

Freya lifted the raven off her shoulder and settled him on Archie. "Orus, you'd better wait here. I don't want you hurt."

"Please be careful. Don't expose yourself."

"I won't," she promised as she trotted forward. "Leo Max, there you are!" She pushed between the bullies and reached for the frightened boy's arm. "I've been looking all over for you. You promised to help me with math."

"Hey, hey, hey, who are you?" JP demanded, stepping forward.

"She's the new girl I told you about," one of the boys answered. "The one from my English class. What a freak!" He put on a whiny voice. "She needs to sit at the back of the class 'cos she's got a bad hunch. No one can touch her or she'll get sick. She's been hanging around with that loser Archie."

JP approached Freya and caught hold of her coat lapel with his unbroken left hand. He leaned in close to her face. "No one can touch you, eh? No way. If I want to touch you, I'll touch you," he threatened.

If he moved a couple of inches closer, his cheek would touch Freya's face and he would die. Then her mission would be ruined. "Back off," she warned. "Let go now before I lose my temper."

JP loomed over her, and his eyes burned with fury. She could feel all the bad things he had done resting behind those dark, hate-filled eyes. "Are you threatening me?" he spat.

Freya leaned further back. "I don't make threats. It's a promise."

"Look, new girl," JP pressed. "It's time you learned the rules around here. This is my school. I run things. Now, hand over your money and cell phone."

His hot breath on her face was making her angrier. "And if I don't?"

"Then we're gonna have a big problem."

"We already have a problem," Freya said. In a move too fast to follow, Freya snatched JP's hand and wrenched it away from her face. She started to squeeze, using her Valkyrie strength.

"You run this school, is that what you're saying? Well, not anymore. Leo Max, Archie, and anyone else you torment are now under my protection. Do you hear me?"

JP tried to pull his hand free, but Freya only squeezed harder. "I have been trained in ways you can't imagine. . . ." She drove the bully to the ground as tears of pain rushed to his eyes. "I could break you in two without a pause. So heed my warning. You and your gang of bullies are finished at this school."

JP whimpered in pain. He looked around and called to his gang for help. But when the first member came within her reach, Freya swatted him across the yard with the back of a gloved hand. Then she kicked another away with her boot.

She turned her anger on JP. "Listen to me!" she cried, squeezing until the bones in his hand creaked. "I was raised on the battlefields of war. You can't win against me. Leave the students of this school alone, or I might actually let you touch me—then you'll discover the true meaning of terror!"

"Gee, no!" Archie cried, running forward. "That's enough. He gets the message. Let him go."

Freya looked at Archie in disbelief. "After everything he's done to you, you want me to stop?"

"Please, Gee," he said. "Not for me or JP, but for you. Remember who you are and where you are. . . ."

Freya paused. He was right. She gave the bully's hand one more warning squeeze before releasing him. "Remember what I said, JP. They are all under my protection."

The bully staggered to his feet. "This ain't over, freak," he raged. "You hear me? It ain't over. You're gonna pay for this."

Freya made a move as if to chase JP, and he started to run. When he and the gang were gone, she looked back at Leo Max. Archie was picking up his glasses and a small velvet skullcap from the ground and handing it to him.

"It's over," Archie said. "I don't think they'll bother you again."

Leo Max pulled on his glasses and reached for the skullcap in Archie's hand. "Don't count on it. They've been picking on me for years."

"Me too," Archie said. "What's that for?"

"It's my yarmulke." Leo Max pinned the small black skullcap to the top of his head. "They're always taking it from me." His warm green eyes settled on Freya with nothing less than adoration. "Why did you do that for me? You don't even know me."

"I don't know you, but I do know them," she said. "I've watched their kind for centuries. Brutalizing people and ruining lives for no reason. It sickens me."

"Centuries?" Leo Max asked.

Archie quickly corrected, "She meant it *seems* like centuries. Didn't you, Gee?"

"Of course," Freya agreed.

Orus flew from Archie's arm to her shoulder. He gave her ear a soft nip. *"If I didn't know you better, Freya, I'd say you are developing a soft spot for some of these humans."*

Freya patted him playfully.

"Wow," Leo Max said. "Is that your raven?"

"I don't own him. Orus is free to go where he chooses. But he and I prefer to stay together."

"That is so cool!" Leo Max cried.

Freya asked Archie, "So, how many other kids are in the Geek Squad?"

Archie and Leo Max counted off the other students being bullied by JP and his gang. Altogether there were seven.

"That's enough to start with," Freya said. "Leo Max, I want you to find everyone who's being picked on by JP and his gang. Tell them I want to meet them all right here tomorrow after school."

"Why?" Leo Max asked.

"Because it's time you all learned to defend yourselves."

12

AFTER LUNCH FREYA WALKED BACK INTO THE SCHOOL.
Saving Leo Max from JP and his gang had been almost as
good as saving the couple in Chicago, with the added bonus
of no Loki to ruin things.

But those feelings faded quickly as she moved from one
class to another. This time it was history, science, and social
studies. Once again there was a series of uncomfortable
introductions and shuffling of seats as students were moved
from their desks at the back to accommodate the newcomer.

For her final class of the day, Freya was separated from
Archie. While he went on to phys ed, due to her supposed
physical disability, she had been assigned to Expressive Arts.

Freya finally discovered a class she enjoyed. The
Monday-afternoon session was music. Before she took her

seat, the teacher, Mrs. Breen, stopped her and stood her before the class.

"I'm going to ask you to sing something for me. I need to find out what music group you should be in."

Freya was used to singing with the other Valkyries at Valhalla, but she'd never performed before living humans. Closing her eyes, she imagined Maya at her side and started to sing. Soft and haunting, it was an ancient song, sung in the tongue of Asgard.

When she finished, the only sound in the classroom were gentle sniffs as tears shone in the eyes of her classmates.

Beside her Mrs. Breen blew her nose in a tissue. "Greta," she said softly, hardly daring to break the spell. "That was enchanting. What's it called?"

Freya shrugged. "It has no name. It's an old folk song my mother taught me. It tells the story of a great love between a young Valkyrie and a valiant warrior. So beautiful was the warrior's face that the Valkyrie fell instantly in love with him and couldn't bear to reap him. So she went to Odin and begged him to spare the warrior's life. Unable to grant the request, Odin took pity on the lovesick Valkyrie and told her to give the warrior her name before he died. In doing so, they could be joined together forever in Asgard."

When she finished, Freya looked around the room and saw, once again, the expressions of confusion. Did no one in this world know what a Valkyrie was?

"You have a lovely voice," Mrs. Breen continued.

Everyone in the class was nodding in agreement. Walking to her seat, she felt the warm emotions directed at her.

When the final bell rang, Freya was surrounded by her new classmates and asked lots of questions. As they pressed closer, Freya could feel Orus squirming under the coat as he was squashed. His soft caws of protest turned to louder curses.

"I'm sorry," Freya said quickly, moving free of her classmates, "but I must go. . . ."

Making it outside, she was left in a daze. She'd never imagined they would react to her singing like they had.

"*Freya, let me out!*" Orus cawed.

Freya opened her coat, and the raven flew out. After a quick circle in the air, he landed on her arm. His feathers were bent and tousled, and he was panting heavily.

"*Never again!*" he cawed. "*You can't pay me enough to go back into that coat. I nearly suffocated. And what was going on with all those students? They nearly squished the life out of me!*"

"I'm so sorry, Orus," Freya said. "I didn't mean for that to happen. They just came at me. I was surrounded."

"*That's the price you pay for being popular,*" he said. "*But, Freya, they were dangerously close to you. It could have been a disaster if one of them had touched you. You mustn't let them get that near you again.*"

"I'm not popular," Freya insisted. "This is just my first day. They were being nice."

"Not popular? What about that singing? You had everyone in that class enchanted."

"How do you know?"

"I couldn't see them, but I could hear them," Orus said. "You bewitched them all."

"I didn't mean to," Freya said defensively. "Besides, it's Mrs. Breen's fault. She made me sing."

"Hey, don't get mad at me because they liked you. If anyone has a right to be angry, it's me. I nearly died in your coat," Orus huffed. "All I'm saying is, you've spent so long hating humans that when they're nice to you, you don't know what to do. Enjoy this moment, Freya. You know it can't last."

Freya stroked the raven and considered his words. Orus was right. She was only a visitor here. She could not stay. Once Tamika's family was safe and Archie was protected from the bullies, they had to leave.

"So?" Archie asked as he descended the school steps. "How was your first class alone? Music, wasn't it?"

"Fine," Freya said, almost too quickly. "Everything went fine."

After they dropped Tamika off, Freya and Archie spent the afternoon together. She was grateful to finally be able to take off her coat. As she and Archie sat at the kitchen table to start their homework, Freya stretched out her cramped wings.

"I've never kept them folded for so long," she complained

as she massaged an ache in the long muscle of her right wing. "If I keep that coat on much longer, I'll cripple myself."

"Not to mention the damage it's doing to your feathers," Orus added. *"Not that you keep them well preened anyway."*

Freya stuck out her tongue at the raven and refused to tell Archie what he'd said.

"A few cramps are better than being seen," Archie remarked. Then a dark twinkle rose in his eyes. "Though I'd pay almost anything to see JP's reaction if he saw them."

Freya grinned. "Me too. It would almost be worth it to show him!"

Later, while Freya and Orus were tackling her math homework, Archie ran back into the kitchen, bursting with excitement. "Got it! I just found this on the Internet." He waved a printed piece of paper in front of her. "This is the answer to the Orus situation."

"What Orus situation?" Freya asked.

"Keeping him under your coat," Archie continued.

Orus's nails clicked across the table, and he hopped up onto Archie's arm. *"Thank you,"* he cawed. He looked at Freya. *"See? At least someone here cares about me!"*

"Oh, Orus, you know I care," Freya shot back. She picked up the paper and started to read, but the legal terms made no sense to her. She finally put the paper down. "I don't understand. What does it mean?"

"It means," Archie said, "that since you already have a sick note from Alma saying you wear a back brace and can't let anyone touch you, you can take Orus to school without hiding him under your coat. He's your 'service animal.' They can't stop you from bringing him to school, because you need him to warn you if someone is getting too close. All you need is a medical note with a doctor's signature, and I can do that for you. It's all right here, nice and legal."

"*Perfect!*" Orus cawed. "*No more suffocation!*"

Freya reached out and grasped the raven. She brought him up to her lips and kissed him on the end of his black beak. "No more sharp claws cutting into my side!"

The next morning, after delivering their newspapers and picking Tamika up, the three of them marched into the school office. Orus was seated on Freya's shoulder and had received more than a few stares as they'd walked through the halls.

The school secretary's eyes flew wide when she saw the large black raven. "What's going on here? You can't bring that bird into the school!"

"Good morning, Mrs. Bergquist," Archie said brightly. He handed over the doctor's note he'd forged. "Yesterday Greta tried coming to school without her service animal. But she became frightened when some of the kids in her music class got too near. She normally keeps Orus to warn her if people get too close behind her."

"I don't know about this," Mrs. Bergquist said. "I've never heard of a raven as a service animal before."

Archie then pulled out another paper. It was from the Illinois General Assembly website. He pointed to a clause in the paperwork. "See right there, it even says miniature horses are recognized as service animals. And ravens are way more intelligent than them."

Mrs. Bergquist became flustered as she read the document. "Wait here." She disappeared into the principal's office.

She returned moments later. "Dr. Klobucher would like to see you." The secretary directed Freya, Archie, and Tamika into the principal's office.

"That's fine, Cheryl," said the principal gently. "You can leave us now."

Dr. Klobucher rose and closed the door after the secretary. Her eyes lingered on Orus. "You have a raven as a service animal?"

She was average height with short, styled hair that reminded Freya of fine birds' feathers. But it was her kind eyes and her warm smile that struck Freya most.

"Yes," Freya agreed. "He tells me when people are behind me and warns when they get too close."

"Is he friendly?" Dr. Klobucher asked.

Freya nodded. "He'll let anyone touch him. He just caws if they get too close. Here, you can hold him if you like. He loves to be stroked."

Orus gave Freya a sharp, accusing look but allowed himself to be handed over to the principal and endured her hand stroking the smooth black feathers on his back.

"Well, he seems friendly enough, but I have to consider the safety of all the students in the school."

"Orus is my companion," Freya said. "We've been together for a very, very long time. He poses no danger to anyone here."

The principal handed the raven back to Freya and shook her head, chuckling. "Well, this is a first for me. Legally, I can't say no to a service animal. But if there's a problem with the teaching staff or students, we may have to look at it again. Just keep him under control, and we'll see how it goes."

Moments later the first bell rang and Dr. Klobucher ushered them out. "I'll escort you to your first class to let the teacher know what's happening, and then I'll inform the others."

Freya's morning classes went without a hitch. At first Orus caused a lot of gasps, but after a while the other kids got used to the presence of the large raven on her shoulder.

At lunch Freya and Archie met up with Tamika and Leo Max. Orus remained on Freya's shoulder and was glad for the treats he was handed by the others. Throughout the lunch period, students from Freya's music class came up to her. She was invited to a birthday party and asked to join the after-school glee club.

"You've become really popular," Leo Max commented.

Freya shrugged. "It's not me—it's Orus they like."

Leo Max laughed. "Are you kidding? Greta, boys I've never met are coming up to me and asking questions about you. They want me to introduce you to them. You're the most beautiful girl in school, and because you're my friend, they're talking to me."

Freya was too stunned to respond. They seriously thought she was beautiful?

"I've heard Jim Gardner was asking about you," Tamika added. "He's really cute, and all the girls have a crush on him. I bet he asks you out to the dance."

"What dance?" Freya finally asked.

"You know, the winter dance next month," Tamika said. "Everyone's going."

"Except me," Leo Max said.

"And me," Archie agreed.

Freya turned to Archie. "Why aren't you going?"

"JP says if any of us show up, he'll pound us into the ground." Archie paused and grinned again. "But you can go—especially if Jim Gardner asks you!"

Freya was starting to feel very uncomfortable at the turn in the conversation. "Don't be foolish. Why would I go to a dance with a bunch of humans when everyone knows I don't like them?"

Tamika and Leo Max both looked at her strangely.

"*Freya!*" Orus warned. "*Be careful what you're saying.*"

"Gee!" Archie joined in. He looked at Tamika and Leo Max. "Ignore her. She's crazy."

Freya finally realized what she'd said. "Yes, I am," she agreed. She looked at Archie. "Sometimes I think I must have been crazy to come here."

13

AT THE END OF THE DAY, FREYA AND ARCHIE WAITED outside the school. A short time later Leo Max arrived with a group of other kids. Their eyes darted around, and they all looked ready to bolt.

"This is it," Leo Max said. "This is the Geek Squad. We've all been robbed and bullied by JP." Leo Max turned to the group. "Everyone—this is Greta. She's the one I told you about. She beat up JP and saved me."

All eyes turned to Freya as if she were exposing her wings.

"Really?" a young girl asked, in a voice that was barely louder than a whisper. "But you're a girl!"

Freya approached the timid girl. She was small and thin for her age but very pretty. She had long brown hair with caramel streaks and an exceptionally fair complexion that blushed easily. She kept her large gray-blue eyes cast down to the ground, not daring to look at anyone.

"What's your name?" Freya asked.

"Elizabeth."

Freya bent down to her level and lifted her chin with a gloved hand. "Elizabeth, you mustn't ever think that because you're a girl, you can't defend or protect yourself. If someone is hurting you, you do what you must to survive."

Elizabeth looked on the verge of tears. "But I don't know how."

"Me neither," added a tall, thin boy wearing glasses. His wispy, curly hair fell into his blue eyes; eyes that constantly scanned the area, looking for danger. Archie had told her about him. His name was Kevin, and he was the smartest boy in school—but because he wouldn't share his homework with JP, he was picked on the most.

"Maybe not now, but soon you will." Freya looked at the students. "I asked Leo Max to bring you all here for a reason. I want to tell you that you don't have to be afraid of JP or his gang anymore. If you stand up to them, they will leave you alone. Now, how many of you want to go to the school dance but won't because you're afraid to?"

Everyone put up their hands.

An overweight girl with acne stepped forward. Like Elizabeth, she wouldn't raise her eyes to meet Freya's.

"I really want to, but JP said he'd hurt me if I went. He says fat, ugly girls aren't allowed."

Freya looked at each of them, and they all nodded. "What else has he done?"

One by one the students shared stories of what JP had done. From stealing cell phones and taking their money and jewelry, to beating them up for no reason.

"While I'm here," Freya continued, "I'll protect you. If JP or any of his gang approaches you, just tell them they'll answer to me. I promise you'll all go to the dance. But I must warn you, I won't be here forever." Her eyes darted to Archie, and he dropped his head. "When I leave, you'll have to fight for yourselves."

"How?" the overweight girl asked.

"I will show you everything you need to know. But you have to want this. I won't force you to do anything you don't want to. If you are interested in learning to defend yourselves, meet me here tomorrow after school. We'll find somewhere to go where you can train."

"We can use my backyard," Leo Max offered. "It's close to school."

"Perfect," Freya said.

"How much will it cost?"

Freya looked at the boy who had spoken. He wasn't very tall, but he was stocky. She could feel his fear and desperation. He had been a particular target of the bullies.

"It won't cost you anything," Freya said. "If you want to learn, just come along and I'll teach you."

Moments later Tamika arrived, and Freya could tell from her facial expression that something was wrong. "That's all for today. Remember, meet me here tomorrow if you want my help."

When they were gone, Freya turned to Tamika. "What's wrong?"

"I don't know. Grandma called me. She says we have to come home right now. She sounded frightened."

They found Alma in the living room. Pacing the floor, she was shaking her head and clutching papers in her trembling hands.

"Grandma, what is it?" Tamika said.

Alma's pleading eyes landed on Freya. "We're in trouble."

"What's wrong?" Freya asked.

The old woman handed over the papers. Freya could make no sense of the complicated paperwork. "What does this mean?"

"They're taking our house," Alma said. "Somehow the developers bought our mortgage from the bank. They're demanding full payment immediately or they'll evict us. I don't have that kind of money."

"What!" Tamika cried. "They can't do that!"

Alma nodded. "I think they can. The papers seem to say so. We need a lawyer, but I can't afford one." Her pleading eyes landed on Freya. "Angel, tell me what to do."

Freya looked over to Archie. "I've heard that term before. What is a lawyer? How can they help?"

"A lawyer works as an advocate. So if something is wrong with the paperwork, they'd find it and stop the eviction."

"Please help us," Alma begged.

"Greta's got her own problems. She can't help us," Tamika said furiously. "We just won't go. They can't make us."

Freya approached the old woman and took her hands. "I told your son I would protect his family. I won't break my promise. Those men will not take your home."

"Gee!" Archie cried, indicating Tamika.

"What do you mean, you spoke to my dad?" Tamika asked. "When?"

"What Gee means—" Archie started.

Freya shook her head. "No, Archie, don't make excuses for me. It's time we told Tamika who I really am." She looked at Orus. "What do you think?"

The raven nodded. "*Show her.*"

"Will someone tell me what's going on?" Tamika demanded.

Freya pulled off her velvet coat. When it fell to the floor, she reached back for the slipcover Alma had made for her wings. "I am not what you think I am. Please don't be frightened. I'm not here to hurt you."

"What are you talking about?" Tamika demanded.

Making sure she was standing well away from them, Freya opened her wings.

14

MAYA CONTINUED TO SEARCH FOR HER SISTER. THERE was very little time left before dawn, but still she could find no trace of her. Finally she headed to the one place she prayed Freya hadn't gone: Bifröst. The Rainbow Bridge was shimmering brightly in the cold, clear night. At the entrance Heimdall stood guard.

Maya landed before him. "Greetings, Heimdall." She bowed her head formally.

"Greetings, Valkyrie," Heimdall responded, also bowing. "What calls you to Bifröst so early?"

"Heimdall, you're a friend of Freya's, aren't you?" Maya approached him gently.

The shy Watchman smiled and nodded. "She comes here often, though usually it's late at night. We walk out onto

Bifröst and watch the realms. Most times, we do not speak. I can feel a great sadness in the child. She is restless. I do what I can, but nothing seems to calm her troubled mind."

Maya nodded. "I know what you mean. Did you see her tonight? Has she come this way?"

Heimdall frowned. "Not tonight. Why? What concerns you?"

"I can't find her," Maya explained. "She left Valhalla before me, and when I got home, she wasn't in her bed. I've searched everywhere. Normally I get a feeling for her. But now I feel nothing. I fear something may have happened to her."

The Watchman's fair eyebrows knitted together in a frown. His face revealed he was deeply troubled.

"What is it?"

He shook his head. "It may be nothing, and I beg you not to tell Odin. But sometimes I have episodes. I am at my post one moment; the next, I am on the ground. Nothing around me has been disturbed and I have seen no one. You know I require very little sleep, and I am certain I have not dozed off. But when I wake, I find a fraction of time has passed."

"Did you have a similar episode tonight?"

Heimdall nodded. "It wasn't long. But I awoke on the ground again." He paused and rubbed his chin. "Wait, I remember. Loki was here not long after. He said he caught me sleeping on the job and that he was going to tell Odin."

"Loki?" Maya said. "What did you say to him?"

"I told him if he said one word to Odin, I would squish him like a bug."

Maya bowed again. "Thank you, Heimdall. You have been most helpful."

Maya turned to walk away, now convinced something was wrong. First Grul had seen Freya with Loki, and then Loki had been at Bifröst causing grief for Heimdall. It was too big a coincidence for such a short time.

"Maya, wait!" the Watchman called.

The ground around him shook as Heimdall jogged over to her. "Go to the stables. The Reaping Mares are bound to their riders. Take Freya's mare. She can lead you to your missing sister."

Maya felt like an idiot for not thinking of that first. Sylt was devoted to Freya, just as her own mare, Hildr, was devoted to her. "Thank you, Heimdall. I'll do that."

Opening her wings, Maya launched into the air and flew to the stables, with Grul at her side. Sylt's stall was at the very end. Just as Freya was the youngest Valkyrie, Sylt was the youngest Reaping Mare.

"Easy," Maya said as she entered the stall and stroked the mare's smooth chestnut head. "Sylt, I need you to find Freya."

The mare nickered softly.

"Freya," Maya repeated as she put the reins on the mare and climbed up onto her back. "Take me to Freya."

Sylt nodded her head and pulled at the reins. She trotted out of the stables, opened her large dark wings, and took to the air.

Moments later she landed before Bifröst. Sylt pawed at the ground, shook her head, and snorted in distress. None of the Reaping Mares would dare cross the Rainbow Bridge without permission. To do so would mean their death.

Maya climbed down from the mare and stood at the entrance to Bifröst. The sparkling colors reflected in her pale eyes as a cold chill ran down her spine.

Moments later Heimdall reappeared. "It is as I feared," said the Watchman gravely. "Freya has broken the law. She has left Asgard without permission. When Odin learns of this betrayal, I fear nothing will save your sister. Freya has sealed her fate."

15

TAMIKA WOULDN'T STOP SCREAMING. ·

"Maybe that wasn't such a great idea after all," Orus admitted while Alma and Archie tried to calm her.

"Tamika, please." Freya pulled on her coat. "It's still me. You know me and Orus. We'd never hurt you, and we can help."

"What are you?" Tamika demanded.

"She's an angel," her grandmother said. "Your father sent her to us when he died. She's here to help."

"Angels don't have black wings!"

Freya sighed. "If you must know, I'm a Valkyrie. Do you know what that is?"

Tamika shook her head.

Freya threw up her arms in frustration. "Why does no

one know what I am?" She looked at Tamika. "I was with your father when he died. All he cared about was his family. He was frightened for you and begged me to come here and protect you. Which is what I intend to do."

Then Freya approached Archie. "Would you give me the keys to your house? I need you to stay here with Tamika and Alma."

"Where are you going?" Archie handed over the keys.

"I've got an idea. Hopefully, I won't be long."

"Be careful," Archie called after her.

Freya dashed to Archie's house. She pulled her winged helmet from the bottom of the closet and put it on. Then she reached for her dagger and went out to the backyard, carrying her coat.

"Freya, talk to me," Orus begged. *"What are you doing?"*

Freya stopped. "This is all about money, right? I can't fight that, not with my powers. We need a lawyer. And we both know a man who is married to one."

"You're talking about the man we met when we first arrived!"

Opening her wings, Freya launched into the sky. "That's right. Curtis Banks offered to help, and that's just what we're going to ask him to do."

They headed into Chicago. It was late afternoon, but the sun was still bright enough that she needed the protection of her helmet.

They flew toward the building they'd visited when

they'd first arrived in Chicago. Freya and Orus circled it a couple of times but did not see Curtis or any of his employees there. Moving from that building to the next, they scanned it, too. And then the next. Finally, at the fourth building, Freya brightened. She saw Curtis Banks talking to a group of men as they prepared to go down on the scaffold to clean the windows.

Freya landed and listened to him giving instructions to two men in the scaffold bucket. "Remember, safety first. Keep your equipment clean and safe and don't overreach." He turned to the others. "You two, take the other scaffold down, and start on the fourteenth floor and work your way up."

The men nodded and started to cross the roof. Just as Curtis was making his way to the exit, Freya crept up behind him and whispered, "Curtis, it's me, the Valkyrie. Please. I need to speak with you."

Curtis jumped and fell over backward. He caught himself on the railing and panted to catch his breath.

"Hey, boss, what's wrong?" One of his men ran back and helped him to his feet again. "You okay? Do I need to call a doctor or something?"

"I'm—I'm all right, just lost my balance," Curtis said. "It's fine. Look, you get to work; I'm heading back to the office. Keep an eye on the new guys, will ya?"

"Sure. But what about you? You've gone kinda pale."

Curtis patted the younger man's arm. "Really, I'm fine. Go on now. I'll see you tomorrow."

When Curtis made it to the stairwell, Freya pulled off her helmet. "I'm so glad I found you."

"Damn, girl, you nearly scared the life out of me! Think I just lost ten years!"

"I'm so sorry. I didn't mean to frighten you, but I really need to talk to you."

Curtis squinted at her. "You look so different. What have you done to your hair? And where's your armor and sword?"

Freya knocked on her breastplate. "It's still here, just under my shirt. I've left my sword and gauntlets at home."

Curtis shook his head and chuckled. "You know, I told my wife all about you. She thought I'd been drinking and seeing things. But you ain't no apparition."

"Not quite," Freya said. She stepped closer. "Curtis, do you remember I told you why I was here?"

"Sure, to help that soldier's family."

She nodded. "It's worse than I thought, and I don't know what to do. I really need your help."

Freya filled him in on Tamika's family situation, including Alma's illness and the threat to their home from the developers. "I can fight," Freya added. "I was raised on the battlefield. But this is different."

Curtis shook his head. "That's a lot of tragedy for one family. You know, sometimes I think the next big war will be fought with banks and computers and not weapons. What can I do to help?"

"You told me your wife was a lawyer. Could she take a look at the paperwork? Maybe there's something she can do."

Curtis looked around. "Look, why don't we head back to your friend's place and let me see those papers? Then I can talk to my wife."

"There's something else. They need money to pay off their house before the end of the month." Freya held up her dagger and pulled the blade from the cover. She handed over the heavily jeweled, golden scabbard. "I've heard that humans value jewels. I would give these to Alma to sell, but she'd never accept it. Would you sell them for me? I don't think she'd refuse the money if it meant saving the house. But will it be enough?"

Curtis's eyes went wide. "That looks like enough to buy half of Chicago! But I don't think I can sell them."

"Why?"

"Because I'd need to explain where they came from. I can't exactly tell them that a Valkyrie gave them to me to sell."

"But Alma needs the money!"

"Look, don't panic. We'll figure something out. Heck, it's the least I can do after you warned me about Joe. I got my nephew to look into him, and it turns out he was wanted for doing some pretty bad things. No telling what could have happened if you hadn't said something. But from what you tell me, it sounds like those developers want more than money. They want that property for their big development."

Freya dropped her head. "I know. If this doesn't work, I'll have to do it my way. I don't want to hurt them, but to stop them, I will."

"Let's hope it won't come to that. I'm sure we can find a solution."

Freya had never ridden in a human vehicle before and hoped never to do so again. Trying to sit in the front of the van was more painful than she could have imagined. She needed to keep her coat on to hide her wings, which meant she had to sit on them in order to fit in the front seat.

"You okay?" Curtis asked as he helped her from the van when they arrived at the Johnsons' house. "You look like you're gonna be sick."

"I'll be fine once I get this coat off," Freya complained "I never realized sitting on my wings could hurt so much. I'm shaking all over."

When they walked up the steps, Freya paused. "Curtis, here they call me Greta. Would you do the same?"

"That's not your real name, is it?"

"No. But I like it."

When they knocked, Tamika answered. Her eyes were still big, but at least she wasn't screaming.

"Are you all right?" Freya asked. "May we come in?"

Tamika nodded sheepishly and stepped aside. "I'm really sorry, Greta. I didn't mean to scream like that. But when you showed me your . . ." She paused and looked at Curtis.

"Wings," Freya finished. "This is Curtis. He knows all about me."

Curtis laughed. "I wouldn't say *all* about you. But I've sure seen plenty." His eyes landed on Tamika, and he smiled brightly. "Greta here has told me all about you and your baby sister."

A sad smile crept to Tamika's lips. "Greta, were you really the last person to see my dad?"

Freya nodded. "He was a good man, and I really liked him. He earned a place in Valhalla but wanted to go on to be with the rest of your family."

"So he's with my mom?"

"I believe so," Freya said as she walked into the house.

Freya introduced Curtis to Alma and explained how they had met. The old woman was busy feeding Uniik. When she finished, Curtis asked to hold the baby.

"My wife and I couldn't have kids," he said, making funny cooing sounds to the baby. "Nearly broke our hearts. Now we're too old to adopt." As Uniik started to cry, he reluctantly handed her back to Alma. "Show me those papers Greta told me about—maybe I can help."

Alma handed over the paperwork. As Curtis read every

page, he shook his head. "I'm no expert, but something is very wrong with all of this."

"Of course it's wrong," Tamika said. "They're trying to steal our house."

Curtis smiled at her. "Well, we aren't going to let them." He looked toward Alma. "My wife is a lawyer. Can I take these to show her?"

Alma shook her head. "I can't afford a lawyer."

"Don't worry. She does a lot of pro bono work for a public advocacy group. She loves a good cause," Curtis said. "I promise it won't cost you a dime." He held up the papers. "Men like these have to be stopped before they take over the world." He stood up. "I better get back to the office—but I'll show these to my wife tonight."

As he made for the door, he leaned closer to Freya and whispered, "And don't you worry either. We'll take good care of these folks. That soldier friend of yours can rest easy knowing his family will be safe."

"Thank you, Curtis."

He grinned. "Don't thank me yet. This fight is just getting started."

16

MAYA WAS SHAKING IN FEAR AS SHE STOOD BEFORE
the shimmering Rainbow Bridge. Sylt had confirmed her
worst fears, that Freya was no longer in Asgard. She looked
back to Heimdall and went down on her knee.

"Please, Heimdall," she begged. "Please, let me pass. I
must save my sister. Sylt will lead me to her. I will bring her
back. Odin need never know."

"You want me to lie to Odin?" boomed the Watchman.

Maya quickly shook her head. "No, Heimdall, not lie.
But if he doesn't ask, please don't tell him. I know you care
for Freya, just as I do. Please help me find her."

"Freya is one of the few who is nice to me," Heimdall
said. "She cares not that I am a lowly watchman."

Heimdall was a mystery to everyone. He'd been born of

nine maiden mothers and had no known father. This caused suspicion in most in Asgard. But he had always been exceptionally loyal to Odin and had been happy to take on the mantle of Watchman of Bifröst when asked. Once Heimdall befriended you, he was your friend forever.

"Please," Maya continued. "I do not ask that you come with me or abandon your post. Only that you let me cross Bifröst to see if she's in Midgard. You know I do not do this for myself. It's for Freya. When I find her, I'll bring her right back."

Heimdall looked at the sparkling Rainbow Bridge and then back to Maya. "I will do this," he said, "on one condition."

"Anything," Maya said. "Just ask."

Heimdall's cheeks reddened, and he shuffled awkwardly on his two large feet. "I like your sister very much. She has such spirit. But you are the fairest Valkyrie in Asgard. If I let you go, if I say nothing, will you dance with me at Valhalla?"

Maya was stunned into silence. She'd had no idea he'd even noticed her, let alone wanted to dance with her. "You want to dance with me?"

"Does my request repulse you?" he asked, sounding wounded.

"No," Maya said quickly. "Not at all. Heimdall, I would have danced with you anyway. You need only have asked."

"I am asking now. Do we have an agreement?" he asked.

"*Don't do it, Maya,*" Grul warned. "*Don't follow Freya into disaster.*"

Without hesitation Maya nodded. "Of course. If you let me pass to search for Freya, I will dance with you at Valhalla and be happy for it."

Heimdall gave Maya the biggest, brightest grin she had ever seen. He bowed to her. "Then we are in agreement. You may pass. But be sure to return before the sun rises fully. Odin would have my head if he knew what I was doing."

Maya climbed back up onto Sylt. "No, Heimdall, it will be my head—and my wings, and my eyes—if he finds out."

"Stay safe, Valkyrie," he called as Maya directed Sylt onto the Rainbow Bridge.

17

WHILE ARCHIE SLEPT, FREYA FELT RESTLESS. SHE CHANGED into her leather trousers and black boots. She took her sword and breastplate and grabbed her long velvet coat.

"I'm going for a flight," she announced to Orus. The raven was on the sofa watching television and pecking at popcorn.

"*You can't,*" Orus cried. "*My movie is about to start.*"

"Fine, stay here. Orus, you don't have to come everywhere with me."

The raven muttered under his breath and released the remote. Finally he flew off the sofa and landed on her shoulder. He nipped her ear. "*This is madness, Freya. What if Loki is waiting for you again? Have you considered that this whole thing could be one of his tricks?*"

Freya nodded. "Of course I have. But the danger here is

real. If we go back to Asgard now, who will protect Archie and the others at school—and what about Alma's family?"

"*Protecting them is one thing. But do you really need to go out tonight? What if you're seen?*"

"We'll be careful. Come on, it'll be fun."

"*Yes, fun. Like having Thor hit us with his hammer!*"

Soaring through the night sky, Orus flew close to Freya. "*I really thought you'd done enough for one day. Between teaching the Geek Squad to defend themselves and helping Tamika's family, how much more do you want to do?*"

"I told you, I don't want to do anything," Freya said. "But unlike you, I can't just sit watching television all night. And I'll go crazy if I keep reading my schoolbooks."

"*What's wrong with television?*" Orus demanded.

Freya looked at the raven and laughed. "Don't get me started!"

When they reached the main downtown core of Chicago, Freya glided closer to the rooftops. She headed to the part of town where she had encountered the couple in danger the other night. She immediately sensed the change from the other side of Chicago. Raw and sinister emotions hit her from every angle. The landscape had changed too. She and Orus were flying above a neighborhood of damaged and burned-out buildings when suddenly they heard rapid gunfire.

"*Not again!*" Orus cried. "*You planned this, didn't you? It's just like Loki said. You like playing superhero! Is there any point in me asking you to ignore it?"*

Freya grinned at him. "Nope!"

As she flew in the direction of the shooting, her ears picked up the sounds of different weapons. Mixed in with the gun battle were police sirens.

"Leave it, Freya," Orus warned. *"The police are here already. They don't need you to help them."*

"You worry too much," Freya teased. Up ahead the gunshots grew louder and more frequent. "It sounds like a war."

Then they saw it. Two police cars were parked askew on a darkened street. Officers were crouched behind their open doors, firing into the shell of a burned-out building.

Freya landed on the rooftop across the street and peered down into the building. She sensed at least fifteen men inside, all determined to keep the police out. As she pressed harder, she understood why.

"They're drug dealers, and that's where they're keeping it all," she said. "Orus, they're planning to kill the police." Her eyes moved back to the street. The four police officers were badly outnumbered, but still brave in the face of danger.

"Freya, listen to me," Orus said. *"This has gone too far. I understand your desire to help, but there are just too many people down there. You'll be seen, maybe even photographed. You've*

seen how all the kids at school use their cell phones to take photos. It will happen here, and it will be a disaster."

"But I'll put my coat on. They won't see my wings."

"It's too dangerous," Orus argued. *"Your heart is in the right place, but your mind is betraying you. I would fail as your adviser if I didn't stop you."*

Moments later an officer was hit and fell to the ground. When his partner ran around the car to help, she too was struck down.

Freya looked at the raven. "How can I ignore this? Those police don't stand a chance. They'll be slaughtered."

"It is terrible, but you must fly away from here. You will be no good to Archie or Tamika if you are captured."

Freya was more conflicted than she'd ever been before. Yes, she would remain unseen if she did nothing, but in doing nothing, innocent people would die.

"Uh-oh," Orus called. *"Look who's just arrived."* An Angel of Death landed close to the first fallen officer. *"It's too late for them, but not for you. Please,"* Orus begged. *"Let's go."*

Freya looked at the raven but then shook her head. "I'm sorry, Orus. I can't. Wait here."

Orus went mad and started cawing. *"Would you listen to me for once in your life and stop being so pigheaded? This is too dangerous! You will be seen or, worse, wounded and captured."*

"I'll be careful. I promise!"

"You're going to be the death of me," Orus cawed in exasperation. *"I'm coming with you."*

Freya grabbed her coat and leaped off the building. Silently she glided down the street, to half a block from the gun battle. She folded her wings, pulled on her coat, and drew her sword.

When she reached the police car, she saw there was nothing she could do for the first fallen officer. The Angel of Death was already with him.

"You shouldn't be here, Valkyrie," the angel warned as he rose. The spirit of the dead officer was standing beside him, staring in wonder. "This is our territory. Azrael will be furious."

"I know and I'm sorry. But I can't let this happen." Freya left the angel and went over to the policewoman lying in the road. She had been shot and was bleeding. Out in the open, she was an easy target for the criminals in the building. But when she saw Freya, she held up her hand.

"Get back," she warned through gritted teeth. "This is police business."

"I'm here to help you." Freya easily lifted the woman and carried her to safety behind the police car.

"Go, get away from here," the officer cried. "I'll be fine. Just get to safety."

The bullet had grazed the main artery in the officer's leg. If Freya didn't act quickly, the woman would bleed to death. She covered the gunshot wound with her gloved hand. "If I leave you, you will die. Just be still."

Freya searched for something to wrap around the woman's leg, but there was nothing. She reached under her coat and tore off her blouse, exposing her silver breastplate. She ripped it into pieces and tied it tightly around the officer's wound.

The woman squinted at Freya. "Are you wearing body armor?"

Freya nodded. "It keeps me safe." She looked up and saw another Angel of Death landing. There was a confused expression on the angel's face when she spotted Freya crouching over the fallen officer.

Freya held up her hand. "Stop! I am sorry, Angel, but this woman will not die tonight. You've wasted your journey."

"Valkyrie, you cannot do this," the angel said softly. "It is her time. I must take her."

Freya shook her head. "I was too late for that man, but not her. Please tell Azrael I've claimed this human for myself and I say that she will live."

"Who are you talking to?" the policewoman asked fearfully. "You said Azrael. I know that name. He's an Angel of Death."

"He's *the* Angel of Death," Freya corrected, turning back to the officer. "But there are others who serve him. Now, just stay calm; you are safe. I won't let her take you."

"Valkyrie, you must not get involved," the angel said, stepping closer. "I am here for this woman. I must do my duty."

Freya looked back at the angel. "She is young, with her whole life ahead of her. Give her that life. We both know she's a good woman. This world needs more people like her. If you must claim a life, go into that building and take them."

"You know we do not touch their kind," the angel spat in disgust.

Fear was increasing in the officer's eyes. "Please, I don't want to die."

"You won't," Freya promised. "But you must calm down. Fear is making you bleed faster. Here, touch my covered arm." Freya offered her arm. "Now you can see her."

The young officer touched Freya's arm, gasping in wonder at the sight of the Angel of Death. She was bathed in a white light, her skin and the feathers of her wings glowing radiantly and a gentle smile warming her face.

"She's so beautiful," the officer said, calming. Tears of joy rushed to her eyes.

"Don't be afraid, my child," the angel said directly to the officer. "I am here to bring you home."

Freya shook her head. "Oh no, you're not. She's going to live."

"This is not right, Valkyrie," the angel said. "You can't be here. There will be consequences. Azrael—"

Freya nodded. "Azrael will be furious with me. But I'll take that chance. We both know I can order you to leave—that's exactly what I'm doing. Leave us now, Angel, and return home."

The angel nodded and bowed. "So be it." She opened her wings and flew away.

"Where's she going?" The officer sounded disappointed.

"Back where she belongs. This is not your moment to die."

The officer's eyes focused on Freya. "Who are you?"

"I'm someone who is tired of all the killing humans do."

An agonized cry filled the air. Freya looked up and saw another officer fall to the ground. No angels arrived, so she knew he would recover.

She peered back up into the building. The men inside were moving—she sensed they were planning to bring the battle to the street. If they succeeded, it was unlikely the officers would survive.

"Listen to me," Freya said quickly. "Those drug dealers inside are coming out to kill everyone. I can't let that happen. Please keep pressure on your wound and don't move. The bullet damaged your main artery. Although the Angel of Death is gone, it won't take much to bring her back."

Freya rose, but the woman caught her arm. "No. Don't go! That armor of yours won't protect you. Please, stay with me and wait for backup. They're on their way."

Freya removed the officer's hand. "By the time they get

here, it will be too late. Stay here and live. I argued for your life tonight. From now on, please do all the good you possibly can."

"I—I don't understand any of this," the officer said.

"You don't have to." Freya rose and reached for her sword. "Just live a good life and do no harm."

She darted across the street toward the building. Bullets continued to fly, and she heard a ping as one cut through her coat and hit her breastplate. Once inside the building, she opened her senses fully. She instantly felt three men descending the stairs from the upper floor, where more men were firing down at the officers. Feeling too constricted, Freya shrugged off her coat and freed her wings.

She lifted her sword and charged up the stairs, releasing the Valkyrie cry they used when approaching the battlefield. The sound rattled the entire building and momentarily halted the gunfire.

The men in the stairwell were stunned when they saw her running at them. Using their momentary confusion to her advantage, Freya launched into battle. Within the tight confines, she attacked and cast them down the stairs. Soon they were all lying in a heap at the bottom.

She charged up to the next floor. To the right she saw a room with shabby furniture and several metal barrels with fires burning brightly. It appeared the men were living here. She heard a shout from another room, followed by the appearance of two men in the hallway ahead.

Freya ran at them, this time with her wings open fully, and she howled with all her might. The men dropped their weapons and covered their ears at the horrific sound. With the men disarmed, Freya was able to kick them to the ground, leaving them unconscious.

"Freya!" Orus called as he flew through a broken window. *"More police are here. There are hundreds of them, and they're surrounding the building. Get out before they see you!"*

"Not yet—there are still men upstairs. Orus, they don't want to be caught. They're ready to kill to protect their drugs. I won't let them hurt the police."

"That's it—you are crazy!" Orus cried. *"If we survive this, I'm telling your mother you're completely insane."*

"Come on," Freya called as she ran for the stairs. "They're this way."

Reaching the top floor, Freya hunted the men down, one by one. She cornered the final criminal in a small room on the top floor. As he fell to the ground, she heard a new voice.

"You in there, freeze!"

Freya turned and saw two police officers entering her level. The officers were holding flashlights, and their guns were raised and pointing right at her. "Drop your weapon!"

Freya lowered the sword and put it back into its scabbard. "I'm on your side. Look around you. I've stopped all these men. If you search, you'll find this is where they are keeping their drugs."

The officers were checking on the unconscious men as they cautiously advanced on her.

"We don't approve of vigilantes around here," the officer said. "You are under arrest. Now take off that sword and raise your hands where I can see them."

Freya looked around. She was in the remnants of a room with no windows. If she was going to get out of here, she would have to get past the police.

"Please," she said. "I'm just here to help. These men were shooting people outside. They wanted to kill everyone to keep their drugs safe. I had to stop them."

"If you really want to help, start by removing that sword. This is your last warning. Do it now!"

Another officer entered the level. "You ain't gonna believe what some of those guys are saying. They claim an angel attacked them. Said she got black wings and all—" He stopped when he noticed Freya in the room. "Whoa, who've we got here?"

"A vigilante with a sword," the first officer said. He focused on Freya. "Last warning, drop the weapon."

"C'mon, kid. Do what we tell you," the new officer said kindly. "You're too young to be caught up in any of this." As he approached, his eyes landed on something resting on the floor. He bent down to pick it up.

Freya realized too late what it was. A large, black flight feather. It was one of hers.

"No! Don't touch that!" she cried.

But her warning was too late. The instant the officer's bare hand touched the Valkyrie feather, his eyes rolled back in his head and he collapsed to the ground.

"No!" Freya howled.

Orus moved. He launched himself at the remaining officers and pecked at their heads and faces. *"Run, Freya!"* he cawed. *"Get out of here!"*

Reacting instantly, Freya ran. She pushed through the officers struggling against the raven. She could hear them cursing and calling for help. Soon other officers appeared and blocked her exit.

"Stop!" they shouted as they raised their weapons.

With no recourse, Freya opened her wings and let out the loudest Valkyrie howl she could manage. The sound shattered windows and drove the officers to the ground. Freya darted past them and without pausing leaped through a broken window and opened her wings.

On the street, the hysterical voice of the woman officer she had helped rose to a shrill. "That's her, that's her—there she is! Look, she's flying away!"

The sounds of gunshots followed Freya as she gained height in the sky and flew as fast as she could from the area.

18

FREYA WAS ON A NEIGHBORING ROOFTOP, PACING frantically. Her eyes never left the sky. She shouldn't have left Orus there, fighting the police. But he'd insisted, ordering her to go.

Her hands were shaking and she was sick with remorse. An innocent police officer was dead because he'd touched her feather. Did he have a wife and children? What would happen to them? In her desire for excitement and wanting to help, she had destroyed a good man and his family.

"Freya," Orus called.

"Over here!" Freya cried, waving her arms in the air. "Orus, I'm here!"

"Thank Odin!" Orus flew straight into Freya's outstretched arms. *"I thought for sure we were done for."*

Freya clung to the raven, grateful that he was unharmed. "I'm so sorry. You were right; I should have left when you told me. Orus, I killed that man. . . ." Her voice was no more than a whisper.

"Who?" the raven demanded. *"Freya, who did you kill?"*

"That man, the police officer. He picked up my feather and died."

Orus squirmed free of her embrace and made it up to her shoulder. *"He did not die."*

"Wha-what?"

"I knew you would be upset, seeing him collapse like that. So I flew up into the rafters and watched. They checked him. His heart was beating and he was breathing steadily. He was just unconscious."

"How is this possible?"

"I thought you knew. Freya, when you shed your feathers, they lose their killing power. It had only just come away from you, so it retained some power, but not enough to kill him."

Freya nearly collapsed with relief.

"Come on," Orus said gently. *"It's time to go home."*

"We can't go back to Asgard yet—we promised to help Tamika."

"Not Asgard," Orus said. *"Our home with Archie."*

It was nearly dawn when Freya and Orus made it back to Lincolnwood. They had just landed in the backyard and entered the house as the first rays of dawn arrived.

Freya was still shaking. It had been a bad night, and they had come so close to being caught. It would be a long while before she'd risk going out again. She was walking into the kitchen to make herself a snack, when she heard a sharp banging at the back door. This was followed by a loud whinny and a scraping sound.

"That sounds like Sylt, but it can't be . . ." Freya ran to the door and threw it open. Standing before her was her Reaping Mare with her sister on its back.

"Maya!" Freya cried. She stood back and invited her sister and the horse into the house. The wings on Maya's helmet grazed along the ceiling as Sylt clopped through the hall. The mare's sides brushed against both walls, and her right wing tip swept everything off a small table and sent the table crashing noisily to the floor.

There was barely enough free space in the living room to hold the large mare.

"Thank Odin we found you." Maya leaped down from the horse and landed on the sofa. "What have you done to yourself? Why are you dressed as a man? Freya, what's happened to your hair?"

Freya threw her arms around her sister and held her tight. "I'm so glad you're here! How did you get over Bifröst with Sylt?"

"Heimdall is a good friend of yours. When I told him you were missing, he let me cross with Sylt to find you.

He is waiting for us to come back before anyone notices we're gone."

Just then, Archie staggered into the living room. He was rubbing his eyes and yawning. "Orus, turn down the television. I can't sleep. . . ."

"Archie," Freya called excitedly. "Come here. I want you to meet my sister!"

"Sister?" Archie mumbled.

Maya removed her winged helmet. Suddenly she, Grul, and Sylt became visible. Stunned, Archie stumbled backward and tripped over a side table.

Freya started to laugh and went over to him. "It's all right," she said, helping him up. "They won't hurt you."

Archie's mouth was hanging open as he looked at the large flying horse in his small living room. "Is that Pegasus?"

"Who?" Freya asked.

"Pegasus—you know, from the Greek myths. He's a flying horse who lives on Mount Olympus."

Freya shook her head. "No, this is Sylt. She's my Reaping Mare. Now, come here—I want you to meet my sister. You can call her Mia."

Archie approached Maya in her shining silver armor. She was taller than Freya, and her hair was in two long braids. Her elegant white wings were folded tightly on her back. "You're Gee's sister? Are you a Valkyrie too?"

Maya frowned. "*Gee?*"

"That's my Midgard name," Freya said.

A dark expression crossed Maya's face. "What's going on here? What have you told this human of us?"

"Everything," Freya said. "I'm staying here. Archie and I go to school together. He's teaching me to be human."

"Why?" Maya demanded. "You're not human!"

"I know," Freya said. "But it was you who suggested I get to know them to understand them."

"I meant by talking to the warriors at Valhalla! Not by coming here and pretending to be one! Do you have any idea what Mother will do when she finds out? Especially when she sees what you've done to yourself."

"I like how I look," Freya replied. "And I don't care what Mother thinks. All she worries about is pleasing Odin! I could never live up to her expectations anyway. I'm not beautiful like you, or as graceful as the others."

"Of course you're beautiful," Archie cut in. "Everyone knows it."

Maya's pale eyes flashed at him. "Don't help her, human."

"That's enough," Freya said to her sister. "I'm glad you're here. But Archie is my friend. I won't let you talk to him like that."

"Your *friend*?" Maya said, aghast. "What's wrong with you?"

"Nothing! For the first time in my long life, I have a friend. Yes, he's human, but so what?"

"But I'm your friend," Maya said. "So are Orus and Sylt. That should be enough."

Freya's shoulders sagged. "You're my sister, and I love you. But we aren't the same. You love dancing at Valhalla with the warriors. I don't. You are content to stay in Asgard; I'm not. I yearn to know more, see more, and do more. I want to understand humanity and the reasons for the things they do. So I came here to see for myself."

Archie was standing between the two Valkyries while they argued. Finally his eyes settled on Freya. He started to frown. Leaning closer, he caught hold of her open coat.

"Gee, is that blood?" he asked. "What are those holes in your coat?"

Maya stopped lecturing her sister and leaned closer. "He's right. These are bullet holes." She sniffed the patch of red. "That's human blood. What have you been doing?"

Freya's eyes darted between Maya and Archie.

"Tell them," Orus said. *"They'll find out anyway."*

Freya sighed. "It's been a bad night, and I need some cocoa." She left the living room and headed into the kitchen. "Anyone else thirsty?"

The sun was up fully by the time Freya finished telling Archie and her sister the events of the past evening. Like her, Maya sat on a back-to-front chair and let her wings hang open.

Sylt was standing in the entrance to the kitchen, enjoying

a bowl of apples. On the table the two ravens glared at each other.

"You left a feather behind!" Maya cried. "Do you have any idea how dangerous that is? Even away from our bodies, our feathers retain power. "

"I know!" Freya cried. "By the time I saw it on the ground, the policeman was already reaching for it. Then he collapsed."

"This is a disaster," Maya said. "We must get it back."

"You can't," Archie added. "Not if the police have it. Besides, after tonight there's no telling what will happen to it. Especially if they realize what it can do. They might even be able to develop weapons from it."

"This is very bad." Maya rose from the table and reached for Freya. "If we can't get it back, then we must get away from here before they trace it back to you. Come, we'll fly back to Asgard and hope nothing further happens with it."

Freya remained seated. "I'm not going back," she said. "At least not yet."

"What? Of course you are. Now say good-bye to this human and let's go."

"I have a name," Archie challenged. "It's Archie, not 'Human,' so use it. And if Gee doesn't want to go, she doesn't have to."

Maya loomed above him, and her white wings opened in threat. "This is not your concern, huma—Archie. My sister does not belong here."

Archie rose and stood before the tall Valkyrie. "What are you going to do about it? Touch me? Kill me?" He offered his bare hand to her. "Go ahead! I don't have much of a life anyway. I'd love to see what excuse you give Odin for me showing up in Asgard!"

"Archie!" Freya warned.

Maya's mouth hung open in shock. She looked at Freya and then back to Archie. Finally she burst out laughing. "Very good," she said softly. "You have spirit. I like that. But whether you like it or not, my sister will return with me."

Once again Freya shook her head. "I'll return to Asgard after I have finished what I came here for. Tamika's family is still in trouble. Archie and the Geek Squad still need to learn how to defend themselves. And . . ."

Maya frowned. "And . . . ?"

"*Tell her,*" Orus cawed.

"Tell me what?" Maya demanded.

Freya sighed. "And we all want to go to the school dance together."

"What?" Maya sat down again in utter shock. "I can almost understand your desire to protect Archie and the others. But I can't believe you're risking everything just to attend a dance!"

"It matters," Freya said. "For the first time in my life, I'm meeting people my own age. I like them and they like me. What's wrong with that?"

"Because they're not your age," Maya insisted.

"You know what I mean," Freya argued. "And I'm going to finish what I started before I go back. Nothing you say or do will change that."

"Fine," Maya said, rising. "I can't force you to return. But I will tell you this. Later today we are going on a reaping, and your name is on the list. If you're not there, others will notice and ask questions. If this reaches Thor or Odin or if they figure out what's happened, there will be nothing to stop their rage. Promise me you will be back before then."

"Yes, little Valkyrie, why don't you promise your sister." Loki strolled casually into the kitchen.

"Loki!" Freya cried. "What are you doing back here?"

Archie stood. "How did you get into my house?"

"Silence, human," Loki said, pushing Archie back down into his chair.

"Hey," Freya warned. "Leave him alone!"

Loki grinned as though he'd caught her in a trap. "Aha, so you do like humans after all. Of course he's just a boy, but then again, you're a very immature Valkyrie."

"How did you follow me?" Maya demanded. "I felt no one behind me."

Loki's eyes narrowed on her. "If I don't want to be felt, I won't be." His eyes trailed over to Freya. "Now, for once, I agree with your sister. It's time you returned home. You've been away long enough. Playtime is over."

"I'm not playing," Freya insisted. "And nothing you or anyone else says will change my mind. I promised I was going to help the kids at school, and that's what I intend to do."

"You would risk your life because of a human school?" Loki said. "What's so special about it?"

"Nothing. But a promise is a promise," Freya insisted. "I'll be home when I'm done here."

Before they left, Loki warned Freya not to use her winged helmet again—explaining that when a Valkyrie wears their helmet, they can be tracked from Asgard.

With that agreed, Maya put on her own helmet. After one final plea to Freya, she sadly shook her head and left, with Loki following right behind.

When they were alone, Archie shook his head. "Your sister is really beautiful, and I can see how she cares about you. But Loki isn't what I expected at all. From the stories I read, I didn't expect him to look so—so ordinary."

"What were you expecting?"

Archie shrugged. "Someone much bigger and more frightening."

"Don't let him fool you. Loki is part frost giant. He's a shape-shifter and can change his size as well as shape. He looks like that to trick others into thinking he's harmless. But he's really not."

"But he came here to warn you. I thought he'd cause trouble."

"Me too," Freya agreed reluctantly. "I hope it's not a trick."

"Gee, what did he mean when he said you were risking your life?"

Freya hesitated.

"Go on," Orus said. *"Tell him what happened to Frigha."*

Freya inhaled deeply and motioned at Archie to sit. She told him the story of the runaway Valkyrie and how Odin sent a Dark Searcher to capture her. Then about the punishment he gave her for leaving Asgard without permission. When she finished, Archie sat speechless, staring at her.

"Finish the story," Orus prodded. *"Tell him about the Midgard Serpent. He's human and deserves to know what Odin will do to Chicago if he finds out."*

"And," Freya continued hesitantly, "after that, Odin released Loki's son, Jormungand—the Midgard Serpent— from his prison. He commanded him to punish those who had helped the Valkyrie. The Midgard Serpent is a terrible monster who can devour worlds. The last time he was released, he destroyed the whole village. The only thing that stopped him from devouring the world was Thor. The two hate each other. But it takes all of Thor's strength just to subdue him."

Silence filled the kitchen.

Finally Archie spoke, his voice no more than a faint whisper. "Gee, you gotta go back—right now."

"I can't," Freya said. "I promised Tyrone."

"I'm sure if Tyrone knew what's at stake, he'd never have asked you. It's too dangerous. Go back before Odin finds out."

It felt like someone had just punched her in the stomach. Archie was telling her to go. His face was red and he was growing angry. His emotions were running wild and coming in waves too fast for her to understand.

"Are you mad at me?" Freya asked in a small voice.

"What?" Archie demanded. "Is that what you think?"

Freya couldn't face him. Instead she just nodded.

"Gee, no." Archie moved his chair closer to her and took her gloved hands. "You're my best friend. I care more for you than anyone else in my life! You're everything to me."

"So why do you want me to go?"

"Because Odin could do to you what he did to that other Valkyrie, and it would be my fault! It'll kill me when you leave, but at least you won't be hurt."

"But I won't be," Freya insisted. "Archie, time moves differently between Asgard and here. In Asgard it is still the same night I left, while days and days have passed here. There's still plenty of time for me to do what I came for. Asgard's afternoon is still Earth weeks away."

"But, Gee, if anything happened to you—"

"Nothing is going to happen," Freya insisted. "And I

know I've got to go back. But can't we have just a little more time?"

"Do you promise you'll be safe?"

Freya nodded. "Just a little while longer, that's all."

Reluctantly Archie nodded.

Freya and Archie realized they had another big problem. A problem that looked like a horse, but one that had black-and-chestnut-colored wings.

"If my mom comes home and sees her, she'll have a freak!" Archie said as he stroked the mare's head.

"But if Sylt returns to Asgard, she could be used to lead others to us. Look how easily Maya found me. Keeping her here is the only way. Besides, your mother hasn't been home since I arrived. Perhaps she won't return until I've gone."

Archie didn't look convinced. "Okay. If Sylt stays, what do we feed her? I don't have money to buy straw or hay or whatever she eats. What about exercise? She can't spend all the time in the house."

"Simple," Freya said. "During the day while we're at school, we can hide her in your garage. We'll leave bowls of whatever we eat, and water. Then at night I can take her out to find grains and grass and other food. We can do this, Archie. I know we can."

Archie was stroking the mare's neck. "I've never ridden a horse before."

"Then tonight, after it gets dark, if you want, you can ride her while we go find food."

Freya's final class before lunch was history. Their assignment had been to write an essay about the American Civil War. Archie had volunteered to write it for her, but Freya had wanted to do this herself. She had attended all the battles in the war and was confident she could write about what she'd seen at the Battle of Gettysburg.

Just as they filed into the classroom and took their seats, her teacher, Mr. Powless, asked Freya to stand. She looked over at Archie, shrugged, and stood.

"I was most entertained by your essay, Greta," he started. "But what was it about the assignment that you didn't understand?"

"I understood everything," Freya answered. "You wanted a description of a battle during the Civil War—I gave you a description."

The teacher had a curious expression on his face. "What you gave me, Greta, is pure fantasy." He opened to the second page of her essay and started to read aloud. "At the end of the third day, the battle was drawing to a close. The air was heavy with the stench of blood, filth, and gunpowder. Men's cries drowned out the roaring of the approaching Valkyries.

"On that final day there were more Valkyries on the battlefield than living soldiers. We spent our time causing mischief with the weapons, teasing the men, and misdirecting cannon fire.

"All told, in the Battle of Gettysburg, thirty-five thousand fighters were wounded, and eight thousand, nine hundred and fifty-two warriors were killed. Of those, seventy-nine were reaped by Valkyries and delivered to Valhalla. The remainders were left to the Angels of Death."

Mr. Powless lowered the essay. "I could go on, but I wouldn't want to embarrass you further. If I could give points for originality, you would get a perfect score. However, this is a history class and not creative writing. Not only are your descriptions of the battle scene inaccurate, but your figures are off as well. You didn't separate your casualties into losses on each side."

"The specifics don't matter," Freya said. "Dead is dead. It doesn't matter which side they fought for. They all died, and valiant warriors from each side earned a place in Valhalla."

As the class laughed, Mr. Powless's face lit with a dark scowl. "Of course it matters. We learn from these statistics, and plan better strategies."

"Humans learn nothing from war!" Freya fired back. "I could cite all the losses in all the battles throughout time, and still you would not change."

Mr. Powless was dumbstruck. He charged back to the whiteboard and picked up a marker.

"All right. You claim you can give me all the statistics? Fine. Give me the details of the Battle at Antietam!"

"Deaths or overall casualties?"

"Both!"

Freya started to speak. "Casualties: twenty-four thousand, two hundred and ten. Deaths: three thousand, nine hundred and six. Of those, two hundred and one were delivered to Valhalla, while the others were left to the Angels of Death."

The teacher scribbled down her answers on the whiteboard. He turned on her. "The Battle of Shiloh?"

Once again Freya recited figures. As she spoke, her teacher recorded the casualties and deaths on the whiteboard. His writing became more erratic as his frustration grew. When he faced her again, he said, "All right. Let's move away from the Civil War. There was a battle fought at Little Bighorn. What can you tell me about that?"

"Gee," Archie whispered frantically. He caught hold of her coat sleeve and pulled. "Stop it!"

Freya smiled at Archie, and then calmly gave the teacher the details of the battle between General George Custer and his men against the Cheyenne and Lakota tribes. When she had finished, she said, "Chief Lame White Man was reaped and delivered to Valhalla. He is still there and is very much respected among the warriors."

"Well, it's good to have friends in high places," the

teacher said sarcastically. He narrowed his eyes. "Let's talk World War Two and the Battle of Stalingrad."

Freya rose to the challenge and recited the figures of one of the bloodiest battles in the war. When she'd finished, her teacher was livid. He stood back from each battle statistic on the whiteboard. "Wrong, wrong, and wrong," he said, crossing out each answer. "These are all wrong, and you are wasting the class's time."

"I'm not wrong; you are, you foolish little man!" Freya shouted indignantly as her temper spilled over. "*Your* records are wrong. I was there! I saw everything with my own eyes!"

"Gee!" Archie cried.

"*Freya!*" Orus cried as he gave her ear a sharp nip. "*Stop now. Say nothing more!*"

Mr. Powless had had enough. "Get out. Get out of my classroom right now. Go to the principal's office. I will be there in a few minutes."

19

FREYA WAITED OUTSIDE THE PRINCIPAL'S OFFICE AND listened to the raised voice of her history teacher within the office. He was demanding an apology and insisting she be punished for her insubordination.

It took all her willpower not to storm in there to defend herself. Mr. Powless was not a bad man, but he wasn't a kind one either. Most of his students were terrified of him, and he loved that power.

When he came out of the office, he glared at her but said nothing. Moments later Dr. Klobucher appeared at the door. "Greta, please come in here."

Freya entered the principal's office and shut the door. Suddenly she felt as though she had been summoned to stand before Odin.

"Please sit."

Freya looked at the small chair and shook her head. "I prefer to stand, if that's all right."

Dr. Klobucher sighed heavily. "I've got a problem, and I'm not sure what to do. Normally I like to give new students at least a month to get settled. But in the short time you've been here, I've received complaints about you from several of your teachers. They say you are argumentative and disruptive in class."

"It's not my fault if some of them are wrong."

"Wrong?"

"Yes, wrong," Freya insisted. "Mr. Powless thinks he knows everything about the Civil War, but he doesn't. But when I correct him, he sends me here."

"He's been teaching a long time. I'm sure he understands his subject better than you do."

"No, he doesn't."

"Freya, be careful," Orus warned.

Dr. Klobucher sat back in her chair and steepled her fingers. "Something's not right with you. I wanted to give you the benefit of the doubt—but that stops now. I've looked into the details Alma Johnson gave me, and they are all lies. Just like this doctor's note about your back and the need for your service animal." She leaned forward. "You're hiding something, and I don't like it. So we can do this one of two ways. You either tell me the truth right now, or I'll call in the police to talk to you. If you're in trouble or a runaway, they'll tell me."

Freya felt cornered. "Please don't do that," she started. "I am not ready to leave here yet. People are depending on me."

The principal rose to her feet and leaned over her desk. "Then talk to me. Tell me the truth. Who are you? Where are you from? Do your parents know you're here? What trouble are you in? Whatever it is, we can deal with it. But I can't help you if I don't know what's wrong."

"I can't tell you," Freya said.

"Yes, you can."

Freya shook her head. "If you knew the truth about me, you'd run out of this office screaming."

Dr. Klobucher shook her head and walked around her desk. "Give me a little more credit than that. There's nothing you could tell me that I haven't heard before."

"Not this."

"Let me be the judge of that."

Freya gazed into Dr. Klobucher's hazel eyes for several seconds. "Do you know what a Valkyrie is?"

"Of course. They're from Norse mythology. You were talking about them in the essay that Mr. Powless showed me."

"Yes, my essay," Freya repeated softly. "Do you believe in them?"

"I don't understand. Why does that matter?"

"It matters to me. Do you believe Valkyries exist?"

"I—I don't know. I've never really thought about it."

Freya faltered before she finally said, "They do." Her hands were trembling as she reached for her coat.

"*Freya, what are you doing?*" Orus warned. "*Stop. This isn't a good idea.*"

"I'm doing what I should have done at the beginning." To the principal she said, "The reason I know all those figures from the war is because I am one."

The principal shook her head. "You've lost me. What are you?"

Freya let her coat drop to the floor. "The reason I can't sit properly in a chair isn't because of my back or a brace. It's because *I am a Valkyrie* and I have these." She pulled off the slipcover and extended her wings.

Dr. Klobucher stood very still and silent for several moments. Finally she lifted her hand and reached out to touch Freya's wing.

Freya pulled it back and folded it tightly. "Please don't touch. If you do . . ."

"I'll die," the principal said softly. "Valkyrie: a reaper of souls from the battlefield, also known as the Battle-Maidens of Odin. I studied mythology in college. You're death."

Freya shook her head. "No, I'm not, although my touch is lethal. And yes, I do reap the souls of the valiant dead and deliver them to Valhalla. But I don't go around randomly killing people."

Suddenly Dr. Klobucher staggered back and started to

collapse. Freya caught her before she fell. At her touch, the principal's eyes went wide with terror.

"Don't be afraid. You're safe while I'm wearing my gloves," Freya said. "And I never take them off in school."

"H-how . . . Why . . . ," the principal stammered. "Why are you here?"

"Because of Tamika Johnson," Freya explained. "I reaped her father when he was critically wounded in battle. When I delivered him to Valhalla, he said his family was in trouble and begged me to help them. So I came here to find them. Then I met Archie when he was being attacked by JP and his gang. I stopped them, and now we're friends. He helped me find Tamika."

"You're saying Valhalla is real?" Dr. Klobucher asked breathlessly. "That you've been there?"

Freya nodded. "Odin and Frigg, Thor, Loki, the Valkyries, we're all very real."

"And the Rainbow Bridge?"

"Yes. Bifröst is beautiful, especially at night."

"I can't believe it. . . ."

"Look at me," Freya said. She turned and presented her folded wings. "I swear it's all true."

"All the Norse myths?"

"You call them myths, but to us they're our history."

Dr. Klobucher returned to her seat while Freya covered her wings and pulled on her long coat.

"You stopped JP from beating up Archie?"

When Freya nodded, the principal continued. "We have a zero-tolerance policy toward bullying, but I know it happens—especially off school property. I've been trying to work with JP for years. He's a deeply troubled boy."

"Your efforts are in vain," Freya warned. "I can feel the darkness within him. He enjoys hurting people and won't ever stop. He's dangerous and will one day kill someone."

The principal nodded. "He worries me, and I know he terrifies the other students."

"This is why I'm going to teach the Geek Squad how to stand up to him. I won't always be here to fight their battles for them."

"Greta, you can't fight any of their battles," Dr. Klobucher insisted. "You're a Valkyrie, for heaven's sake! You could kill someone."

"I know that!" Freya sighed and softened her tone. "Before I came here, my only experience with humans was on the battlefield, and I hated them. But now, after meeting Archie and the others, I don't anymore. I want to help them learn to protect themselves against bullies like JP."

The principal sat back in her chair. "I'm glad you don't hate us, and I'm grateful you want to help. But I can't allow a Valkyrie to run loose in this school. If you make one mistake, someone could die."

"Please don't ask me to leave," Freya begged. "I'm careful.

You know I am. That's why I have Orus with me to keep everyone away. I wear gloves and my coat all the time. No one can touch my bare skin."

"But how can I risk it?"

Freya leaned over the desk. "Dr. Klobucher, you are a good woman. I know that. You care about your staff and your students. I am a student. I may be unusual, but I am still just a student. Please, help me find a way to stay a little while longer. Just until Tamika, Archie, and the Geek Squad are safe."

The principal's eyes went down to the essay Freya had written. "Is this true? Were you really there?"

Freya nodded. "I have been to every battle fought over the past six hundred years. I have seen all the horrors humans are capable of. It is only in the short time I've been here with Archie and Tamika that I am starting to see the good in humanity."

Dr. Klobucher held up the essay. "It's no wonder you hated us. Had I seen all that violence, I would to." She paused, considering. Finally she nodded. "Okay. You can stay, but under a few conditions. You're not to argue with any of your teachers, even if they're wrong. And if you make one mistake, just one, you *will* leave right away and not return. I'm taking a big risk here. Please don't disappoint me."

Freya beamed with excitement. "I promise. You'll see. We can make this work. No one will ever learn the truth about me."

20

WITH A RENEWED DETERMINATION NOT TO CAUSE ANY more trouble at school, Freya walked with Archie to their first class after lunch. They entered the chemistry lab with its large worktables, sinks and water taps, gas pipes, and glass beakers for mixing chemicals.

Taking their usual seats at the rear work station, they watched the back of a substitute teacher writing his name on the whiteboard. His suit was poorly fitting, and the hems of his trouser legs were high over his mismatched shoes and socks. His long dark hair was tied back in a ponytail. Some of the boys were snickering and making comments about his rumpled appearance.

When the teacher finished, he turned and faced the class. His piercing dark eyes sought each boy that had laughed, and he silenced them with a threatening look.

Freya inhaled sharply. Orus cawed, and beside her, Archie fell off his stool. "No way," he cried. "What's he doing here?"

Loki started to pace before the class. "My name is Mr. Jötunn. I will be your substitute teacher until Mrs. Cornish recovers from her unfortunate accident. I'm sure we all wish her a speedy recovery after her tumble down the stairs."

Freya felt the color draining from her face as Loki moved confidently around the room. Occasionally he would look at her, and the corners of his mouth would tilt up. He was challenging her to say something.

"You don't think he pushed old Cornish down the stairs?" Archie asked.

Freya nodded. "That's exactly what he did."

At the front, Loki's mischievous eyes settled on her again. "I hope you will all forgive me, but this is my first time in an American school. I'm quite sure it will be a stimulating experience—though I am curious to discover why some of you would choose to remain here when you could be elsewhere doing *other* things."

A broad grin lit his face. Loki was in complete command and thoroughly enjoying himself. "So would someone like to tell me what you are studying?" He ignored the raised hands and pointed a finger at Archie. "You, blond boy, sitting next to the girl with the ugly black bird—"

"Um . . ."

"Stand up; tell me your name."

Archie looked at Freya and rose from his stool. "I'm Archie Peterson. We're doing experiments on chemical reactions."

"Oooh, experiments." Loki eagerly rubbed his hands together. "My favorite."

"Freya, this is bad," Orus warned.

"Excuse me, you there, young lady," Loki called. "If you can't keep that bird quiet, I'll have him removed from my class."

Freya glared at Loki, and he smiled at her discomfort. She grabbed the raven's beak. "You heard him, nice and quiet." She winced as Orus's claws dug into her shoulder.

"Now, where to begin," Loki started. "Yes, there can be many types of chemical reactions. For example, fear can cause a reaction in your body that makes you sweat and increases your breathing in preparation for your fight-or-flight response. Don't you agree?" He pointed at Freya. "What's your name?"

Through gritted teeth, Freya responded. "I'm—"

"Stand when you speak to me. Now, again, what was your name?"

Freya climbed off her stool, careful not to reveal her wings. "I'm Greta Johnson."

"Really?" Loki burst into laughter. "You're serious? You're calling yourself Greta?"

Archie jumped off his stool. "Her name is Greta."

Loki strode down the aisle and stood before Archie. "Did I give you permission to speak, boy?"

"No, sir, but here in *America*, it's not polite to laugh at people's names."

"Well, well, well, aren't you just the little defender. Allow me to tell you, in none of the realms is it polite to interrupt your elders. What do you think would happen if you did that to, say, Thor or Odin?"

Archie looked nervously at Freya. "I—I don't know."

Loki looked at the other students. "How many of you here know who Thor is? Hands up."

When most of the students raised their hands, Loki pointed to one. "You. Stand up and tell us what you know of Thor."

The boy grinned at his friends. "He's a big, dumb comic book hero who wears a cape and carries a stupid hammer."

"A big dumb hero?" Loki exploded with laughter again. "Yes, that's exactly what he is. Well said. Now, what do you think he'd do if Archie were rude to him?"

The student started to chuckle. "He'd take his hammer and squash him."

"Exactly!" Loki's threatening eyes focused on Archie, and he leaned in close to his face. "He would squash you until you were nothing more than a puddle of gelatinous goo. So next time you decide to speak, consider the consequences."

His knowing eyes passed from Archie to Freya. His eyes

were alive with mischief and defying them to say more. Finally he grinned and returned to the front of the class.

"Where was I? Oh yes, chemical reactions," Loki continued. "Now, there are some very strange things that can happen when you mix three innocuous compounds together." He reached into his pocket and pulled out a small leather pouch. He poured the contents into a glass dish on the workstation at the front. Immediately the room filled with a foul odor.

Everyone cried at the stink and held their noses.

"Gross," Archie cried. "What is that?"

Freya's nose wrinkled at the stench. "It's dried dragon's dung—very old, by the smell of it."

At the front, Loki pulled another pouch from his pocket "Now, I know this doesn't smell nice, but you're going to love what comes next." He poured silver granules into a beaker. Then he turned on the water tap and filled another beaker with cold water.

"*Freya, he's not!*" Orus squawked.

"He wouldn't!"

"Wouldn't what?" Archie demanded.

"*Oh yes, he would,*" the raven cried.

Loki grinned. "I want you all to be quiet; this is where the real fun begins. Here we have some dried animal waste, and in here we have some ground dwarf's silver. If I pour just a bit . . ."

Freya looked wildly around the room. There was only

one door, and that was at the front, near Loki and his mad experiment. There wasn't time to get everyone out. Jumping to her feet, she held out her hand. "Loki, stop. Don't do it!"

Loki paused. "Excuse me? What did you just call me?"

"I mean, Mr. *Jötunn*," she corrected. "Please, stop. The smell is making everyone sick. I think we should all get out of here, now."

Loki put down the beaker of silver. "Science isn't pretty, and it doesn't always smell like roses. But to learn, one must take risks. However, not all risks are good, are they, *Greta?*" His expressive eyes darkened in threat. "Now, if someone had done what they were told to and gone home straight-away, it wouldn't have come to this. But since that someone has defied an order, risking not only their life but the *others* who helped them—we must see what kind of reactions that could cause. You get my meaning?"

"Gee," Archie said, "what's going to happen?"

"Yes, *Greta*," Loki said, emphasizing the name again. "Why don't you tell the class what will happen next if I add silver and water to the dung?"

All eyes in the room focused on her, and she heard echoes of the principal's recent warning not to get into more trouble. But what would Dr. Klobucher say if she knew that Loki had invaded the school? She'd probably throw them both out.

Freya sat down slowly. "Um, I'm not sure. But it stinks. . . ."

"Sometimes life stinks," Loki said. "Now, are you finished?"

"Yes, sir," Freya said.

Loki glared at her for a moment longer, enjoying himself. He picked up the silver-filled beaker. "Now, shall we add a bit more, just for fun?" He poured all the silver onto the dung. "As you can see, we already have a chemical reaction starting as the molecules of silver mix with the biologicals of the dung."

Putrid smoke rose from the mixture, and the stink was far worse than the dung alone. Students started to gag and cough. Several were physically sick and ran from the room crying.

Loki reached for the water.

"Gee, is he going to hurt us?" Archie whispered.

"No," she answered. "But the moment he adds the water, get down and stay down!"

Loki tipped all the water onto the mixture and jumped back. "Oops, too much!"

Freya reached for Archie and hauled him off the stool. They hit the floor to the sound of sizzling. Each second the sound increased, until a large explosion went off at the front of the room.

"Now, that's what I call a chemical reaction!" Loki cried as the mixture billowed smoke and swelled out of the dish. Like a living, breathing thing, it moved across the workstation and continued to increase in size until it poured onto the floor and wove its way down the aisles.

Students screamed and lifted their feet as the living blob wove its way around the whole classroom.

"Get ready!" Freya cried.

"What is that?" Archie cried, coughing and choking from the putrid smell.

Suddenly the mass swelled faster than it could move, and like an overfilled balloon, it exploded. Droplets of the most horrible-smelling pieces of gunk flew around the room and covered the entire class.

Despite crouching under their station, Freya, Orus, and Archie were splattered with the foul-smelling mixture.

"It's an Asgard stink bomb," Freya said, wiping the slimy liquid off her face.

Thanks to Loki's experiment, the school was closed for the rest of the week as work crews in hazmat suits went in to clear up the mess in the chemistry lab. The smell, however, lingered much longer, and that entire section of the school remained closed until further notice. As for Mr. Jötunn, he disappeared. Freya could only hope that Loki had returned to Asgard and would stay there.

During their time off, Freya met up with the Geek Squad in the back of Leo Max's yard. Over the days, word spread of the training sessions, and more of JP's victims arrived.

Freya spoke first about the importance of staying close together. She spoke of strength in numbers and how even the smallest army can succeed in battle with strategy, skill, and stealth. Then one by one she took them through the basics she had been taught about self-defense in her early life.

Despite the seriousness of the training, there was a lot of laughter too. Freya delighted in watching the misfits coming together. Friendships were being forged, and they were learning to watch each other's backs. Soon the name "Geek Squad" was said with pride, not shame.

At the end of the fourth day, Freya, Archie, and Tamika made their way to Alma's house and saw an unfamiliar car in the driveway. Inside they found Curtis and his wife sitting in the living room, drinking coffee while Curtis's wife cradled Uniik in her arms. Her face was glowing as she gazed down on the baby.

"Greta!" Curtis cried when he saw her. "Come, I want you to meet my wife. This is Carol."

Curtis's wife stood. Her dark eyes were wide and carried a trace of doubt. They lingered on the lumps at Freya's back.

Freya grinned at her curious expression. "Curtis told me you knew about me. Do you want to see them?"

Carol blustered. "I—I don't want to be rude."

"I don't mind." Freya removed her coat and freed her wings. "See," she said, opening them, "just ordinary wings."

As Carol inhaled, Curtis reached out and took the baby

from her hands. "It's all right. You get used to them real quick. Soon you'll even forget she's got them." He winked at Freya. "Except for when you try to get her into a car. Then that's all you hear about." He put on a high and teasing voice: "My *wings* this . . . and *my wings* that . . ."

Archie started to laugh. "You sound just like Gee!"

Freya also laughed. "I don't sound like that!"

"Sure you do," Tamika added.

When they settled, Carol explained what she'd learned about the developers. How there were rumors of foul play, but so far no charges against them had stuck.

"Is there nothing you can do?" Freya asked.

"I'm only just getting started."

"You be careful," Alma warned. "These are bad men who will kill to get what they want."

Carol's dark eyes sparkled. "That's just the kind of challenge I like."

When Curtis and Carol left, Freya and Archie stayed for dinner. Freya helped the old woman prepare the meal, while Archie and Tamika practiced their defensive fighting in the backyard.

Alma looked at Freya slyly. "I know exactly what you're doing, Angel."

"What?" Freya asked as she sliced up vegetables.

"I know, and I am truly grateful."

Putting down the knife, Freya looked at the old woman. "I really don't understand."

"Yes, you do. The moment you found out I was sick, you were thinking of Curtis and his wife for Tamika and Uniik."

"You're busted!" Orus laughed.

Freya sighed and pulled out a chair for Alma to sit in. "I promised your son I would see his girls protected. He couldn't have known that his wife would die or that you had cancer. But you do. So when I felt what a good man Curtis was, it seemed the perfect solution."

The old woman chuckled. "It is. They are both good folk and will care for my girls. I couldn't have chosen better."

Freya tilted her head to the side and smiled. "Alma, there isn't an Angel of Death beside you just yet. Take the time to get to know Curtis and Carol better, and then decide."

"I don't have to—I already know," the old woman said. "But I will make sure that Tamika and the baby get to know them."

After dinner Freya and Archie made their way home. Sylt had been made comfortable in the garage and nickered excitedly when Freya approached her.

Archie's eyes were wide with excitement as he stroked her.

"All right, Archie. Sylt has never been ridden by a living human before, so she may be a bit nervous. But if you reassure her, she'll be fine."

Archie did everything he was told to do, and before

long, Sylt opened her wings and invited him up onto her back. Once he was seated, he offered Freya his hand. "Come on up."

"I've got my own wings that I need to stretch. Besides, I can't risk my hair or something else touching you. But I'll be right beside you all the way."

"Me too!" Orus added.

They took off from the backyard. After climbing high into the night sky, they spent hours flying over the open fields and farms of central Illinois. Freya watched Sylt closely. When the mare opened her nostrils and started to sniff, she knew they had found somewhere for her to eat.

Soaring closer to Archie, Freya watched the joy in his eyes. He was having the best time of his life. She hated to end it, but Sylt needed food. Finally she called over to him to let him know they were going down.

As Freya tilted her wings and descended, the Reaping Mare followed. They touched down in the middle of fields that had recently been harvested. Archie slid off the mare and hugged her neck. "Sylt, you're awesome!"

Sylt turned her head back to him and neighed. Then she focused on eating what was left after the harvest.

"I can't believe it," Archie cried. "That was so cool! Riding Sylt is better than riding the biggest roller coaster! We could make a fortune selling rides on her."

Freya laughed. His face was flushed from the chill of the

night air and the excitement. He could hardly stand still. "Can we go out again tomorrow night?"

"Sure. We'll have to do it every night. Sylt needs food and exercise. But, Archie, we can't be out as long as this each time."

"Why not?"

"Because you're human. You need to sleep!"

"I'm not tired."

"You will be."

Archie was still stroking Sylt as she munched on the grain. "You know, you're really beautiful when you fly. That's the first time I've ever seen you do it. You're so graceful in the sky."

Freya's cheeks went hot with a blush. "I love flying. Sometimes late at night in Asgard, Orus and I would go out until it was light."

"I'd sure like to see that."

"I really wish you could too," Freya admitted.

It was getting very late when they brought Sylt back to the garage. Despite the hour, Archie was wide awake. "I can't wait for tomorrow night," he said brightly. "This has been the best night of my life!"

21

LIFE IN LINCOLNWOOD ENTERED A BLISSFULLY QUIET
routine. Curtis and Carol spent more time with Alma and
the family. Carol managed to suspend the foreclosure on the
house while the investigations continued, but she warned
that this could be the calm before the storm and that they
shouldn't let their guard down. Now that the authorities
were involved, it could make the developers even more
dangerous.

After her near capture, Freya stopped going into Chicago
at night. Instead she and Archie would take Sylt out on long
flights as they searched for food for the Reaping Mare.

Despite the calm, the afternoon training sessions with
the Geek Squad continued. Freya marveled at the changes
in her students. They had learned how to defend themselves.

But more than that, it was their growing confidence and friendships that touched her the most. They had all come together and formed tight bonds. As the days ticked by, the Geek Squad began to get very excited about the upcoming winter dance.

Friday afternoon Freya was standing outside the school waiting for Archie and Tamika. She felt more than saw Tamika running toward her, face flushed and a panicked expression in her eyes. "Greta, come quickly! JP's gang is going after Archie again. They've dragged him and Leo Max behind the gym building. Elizabeth has gone to get the teachers, but they might be too late!"

Freya burst into a run and followed Tamika around the school to the secluded area where the older students met up to sneak a smoke. By the time they arrived, JP's friends were attacking other members of the Geek Squad. Archie had two gang members on him, while Leo Max was struggling with another. Kevin was down on the ground, being kicked by another. But a moment later he used a move Freya had taught him, and he gained his feet and was defending himself against his attacker.

"C'mon!" Tamika called, trying to drag her along.

"No, wait." Freya slowed to a walk. "Look at them. They're standing up to the bullies and working together to defend themselves.

"But they could get hurt!"

"Yes, they could, but I can't get involved. You know I can't stay here forever. If they don't do this now, they never will." Freya pulled the raven from her shoulder and handed him to Tamika. "Here, hold Orus for me. If this gets out of hand, I'll join in. But let them go for a moment."

Word of the fight spread fast as more and more kids arrived to cheer on the Geek Squad, who were defending themselves but without becoming the attackers. Their days of being victims were over.

Freya strained to see JP among the bullies, but he didn't seem to be there.

Suddenly a powerful, bone-crushing blow cut across Freya's wings and back. She was knocked forward and driven to the ground. This was followed by a second, more powerful strike across her wings.

Howling in pain, Freya looked up to see JP looming above her with a baseball bat.

"Not so tough now, are ya?" He lifted the bat and brought it down again. Freya raised her arm and blocked the blow. The bat struck her painfully in the wrist, and she yelped.

Orus cawed and flew from Tamika. He launched an attack at JP's head. Using his sharp claws, he cut the bully's scalp and pecked at his eyes, driving him away from Freya.

Moments later JP reached up and caught hold of the enraged bird. He punched Orus in the beak and kicked him away from him. The raven hit the ground several feet away and didn't move. "Orus!" Freya cried.

Tamika ran to the raven and picked him up. Cradling him in her arms, she called, "He's all right, just a little stunned!"

"Gee!" Archie cried when he saw what had happened. "Leo Max, look! JP's going after Gee and Orus!"

Archie broke free of his attackers and charged over. Leo Max was right behind him, and together they pulled the bully away from her.

Freya climbed painfully to her feet. Her wings felt like they were on fire and screaming to be freed from the coat. She had stopped wearing her protective armor to school weeks ago, and now, as her wings throbbed, she regretted that decision. She feared a bone or two might be broken.

Gang members came to JP's aid and pulled Archie and Leo Max off their leader. Within moments JP was holding the baseball bat again and moving straight at Freya.

"This is it. You're gonna die!" he threatened.

"And you are too stupid to live!" Freya responded as she prepared to take him on.

At that moment several teachers arrived on the scene. Most went after the other bullies while Mr. Powless approached JP. "That's enough, JP. Drop the bat!"

The history teacher grabbed the bully's arm to stop him, but JP turned quickly and swung the bat at him.

With little time to think, Freya jumped in front of Mr. Powless and turned her back to the bully, taking another full blow to her already damaged wings. She cried out, as tears of pain rose in her eyes.

"Greta, get back!" Mr. Powless ordered, pushing her aside. "I'll handle this!"

Freya had never been so enraged in all her life. She ignored her teacher and went after JP. Wrenching the weapon away from him, she roared, "I have had enough of you, *human!*" Tossing the bat aside, she lunged forward and caught JP by the coat. Hoisting him easily over her head, she let out a loud Valkyrie roar as she hurled him across the yard.

"Stay here!" Freya ordered her teacher. "It's time I finished this!"

In a full rage Freya charged the bully and, tearing off a glove, exposed her bare hand. But just before she could touch him, Loki appeared and blocked her way.

"Loki!" Freya cried. "Get out of my way."

"And just what do you think you're doing?"

"What I should have done weeks ago!"

Loki started to chuckle and stepped aside. "Oh, well, in that case, go right ahead. Reap him in front of all these witnesses and then try to explain his presence in Asgard."

Archie broke away from the teachers and ran up to them. "You again?" he cried to Loki. "Don't you have anything better to do than harass Gee?"

"I don't like your tone, boy," Loki said. "But if you must know, I'm about to let this Valkyrie expose herself. Then she can come home with me and explain herself to Odin."

"Gee, no!" he cried. "You can't. Everyone's watching you!" Archie held up her glove. "Don't listen to him. Just put this back on and walk away."

Freya saw the anticipation on Loki's face, and then noticed everyone else in the yard staring at her.

"Please, don't," Archie begged. "The teachers have seen what happened. JP and his gang will be expelled. They won't be allowed back here. We won!"

Orus cawed and flew unsteadily to her shoulder. One of his eyes was closed and swollen, and his beak had blood on it. *"It's over, Freya."*

Seeing the damage JP had done to Orus fanned the flame of her rage. She was shaking as she tried to contain herself. She wanted nothing more than to hit something or someone. Preferably JP or Loki—it didn't matter which.

"Greta!" Dr. Klobucher ran between the gathered students and teachers. When she spotted Loki standing with Freya, she frowned. "Mr. Jötunn, where have you been? I've been trying to reach you regarding that disaster in the chemistry lab."

"Dear lady, if you must know, I went home, but came back here to stop this little Valkyrie from doing something particularly stupid."

The principal's eyes went from Loki to Freya and back to Loki again. "Valkyrie? You know about her?"

Loki was equally shocked. "Oh my, it seems you know about her too."

"Dr. Klobucher," Freya said softly. "This isn't a teacher; it's Loki of Asgard."

"Loki?" the principal said. "The real Loki? You're the one who set off that stink bomb in my school?"

Loki bowed at the waist. "At your service."

The sound of approaching police sirens halted further discussion. "I've called the police. I don't think either of you should be here when they arrive."

"I don't know," Loki said. "It might be fun."

The principal narrowed her eyes at him. "You really are trouble, aren't you?"

The grin on Loki's face broadened, and he winked. "Well, I do like to have my fun."

"Loki, that's enough," Freya said as more students came up to them. They were now completely surrounded.

"You two must go," the principal said. "The police will be right here, and I can't explain you away."

"I might hang around for a bit," Loki teased.

"But you can't," the principal said. "It's too dangerous."

"Loki, go," Freya said, "or I might be forced to tell Odin it was you who helped me cross Bifröst."

Loki's eyes darkened. "Are you threatening me?"

Freya nodded. "The way I feel right now, I'm ready to hit you!"

"Not smart, little Valkyrie," Loki said as he turned to walk away. "Not smart at all."

"Do I want to know what that was all about?" Dr. Klobucher asked.

"No," Freya said. "The less you know about Loki, the better."

When two police cars pulled up, Archie caught Freya by the sleeve. "C'mon, Gee, let's get you and Orus out of here before they start asking questions."

Everyone was staring at Freya as she stormed down the school's hall. Word of the fight between her and JP had spread faster than a wildfire, and all the students wanted to see her. Stopping at the girls' bathroom, Archie shoved open the door. "Is anyone in here?"

When no one answered, they walked in.

"Stay at the door," Archie said to Tamika. "Don't let anyone in, including teachers."

Freya checked on Orus first. When she was satisfied that apart from the swollen eye and a few bent feathers, he wasn't seriously hurt, she reached for her coat. "Stand back," she warned Archie as she reached for the slipcover. When it came away, she put both hands on the edge of the sink and leaned forward as she slowly opened her wings. The pain was intense. Freya started to tremble as she carefully extended them fully. She sucked in her breath as the pain soared.

"Gee, you're bleeding!" Archie cried as blood dripped to the floor. "JP broke your wing!"

"*Let me look,*" Orus said.

The raven climbed onto Archie's arm and inspected Freya's right wing. He leaned forward and carefully went through all the feathers until he found the problem.

"*Uh-oh, here it is. It's a ruptured blood feather. One of the big ones,*" Orus explained. "*I'm afraid it needs to come out now.*"

"My wing isn't broken. It's a ruptured blood feather," Freya explained. "When a new feather is just emerging, the shaft is full of blood. Now that it's broken, unless I pull it out, the bleeding won't stop."

She looked back at Archie. "Move further away from me—this could be messy, and I can't risk you touching my blood."

When Archie was standing next to Tamika, Orus directed Freya's hand back to the broken feather. It hurt to even touch it. She closed her eyes, gritted her teeth, and caught hold of the shaft. Fighting to keep in the cries of pain, Freya wrenched the feather out.

Her hands were shaking as she inspected the damaged black feather. "It takes ages to grow primary flight feathers."

Archie peered at the broken feather shaft. "Wow, no wonder it hurt. That's thicker than my finger!"

"Let me see," Tamika called. She came forward and looked at the damaged feather. "Yuck, that's gross." She pulled paper towels from the dispenser. "We'd better clean up that blood before someone sees it."

"I'll do it," Freya said. "You can't touch it. My blood is as deadly as I am."

"Are you going to be all right?" Archie asked.

Freya nodded as she started to clean the floor. "I won't be flying anytime soon, but I don't think any bones are broken."

Tamika shook her head. "I was so scared when I saw JP hit you with the bat. But I was even more scared when you took off your glove."

Freya looked down. "I shouldn't have done that. If Loki hadn't arrived, I would have killed him."

"I'm glad you didn't, but why is Loki hanging around?" Archie asked.

"He's bored," Freya said. "And he knows he'd be in as much trouble as I would if Odin finds out about me."

"Well, I hope he's gone for good," Archie said.

"Don't count on it."

22

IN ASGARD, MAYA HAD ONLY JUST RETURNED TO BED when the sound of loud, angry voices disturbed her rest. She sat up when she realized who it was.

"*Is that—*" Grul asked sleepily from his perch.

"Odin!" Maya cried. She leaped from her bed and reached for her robe.

Maya entered the living area and saw her mother and three sisters standing before the leader of Asgard. Her mother was wearing her light robe, and her long braids hung down to the floor. She was wringing her hands and trembling.

Her sisters were still dressed in their gowns and looked as though they had only just arrived from Valhalla.

Odin's face was stormy as he stood before them. Loki was standing right beside him wearing a self-satisfied expression.

The moment Maya laid eyes on him, she knew he was the reason for Odin's visit.

"Where is she?" Odin demanded. "I do not like to be disturbed during my sleep with news of a runaway."

"Freya has not run away," her mother insisted. She caught sight of Maya and ran to her. "Maya, would you please fetch Freya. Loki insists she has fled Asgard."

Maya shot a threatening look at Loki.

"I am sorry, dear lady," Loki said, "but Freya is not here to be fetched. Earlier this evening, with my very own eyes I saw her and Orus flying across Bifröst."

"That is impossible," Odin said. "Heimdall would never allow it."

"Yes, well, Odin, I do hate to tell you this," Loki said in a voice that dripped with false sadness, "but Heimdall isn't as reliable as you think he is. I often catch him sleeping on duty. Why, this very night, I found him lying on the ground and snoring like thunder. He threatened me when I told him you would be angry."

"That's a lie," Maya shot. "Heimdall is loyal to Odin and his duties!"

Loki gave Maya another knowing smile. "Anyone who is content to spend an eternity watching a bridge can't be trusted. How do we know that he won't allow the frost giants to cross into Asgard to destroy us all? He barely speaks to anyone. Who knows what he's thinking or what plots he's hatching?"

Just as Odin opened his mouth to defend Heimdall, Loki continued. "But if you insist that Freya is here, show her to us and we can end this."

Pressed into a corner, Maya approached Loki. "If you are so frightened of frost giants, what does that say about your very own wife, who happens to be a frost giantess? Are you suggesting that we can't trust her and that she shouldn't be welcomed in Asgard?"

"You leave my wife out of this, Valkyrie," Loki shot back as his dark brows knitted together in a threat.

"Enough!" Odin shouted. "I will not have this bickering."

"Great Odin," Maya said, "are you going to let Loki disturb your rest and lead you around like a mule? He is causing trouble, and you know it!"

A shadow crossed Odin's face. "I do not like your tone, child. Loki told me he saw your sister cross Bifröst without leave. I have no cause to doubt him."

"But it's Loki!" Maya insisted. "You know he's only doing this to discredit Mother."

"Maya . . . ," her mother warned.

Maya was desperate to save her little sister and had to do something to convince Odin of Loki's treachery. "Look what he did to your own son," she suggested. "Everyone knows it was Loki who gave Mjölnir to the frost giants. Then he convinced Thor to dress as a woman and pretend to be the new bride of their leader to get it back. Thor was humiliated, and it nearly started another war with them!"

"Maya, stop!" her mother cried as her pale cheeks went red with embarrassment. "It was never proven that Loki stole Mjölnir. And it wasn't just Loki who convinced Thor to dress as a woman; we all did. It was the only way to get his hammer back without going to war."

"No, it was Loki!" Maya insisted. She looked desperately to her three sisters for support, but they said nothing. They were too frightened to speak.

"Stop!" Odin boomed. "If it is true that Loki is causing trouble, prove it. Bring your sister to me. However, if she has fled Asgard, it is she who is in a great deal of trouble."

Loki grinned, challenging Maya to say more. "Yes, Maya, prove me a liar and a trickster. Produce your little sister."

Maya was trapped. She didn't know what she could say to protect Freya. She cursed Loki with her eyes. But if she said more and told Odin it was Loki who had helped Freya cross Bifröst, that wouldn't help her sister.

"She's not here," Maya finally admitted, trying to sound casual. She looked at her mother. "You know how Freya loves to go flying with Orus at night? Especially before a reaping? Do you remember the First Day Ceremony? She went out again last night and isn't back yet. I suspect Loki saw her out there and is using that to cause trouble."

Her mother nodded. "Yes, of course! Odin, Freya was nearly late for her own First Day Ceremony. Maya found her halfway across Asgard. My youngest daughter has a wandering spirit. She often goes out flying alone."

"Nice try, Maya, but it won't work," Loki said. He looked back at Odin. "I told you she's not here. She's gone to Midgard to be with the humans."

"She wouldn't do that," Maya's mother cried. "She knows the penalty for leaving without permission! Please, Odin, give us some time to find her. She and her sister are very close. If anyone can find her, it will be Maya. Please let her go. You'll see. Freya is just out for a short flight."

The smile on Loki's face broadened. "Yes, Odin. Why don't we let Maya go? I am sure she can lead us straight to Freya—in Midgard!"

Maya felt the noose tightening around her neck. "I can only find her by flight." She turned hate-filled eyes on Loki. "And you don't have wings; you're grounded. You can't follow where I go."

Loki used his shape-changing abilities to turn himself into an eagle, then a hawk, and finally a large black insect. When he returned to his normal shape, he smiled again. "I can follow you anywhere you go, Valkyrie. But I don't have to. Freya is not in Asgard. She has gone to the human world to live among them. She hates it here, and she hates Odin!"

"Enough!" Odin shouted.

He approached Maya and raised a threatening finger to her. "Go now. Fly. Find your sister. But if you do not return with her before the Valkyries gather for the reaping this afternoon, you know what I will do."

Maya's mother brought her hands to her lips. Her wings were quivering in fear. "No," she whispered softly.

Odin nodded and turned furious eyes on Maya. "Find your sister, bring her to me at Valhalla, or, I swear by my sword, I will send out a Dark Searcher to find her and unleash the Midgard Serpent on Earth."

23

"I'VE NEVER BEEN HIT IN THE WINGS BEFORE. I DIDN'T think it would hurt so much."

"At least you weren't kicked in the head," Orus complained. *"My eyes still won't focus properly, I nearly bit through my tongue, and my head is still spinning!"*

Freya, Archie, and Tamika walked more slowly than usual as they made their way home. As the excitement faded and Freya calmed, the throbbing in Freya's wings increased. She was glad she hadn't tried to put the silk cover on them again. The coat was bad enough.

"We'll put ice on them when we get home," Orus offered. *"That will get the swelling down."*

"I'm sorry," Archie said. "This was my fault."

Freya frowned. "Why? You didn't hit me."

"Because JP used me as bait. I should have realized when the gang attacked us and he wasn't there that it was a trick. Ever since you stood up to him, he's been waiting to get you. Now he's hurt you."

Freya stopped. "Archie, this wasn't your fault. And I'm not hurt. Just bruised, that's all. It will take more than a baseball bat to hurt me. Remember, I'm a Valkyrie. We've been shot at and blown up since wars on Earth first started. We've had arrows fired at us, cannons, rifles, and hand grenades. Even without my armor, I'm still pretty tough."

The words were just out of her mouth when they all heard the heavy gunning of an engine. They turned and saw a large blue pickup truck jumping the curb and driving along the sidewalk—straight at them.

Freya had only seconds to see JP behind the wheel. Hatred burned in his eyes, and she felt murder in his heart. He wasn't going to stop.

Tamika screamed. Freya knocked Orus off her shoulder and tried to push Tamika and Archie away. Tamika landed on the ground away from the vehicle, but Archie didn't. He and Freya both received the full impact of the truck's front end.

Freya was knocked high into the air. She instinctively tried to open her wings, but couldn't because of her coat— although her strength did manage to tear off the closed buttons. She crashed to the ground hard, landing on her back and damaged wings.

With the wind knocked out of her, Freya was barely aware of the sound of screeching brakes and a truck door opening. Still trying to catch her breath, she saw JP running over. He was clutching his baseball bat, but when he saw her lying on the ground, he stopped. His mouth hung open in confusion and disbelief.

Freya was furious to realize her coat was wide open and her wings fully fanned out on the ground beneath her. JP could see everything.

"What are you?" He kicked the side of her left wing and gasped as it moved, and she folded it in tighter.

"What am I?" she repeated as she climbed, slowly and painfully, to her feet. She pulled her wings in and closed her coat. "I'm the last thing in this world you should have crossed. You've just made your last, fatal mistake!"

"You're an alien!" JP cried as he backed away. "That's what you are, a freakin' mutant!"

"No, not an alien—a very angry Valkyrie!"

Freya started to advance on him. JP threw the bat at her, and she easily deflected it away. "Do you remember when you broke your wrist? You did that trying to hit me."

The sudden realization showed on his face. "That was you? You were invisible?"

Freya nodded and caught him by the coat. She pulled

his face close to hers. "Angels of Death bow to me," she said tightly. "Kings cry before my kind. You, JP, have just sealed your fate!"

"*Freya,*" Orus called. "*Leave him and come quickly. It's Archie. I think he's dying!*"

24

ARCHIE WAS LYING VERY STILL IN THE STREET. THERE WAS a spreading pool of blood underneath him. Orus was hopping around him frantically, while Tamika took off her coat and used it to apply pressure to a large, open gash on his head.

Freya tossed JP aside and ran to Archie. He was unconscious. Despite Tamika's attempts to stop the bleeding, he was still losing a lot of blood.

"Freya, help him!" Orus cawed.

"How?" She had never felt so helpless before. Her best friend was lying in the street, possibly dying. He needed help, but what could she do? Her touch meant death to him, not life.

"Greta, here," Tamika called. "Be careful not to touch him, but hold this coat over his wound. I'm calling an ambulance."

While she kept pressure on his head, Freya looked wildly around. She searched the sky for an Angel of Death. But so far, none had come. Archie had a chance. But as she held the coat to his head wound, she could feel him starting to fade.

"Hold on, Archie," she cried. "Just hold on!"

The police and an ambulance arrived within minutes. Freya was shooed away from Archie as the paramedics started to work on him. She stood back with Tamika, arms crossed over her chest and trembling as she watched them trying to save his life.

Soon Archie was loaded onto a stretcher and lifted into the back of the ambulance. Freya charged forward and tried to climb in after him, but the paramedic stopped her.

"I must stay with him," she cried. "I can keep the angels away!"

"We'll keep the angels away," the paramedic promised. Then he looked at her. "Were you hit too? You look a little rough. Your cheek is cut, and there's blood on your coat."

Freya looked down at the wide, wet stain on her torn velvet coat. "It's Archie's blood, not mine. Please, I must stay with him!"

A second paramedic shook her head. "I'm sorry, but we need to work on your friend. There's no room in the ambulance for you. We're taking him to the hospital. You can follow behind us."

A police officer came up to Freya. "Let them go. I need you to tell me what happened here."

Freya shook her head. "Not now. I have to stay with Archie." She focused on Tamika, who was standing back with a haunted expression on her face. "Will you tell them what happened? I'm going to get my helmet!"

Freya darted from the scene before the police could stop her and ran the short distance to Archie's house. After tearing inside, she left her breastplate and weapons in the closet but reached for her winged helmet and pulled it on. As the world turned to black and white, Orus called to her, "*Hurry. They're taking him away.*"

Freya threw aside her coat and dashed outside. She opened her wings, but when she tried to fly, she found they were too sprained to work.

"*Try again!*" Orus ordered. "*Hurry!*"

On the second attempt Freya only climbed a few feet off the ground before her wings failed and she fell from the sky.

"I can't fly!" she cried.

"*Then run!*" Orus cawed.

While the raven soared above her, Freya ran as fast as she could to catch up with the ambulance. She darted around cars and wove through traffic as she followed Archie to the hospital. Her eyes never left the sky as she watched and waited for an Angel of Death.

"*Archie will live,*" Orus called. "*He wouldn't dare die on us.*"

25

FREYA KEPT HER HELMET ON WHEN THEY REACHED THE
hospital. Invisible, she watched the doctors work on Archie,
and kept out of their way as they took him into surgery. Orus
remained at her shoulder, offering what little comfort he
could.

The surgeons had only just started to work on his head
when an unwelcome visitor entered.

The most stunningly beautiful angel Freya had ever
seen drifted into the operating theater. He was tall and
lean, with immaculately groomed feathers on his neatly
folded wings. He wore a soft, warm expression on his painfully handsome face.

Freya approached and held up her hand. "Go back," she
warned the Angel of Death. "You are not taking him."

The angel smiled. "I'd heard that there was a Valkyrie in this place. You don't belong here, child, and you know it."

Freya nodded. "I do know it. And I know I've caused trouble with the other angels and that Azrael is going to be furious with me. But please, I am begging you. Go back. Archie means everything to me. I can't let you take him."

The angel chuckled softly, and the sound was like soft bells. "You think Azrael will be furious?"

Freya nodded. "That's what the others say."

"Well, I've heard he can be very understanding."

"Not about me being here. But this time it's different. Archie is my best friend; I can't lose him."

"I am sorry to disappoint you, young one," the angel said. "But it is his time. He was meant to come weeks ago, but you intervened and stopped that other boy from killing him. You gave him extra time. But that time has run out. He must come with me now."

Freya gasped. "Archie was going to die that day?"

The angel nodded. "You saved his life then. But there is nothing you can do for him now. It is as it must be. There is no future for Archie, only the past. Take your precious memories of him and return to Asgard."

Freya opened her arms and her pain-filled wings to block the angel. "No. I'm sorry, but I won't let you take him. He has lived a hard life. He deserves better."

"And he will have it. This you already know."

Freya shook her head. "No, I mean here and now, in this life. For the first time, Archie has friends and people who care about him. I won't let you take that away."

"You can't stop me," the angel said softly.

"Actually, I can, and you know it," Freya said. "Valkyries get first pick of the dying. You cannot reap until we go. I will not leave him to you."

"But you cannot stay here indefinitely. You have your own duties to attend to and will have to go eventually. When you do, I will be waiting."

"We'll see about that," Freya challenged.

The Angel of Death chuckled softly, bowed, and walked through the wall. Freya could feel him waiting just outside.

"I don't think he's going to go," Orus said. *"He could cause some trouble for us."*

Freya shook her head. "I don't care. I am not going to let him take Archie."

True to her word, Freya remained with Archie all through his surgery. As long as she was there, the Angel of Death had to stay away. She watched the surgeon slowly putting her friend back together again and then followed Archie into the recovery room.

Freya stayed with Archie as he was wheeled into the intensive care unit. As the long night wore on, she kept a vigil at his bedside. He was hooked up to so many machines that she could barely see his bruised face under all the tubes that fed into him. The sighs of mechanical breathing mixing with the beeps of his heart monitor were the only sounds breaking the silence in the room.

His surgeon, Dr. Taylor, came to check on him several times, but Archie's face never changed—it was as if he were in a deep sleep. Freya remained at his bedside and could feel the doctor's deep concern for his patient.

The world outside seemed to still, as night turned to day and then back into night again. As yet another dawn approached, Freya refused to leave. She couldn't risk it. Gazing toward the door, she saw Archie's Angel of Death patiently waiting to enter. He would nod to her when she gazed in his direction. He was leaning casually against the doorframe, with his arms folded across his chest. Never moving, always just watching and waiting.

"*He's almost as determined as you are!*" Orus said. "*Do you want me to go and peck him?*"

"No. He's just doing his job," Freya said tiredly. "At any other time we might have been friends. He can't help what he is any more than I can."

Late in the afternoon Freya heard a voice she recognized. She looked up and saw Tamika standing outside the unit. Curtis was with her, holding her hand. The nurse pointed to Archie's bed and said, "You can only stay a few minutes."

"Greta, are you here?" Tamika called softly.

"I am," Freya answered.

"Where? I can't see you."

"I'm here, in the corner up by Archie's head."

"How is he?" Curtis asked.

"Not good," Freya answered softly. "It's like this terrible waiting game. As long as I'm here, Archie will live. But if I go, the Angel of Death will take him."

"The Angel of Death is here?" Curtis asked fearfully. "I can't see him."

"He doesn't want to be seen, so you won't be able to. He's standing right beside the door. He can't come in with me here. He's looking at us right now."

Tamika looked at the doorway. "Please go away," she called softly. "Archie has to live."

The angel smiled gently at her but shook his head.

"He still won't go," Freya said.

"Greta, you can't stay here all the time," Curtis said. "You'll have to go eventually. What about food?"

"I won't leave him," Freya said stubbornly. "I will eat when I know he's safe."

Curtis looked down at Archie. He was deathly pale and unmoving in the bed. The machines were all that kept him alive. "Maybe it's his time," he said softly. Tears sparkled in his eyes.

"No," Freya shot back. "I won't allow it. I can't lose him."

"Has his mother been told?" he asked. "I know this is

very difficult for you, but it's her decision whether to turn the machines off or not."

"She doesn't have the right to make that decision," Freya spat. "Not with the way she neglects him. It doesn't matter anyway; no one knows where she is."

A nurse entered the unit. "I'm sorry, but you need to go now. Archie needs his rest."

Tamika was reluctant to leave. She whispered, "Don't die, Archie—I've lost enough people in my life." Wiping away tears, she called, "Bye, Greta. See you later."

"Who's Greta?" the nurse asked as she escorted them out.

As evening turned to night, Freya remained at Archie's side. She reached out with her gloved hand and took hold of his hand. Saying nothing, she stood still, keeping a protective vigil over her friend.

26

MAYA WAS FRANTIC. AFTER THE CONFRONTATION WITH
Odin, she dashed to her bedroom, picked up her winged helmet, and flew out the window. Checking that Loki wasn't
following her, she headed straight to Bifröst.

Heimdall was at his post, and his face showed alarm
when she landed before him. "Maya? What brings you back
here so soon and dressed like this?"

Maya realized she was still dressed in her nightgown. "It's
Loki," she cried. "He's betrayed us and told Odin that you
were asleep on duty and allowed Freya to cross the bridge. I
have been commanded to bring her back before the Valkyries
leave for the reaping, or he'll send out a Dark Searcher to
find her and release the Midgard Serpent!"

"No!" Heimdall cried. "This is my fault. Freya will be

punished, when the crime was mine. I must tell Odin."

"It was Loki, not you!" Maya insisted. "But all is not lost yet. I have until the reaping to find her. Please, I beg you, let me cross Bifröst. I will go to Midgard and bring her right back. Then we can go to Odin together and tell him of Loki's treachery."

Heimdall nodded and stepped aside. "Go, find your sister. I will do what I can from here."

Filled with relief, Maya went up on her toes and kissed the Watchman lightly on the cheek. "Thank you, Heimdall. I will be back soon."

"Fly safe, Valkyrie!" Heimdall called as Maya leaped up into the sky.

As though the Rainbow Bridge understood the urgency of the situation, Bifröst released Maya over the central United States. It was dark out, and she was grateful for the cover of night.

Flying as fast as her wings could carry her, she flew down into Lincolnwood and landed in the backyard of Archie's house. She stormed up to the door and shoved it open.

"Freya!" she shouted. "Freya!"

Silence.

"*Maybe she's in the city helping people again*," Grul suggested from her shoulder.

"I hope not." Maya ran into Freya's bedroom to look for clues.

"*Maya, look,*" Grul cawed. "*That's Freya's coat.*"

Her sister's velvet coat was in a heap on the floor. When Maya picked it up, she saw that it was torn and covered in fresh blood. She sniffed the red patch. "Oh no."

"*What is it?*" Grul demanded.

"This is mainly Archie's blood, but I can smell Freya's, too."

"*But there's so much of it,*" the raven cried.

Panic gripped Maya's heart. Her sister was missing, and her coat was covered in blood. She took several deep breaths to slow her pounding heart and closed her eyes and opened all her Valkyrie senses. She felt nothing of Freya or Archie in the house, but she did find something that might help.

"Sylt!" she said. "Grul, Sylt is still here."

Maya found her way to the garage and opened the door. The Reaping Mare was inside and whinnied excitedly when she entered.

Without pausing, Maya leaped onto the mare's back and directed her out of the garage. "Find Freya," she ordered. "Sylt, take me to Freya."

The Reaping Mare nickered, opened her wings, and launched into the sky. Keeping low, she soared over Lincolnwood and headed toward a large building. Maya read the lit sign on the front. LINCOLNWOOD HOSPITAL.

She looked at her raven. "This is where they treat wounded humans."

"*Archie's blood,*" Grul offered. "*He's been hurt and brought here.*"

"I just hope Freya hasn't done something foolish."

"*You mean more foolish than running away from Asgard to come here?*" Grul asked.

Maya had the Reaping Mare land on the roof. "Sylt, stay," she ordered as she climbed down. "We won't be long."

"*Is it wise to leave a young Reaping Mare here unattended?*" Grul asked.

"No, it's not," Maya admitted. "But we don't have much choice. It's still dark out, so there's little chance of her being seen."

"*You hope.*"

Maya looked at her raven. "Yes, I hope. Now, let's get in there and find that sister of mine!"

27

ARCHIE WASN'T GETTING ANY BETTER. AS THE LONG
night progressed, the surgeon came in for several short
visits. But each time he looked less hopeful.

Hours before dawn, Freya heard a voice.

"There you are!"

She looked up and saw Maya. Her sister approached the
Angel of Death and bowed before storming into the intensive care unit. She was wearing her winged helmet and
nightclothes.

"I have been searching all over for you!" She caught hold
of Freya's hand and started to pull. "Come, we must go. Odin
is in a fury. He knows you've run away. Sylt is on the roof; she
will bring us home."

"Odin?" Freya cried. "How?"

"How do you think? Loki told him. You must come back now, before the Valkyries gather for the reaping. Odin doesn't know I've left Asgard. I told him you were out flying. But if he finds out, he'll send a Dark Searcher after both of us."

Freya's eyes went from her sister to Archie and then to the angel at the door. "I can't go." She pulled free of her sister's hand and moved back to Archie's side.

"What? Why?" Maya demanded.

"Because of him!" Freya pointed to the angel. "He's here for Archie."

Maya frowned in confusion. "So, let him have him."

"No!" Freya cried. "Archie is my friend. If I let the angel take him, I'll never see Archie again."

"Then reap him, and we can go."

"I can't do that, either," Freya said. "He won't have died in battle. Odin will never allow him to stay in Asgard. He'll send him through the Gates of Ascension and I'll lose him forever."

Maya pulled off her helmet and became solid. "Freya, you're going to lose him anyway! If Odin sends a Dark Searcher after you, you will lose everything. So will I. I begged Heimdall to let me cross Bifröst again. He'll get into trouble as well."

Freya removed her own helmet. "I'm sorry, Maya. Go back to Asgard. I don't want you to get into trouble for me.

Tell Odin what I'm doing. Tell him I promise I'll come home as soon as I know Archie is safe."

"Are you insane?" Maya cried. "I can't tell Odin that!"

"I don't care what you tell him," Freya continued. "I'm not leaving Archie!"

"But he's just a human!" Maya exclaimed. "You hate humans! Why would you risk yourself for one?"

"Valkyries," warned the angel at the door. "I believe you should cover yourselves again. The doctor is coming!"

But it was too late. Freya and Maya watched Dr. Taylor enter the intensive care unit. His surprised eyes landed on them by Archie's bed. "You there," he called. "What are you doing in here? It's late—visiting hours are long over."

Maya stepped forward and gave the doctor her most devastating smile. The surgeon was stopped in his tracks and stared at her with his mouth open.

"Wait here," Maya told Freya. "I'll take care of him."

"No!" Freya wailed. "Don't reap him. He's trying to save Archie!"

"I'm not going to," Maya said. "Would you please trust me?"

She approached the surgeon and placed her hand on his covered shoulder. "What's your name?"

"P-Peter," he stammered. "Peter Taylor."

"Well, Peter, I need to speak with my sister," she said softly. "Would you please check on your other patients and leave us be for just a little while?"

"I—I . . . ," Dr. Taylor muttered.

"Please . . . ," Maya said coyly, giggling softly. "I promise we won't be long."

Freya watched her sister use her beauty like a weapon against the unsuspecting surgeon. His eyes were huge, and his face turned bright red. He didn't stand a chance against her. Maya's ability to charm was renowned in Asgard. No human could resist her.

"Of course," the surgeon finally said. "Take all the time you need." He drifted out of the intensive care unit as if in a dream.

The Angel of Death took several steps into the room. "That really wasn't very nice of you, Valkyrie. He will come out of your spell very confused. Peter Taylor is a truly gifted surgeon. It won't be good for him or his patients if he starts to question himself."

"It's better than me reaping him," Maya shot back. She focused on Freya. "Now can we go?"

As they talked, the Angel of Death took several more steps closer.

"Stop!" Freya said, blocking his way. "I told you, you're not taking him."

"It is his time to die," the angel said softly. "It grieves me that his passing will cause you pain, but it is unavoidable."

"And I say he is going to live," Freya insisted. "Angel, you have so many others you must take. Go to them. Let me have Archie for a while longer."

"I am sorry, Valkyrie," the angel said softly. "This is not my decision. I do only what I must."

The angel took one more step closer and focused on Maya. "Would you please tell your sister that there are times when we must all do things we don't want to?"

Maya reached for Freya's hands. "I know how much you care for Archie, but you must let the angel do his job." She paused and drew her sister closer to Archie's head. "Look at him. He is suffering. The longer he lives, the more he will suffer. He wouldn't want this half existence between life and death while you and the angel fight over him. There is no recovery for him, and you know it. Let Archie go."

"No," Freya cried. "Please," she begged the angel. "Please just give us more time together."

"Freya, you can't stay," Maya insisted. "Odin is going to send the Dark Searcher after us."

The angel inhaled sharply. "A Searcher is coming for you?"

Maya nodded. "If my sister doesn't return to Asgard with me right now, Odin will send him after both of us."

"Child, listen to me," the angel said. "Dark Searchers are not to be taken lightly. Please, do as your sister asks. Save yourself and return to Asgard. Your loyalty to your friend is admirable, but it will get you killed."

Freya was desperate. "One week, that's all I'm asking for. Please, just give us one more week."

"Why one week?" Maya asked.

"Because that's when the school dance is," Freya explained. "Archie was so excited about it. All of the Geek Squad are going." She turned, imploringly, to the angel. "Angel, I know it's within your power to grant Archie one more week. Please, you must do this for him. He and the Geek Squad have been denied so much; can't we give him this one dance?"

The angel frowned and stepped closer. "You, a powerful Valkyrie, would risk your own life so this boy can attend a simple dance?"

"It's more than a simple dance; it's a triumph. You don't understand how it is for Archie and the others like him," Freya continued. "They have been picked on, beaten up, and bullied just because they're different. But they are all wonderful, caring people. This one dance doesn't mean much to most, but to them it's everything. They are just learning to stand up for themselves, and coming to this dance will prove it. If Archie and I don't go, they won't. How can we deny them this victory over their fears?"

The angel considered a moment. Then he looked at Maya. "One week will be but a short time in Asgard."

"But Loki is out for blood," Maya cried. "There is no telling what poisonous words he is feeding to Odin right now. It is too dangerous."

"I'm not leaving," Freya insisted stubbornly. "Please, Angel, give Archie one more week."

The angel looked over at Archie. Then he approached

Freya. Standing before her, he rested his hands on her shoulders and leaned closer to her. "If I do this, you must swear that the day after the dance, when I come back for Archie, you will not stop me."

"Don't do it!" Maya cried. "One week is still too long. Loki has betrayed you. Odin will send the Dark Searcher. I know he will. You must come with me now before it's too late."

"I can't," Freya insisted. "I'm sorry, but you still don't understand. I must stay for Archie, Tamika, and the others. Go back to Asgard. I will return right after the dance."

"But the Dark Searcher will find you."

The angel shook his head. "No, he won't. Not if she doesn't wear her helmet. That's how he'll track you. When he arrives, we will do what we can to distract him."

Freya looked at the angel in shock. "You would do that for me?"

"You are risking Odin's wrath for this human boy. How could I not? Now, do we have an agreement?"

Freya nodded. "I swear, after the dance, I will not stop you."

"It is agreed," said the angel.

Freya stepped aside and let the Angel of Death pass. Her heart was pounding ferociously in her chest. She knew angels could be trusted. But seeing him so close to Archie set her nerves on edge.

The Angel of Death stood beside the bed and waved his hand over Archie's head. "It is not your time, child. Sleep now and heal. When you wake, you will grow stronger. Go to the dance. Live your whole life within this next week."

When he finished, he looked at Freya. "It is done. He is yours—for now. You are risking everything. Use this time wisely, Valkyrie."

The angel bowed and then vanished.

When he was gone, Maya faced her sister. "Freya, what have you done?"

28

MOMENT BY MOMENT ARCHIE IMPROVED. AN HOUR LATER
Dr. Taylor and a nurse returned, but with the Valkyries wearing their helmets, they remained invisible.

The doctor checked and rechecked Archie's vitals. He scratched his head in complete puzzlement. "I don't know how, but this boy is recovering at an amazing rate. I'm sure he can breathe on his own now."

"It's a miracle," the nurse said as she helped the surgeon remove Archie's breathing tube.

When they left, Maya shook her head. "So, the angel has done what he promised. Archie will live one more week. You're risking everything for him. Is he really worth it?"

Freya nodded. "He is. If you knew him, you'd understand."

She looked out the window. "It's still dark out. You'd better get going. Take Sylt back to Asgard with you. I don't want her blamed for my actions. "

Maya shook her. "I'm not going anywhere. If you are staying, so am I, and if the Dark Searcher comes, we'll face him together."

Freya was awash with gratitude for her sister. She threw her arms around her and hugged her tightly. Together, she knew they could face whatever Odin threw at them.

They stood at Archie's bedside waiting for him to wake up. Just before dawn, he started to stir.

Orus flew down from her shoulder and landed on Archie's chest. He marched up to his chin. *"Come on, Archie,"* he cawed loudly. *"Wake up!"*

Finally Archie opened his eyes.

Freya removed her helmet, and Maya did the same. "Gee," he rasped softly. "What happened?"

"JP hit us with a truck. But you weren't struck very hard. You're going to be fine."

A frown knitted Archie's brow. "I don't remember. Are you okay? There's a cut on your face. Did he hurt you?"

Freya smiled gently at her friend. "I'm fine; the cut's almost healed. But he did hurt my wings again."

"Guess this means you'll have to ride with me on Sylt until they heal."

"Ride Sylt?" Maya asked. She looked at Freya. "Have

you been letting him ride your Reaping Mare?"

Freya nodded. "Every night. We take her out and go flying together, don't we?"

Archie nodded. "I love Sylt. She's so cool."

Freya reached for the covers. "Come on, then. Get up. It's time to go home."

Archie pulled the covers back. "I can't leave. This is a hospital. I need to be released."

"What?" Freya cried. "Of course you can. You're healed, and I release you."

Archie laughed. "You can't release me. We need a doctor to let me go, and because I'm a kid, an adult needs to bring me home. They won't let me go on my own."

Freya looked out the window at the rising sun. "I don't understand, but all right. I'll be back later with Alma or Curtis and Carol; they should be able to get you out."

As the two Valkyries put their helmets on to leave, Archie called after them. "Ask them to hurry. I'm starving!"

29

IT WAS MIDAFTERNOON BY THE TIME CURTIS AND CAROL were able to get Archie checked out of the hospital and back home. After they left, against all orders to take it easy, Archie ordered pizza with everything and devoured more than half the pie by himself.

Freya watched with deep pangs of sorrow as her friend enjoyed his food. Archie was running out of time but didn't know it.

She caught Maya watching her and smiled weakly.

"I'll be here with you for it," Maya said softly.

"For what?" Archie asked, stuffing another piece into his mouth.

"The dance," Maya said. "Greta told me all about it, and it sounds like fun."

"You're coming to the dance?"

When Maya nodded, Archie grinned. "I'm going to the dance with two Valkyries? How cool is that!"

Later in the day Freya and Archie convinced Maya to put on some of Freya's clothes and join them in going to Tamika's house. Archie wanted to show them he was all right, and Freya wanted to introduce her sister. She also wanted to quietly thank Tamika and Alma for cleaning and repairing her velvet coat. With the bloodstains gone, she didn't have to worry about Archie seeing them and asking awkward questions.

When they arrived, everyone was shocked and thrilled to see how much better Archie really was.

Alma grinned at Freya. "Angel, did you have something to do with his sudden recovery?"

She shrugged. "What could I do? I'm just a Valkyrie." Freya then introduced her sister, using the name Mia.

Alma smiled radiantly at Maya. "Aren't you the pretty one!"

Maya returned the smile. "It is a pleasure to meet you."

Tamika was bursting with excitement and could hardly contain herself. "We've got so much to tell you! We're moving!"

"What?" Freya said.

"Curtis and Carol are buying a big house near here, and we're all moving in together. I won't have to change schools!"

Freya frowned in confusion. "But what about this house? You said you didn't want to leave it."

Alma came forward. "This place? It's just an old, run-down house. We were fighting to protect our home. We'll still have that. And thanks to you, our family has grown."

"I—I don't understand," Freya said.

"Come into the kitchen and help me finish making dinner."

Leaving the others, Freya and Orus followed the old woman into the kitchen. When they were away from Tamika's hearing, Freya watched the old woman struggle to sit down. Instantly at her side, Freya helped her into a chair. She could feel her increasing weakness. Alma didn't have long.

"The doctor says the cancer's grown. I don't need any doctor to tell me that. I can feel it in my bones."

Freya felt the oddest sensation clutching her heart. It was something she'd only experienced once before—when the Angel of Death had said Archie's time had come. She suddenly realized she was feeling grief. Though she had only known Alma for a few weeks, the thought of losing her was painful.

"Is there nothing they can do?"

The old woman shook her head. "They've done all they can. It's my time, and I'm getting tired of fighting. You once told me there wasn't an Angel of Death standing at my side.

He may not be beside me, but you can bet he's knocking at my door. I can feel him."

Freya heard Tamika's laughter from the front room. "Does she know?"

Alma shook her head. "Not really. She's so excited for the dance, I couldn't tell her."

Freya dropped her head and walked over to the sink. She peered out the kitchen window at the burned-out wreck of the house next door. "I've failed," she said softly. "I promised your son I would take care of his family, and I have failed."

"What?" Alma cried. "You've done everything you promised Tyrone and so much more."

"But I didn't save this house—you're leaving it. The girls will be left alone without you."

The old woman struggled to rise and approached Freya. She put her hand lightly on Freya's arm. "You listen to me, and you listen good. I was going to die whether you came or not. But now, thanks to you, I can rest easy knowing my girls will be safe with Curtis and Carol. We're making all the arrangements. They're going to adopt the girls when I'm gone. Tamika and Uniik will have everything they need to live good lives."

"But—" Freya said.

"No buts. You've fulfilled your promise to my son in more ways than even he could have imagined. Maybe not in the way you intended, but you have. Child, listen to me.

I understand what you are and what you've gotta do in your life. But here and now, you have saved all of us. Tamika has friends she never had before. She and her sister will grow up with parents who adore them. What more could you possibly give them?"

"You," Freya said softly as she peered into the old woman's fading eyes. "I should be able to give them you."

Alma smiled gently. "I don't think even a Valkyrie could do that. Death is natural for us folk down here on Earth, and I'm ready to go." She reached for her cooking pot. "Now, why don't you spend some time with Tamika and Archie, and leave me to finish dinner?"

"But I want to help," Freya argued.

"You can help by staying out of my way." As she shooed Freya out of the kitchen, the old woman laughed. "And tell your sister I want to take her measurements later. By the looks of things, I have another dress to make for the dance."

Dinner was loud and filled with laughter as they all sat together enjoying their meal. At first awkward, Maya soon relaxed and sat beside her sister, telling stories of their life together in Asgard and sharing with the others the details of Freya's First Day Ceremony.

"I wish I could've seen it," Archie said. "Valhalla sounds awesome."

"It is," Maya said. "But this world has its own kind of magic. I think my sister is just discovering that for herself."

Freya nodded and then looked at Alma. "When I came here, I really didn't like humans."

"And now?"

Freya grinned. "I really like them."

"That's just too sweet." Archie put his finger down his throat and pretended to gag.

"I like *most* humans," Freya corrected as she whacked him lightly on the arm.

When Monday morning arrived, Freya tried to convince her sister to join them at school. But nothing she said could induce Maya to come.

"Spending a day at a human school?" Maya cried in disgust. "I'd rather marry a Dark Searcher."

Freya shot a look at her. Dark Searchers were a subject she'd rather not think about.

"Sorry," Maya said quickly. "My words got away from me."

Archie looked suspiciously between the two. "Is there something you're not telling me?"

Freya put on a forced smile and shook her head. "Nope. Everything's fine." She waved good-bye to her sister. "We'll be back by four."

Outside, Archie looked back at his house. "Will Mia be okay on her own?"

Freya nodded. "Orus taught her how to use the television

and remote. He's told her all about his favorite shows. I'm sure we'll find she hasn't moved from the sofa all day."

Archie's return to school was met with loud shouts of greetings from the members of the Geek Squad.

"Boy, I thought I'd never see you again!" Leo Max said. "We tried to visit you at the hospital, but the battle-axe on the desk wouldn't let us in."

"It wasn't serious anyway," Freya said quickly. "It was just a bump on the head."

Archie nodded. "It's going to take more than JP in a pickup to keep us down. Isn't it, Gee?"

Freya nodded as once again pain stabbed her heart. JP had gotten him down. It was only the deal with the angel that was keeping him alive. Hoping to change the subject, she asked, "What happened to JP? Did the police get him?"

Kevin shook his head. "He knocked Dr. Klobucher down and then started pounding on Mr. Powless. He ran just as the police got here. Then he stole his dad's pickup truck. That's what he hit you with."

"Yeah," Leo Max added. "He busted up Mr. Powless's lip good and broke his nose. He's been away on medical leave."

"Where is JP now?" Archie asked.

Leo Max shrugged. "The police are still looking for him, but they think he's run away. His gang has been expelled permanently from school."

"Finally!" Archie cried.

The bell rang, and everyone headed toward their classes.

"Aren't you coming?" Archie asked as Freya stood back.

Freya shook her head. "I'll be right there, but I've got to see the principal first. I want to let her know that you're back and to ask permission for my sister to come to the dance." She paused and looked sadly at Archie as he went off with Leo Max and Kevin. She couldn't tell him that she was also going to let Dr. Klobucher know that this was their final week at the school. It was time she returned to Asgard.

30

MAYA WAITED BY THE WINDOW AND WATCHED THE street. She needed to be sure Freya and Archie weren't coming back. When she was convinced, she picked up the large coat Alma had given to her.

"*What are you planning?*" Grul asked as she pulled it on.

"I don't think Freya realizes just how much danger we're in. If Loki convinces Odin that I've come here, there will be no stopping him. I've got an idea, and I just hope it works."

"*I don't like that look on your face,*" Grul warned.

Maya smiled at her raven. "Then you're especially not going to like what I've got planned."

Leaving the house, she walked down the long street. The air was cold, and it felt as if it might snow at any minute.

"*Will you at least tell me where we're going?*"

"I saw a park not far from here when we first arrived. There are some trees in it. I hope they are dense enough to hide in. I can't wear my helmet, but I need to get back up into the air."

"*Where are we going?*"

"Asgard."

Halfway to the park, Maya paused. She had a feeling they were being followed, but she hadn't spotted anyone around her. Using her senses didn't work—there were too many people in the area.

"*What is it?*" Grul asked.

Maya's keen eyes searched for movement behind parked cars or in the bushes in people's front yards. But she couldn't see anything specific.

"Nothing," she muttered. "I just have a feeling that we're being watched."

"*Do you think it's Loki?*" Grul asked fearfully.

Maya shook her head. "No, I can never sense him. Besides, he'd come at us straight on, with Odin in tow. What I'm feeling is very earthbound." After a moment she started walking again.

Reaching the park, they made their way over to a dense cluster of trees. "Perfect," Maya said. She pulled off her wool coat and hid it in the trees. Extending her wings to fly, she suddenly felt someone behind her. Turning sharply, she saw a tall, stocky boy approaching her.

"Well, well, well," he said as he casually came forward. "What have we got here? It's another winged freak."

Maya sensed a darkness coming from the boy. Hatred so deep and intense, she could almost taste its foulness in her mouth.

"Who are you?" she demanded.

"Don't you know? I'd have thought that other winged freak would've told you all about me. The name's JP. Who are *you*?"

"Not someone you want to know," Maya said darkly. "Yes, I recognize your name. You tried to kill my sister and Archie."

"That black-winged demon is your sister?"

Maya inhaled deeply. "I would tread very carefully, *human*," she warned. "I care a great deal for my sister. I won't tolerate you calling her names."

"What are you gonna do about it, *Valkyrie*," JP shot back. A cruel, triumphant smile rose to his lips. "Yes, I know what you are. That black-winged freak told me, so I looked it up. I know what you do and where you're from. You kill people. But you can't kill me. This isn't a battle-field. Thor wouldn't like it."

"Odin, actually," Maya corrected. "Thor wouldn't care who I killed." She used her Valkyrie speed and strength to catch JP by the coat before he could move. She hoisted him into the air with one hand and slammed him against a tree. When he fell to the ground, she put her boot on his chest.

"Did your research also tell you that Valkyries can punish whomever we feel deserve it? And you, boy, deserve it more than anyone else I've met in hundreds of years. I should break every bone in your body for what you've done."

"Go ahead!" JP challenged. "Then I'll tell everyone what you are. They'll catch you and your sister and lock you up so far away that not even Odin will find you."

Maya was stunned by his arrogant defiance. The boy was as fearless as he was dangerous. She hauled him to his feet and pressed him against the trunk of the tree. JP struggled in her grip and tried to hit her. But Maya was faster and caught his arm.

"What happened to you, boy? How could one so young be so angry?" Her eyes bored into him, searching for answers. "No one is born evil. Who hurt you so badly that you have become this monster?"

"No one touched me. They wouldn't dare!" JP shot back. "I do what I want. Always have, always will, and nobody can stop me."

Maya shook her head sadly and lifted the bully until his feet dangled off the ground. "Now you listen to me. I don't think you fully comprehend who you are dealing with. I could break your body or I could destroy your mind. Then you wouldn't be able to hurt anyone ever again."

For the first time, uncertainty and then fear rose in his eyes.

"Would you like that, JP? Would you like me to destroy your mind? Because I can—right here, right now."

JP shook his head.

"Say it!" Maya commanded.

JP slouched in her grip. He dropped his eyes. "Please don't hurt me."

Maya leaned in closer to his face. "If I didn't have somewhere very important to go, I would make you beg. So hear me well, human. Leave this town. Go as far away from here as you can. If I ever see you or hear anything of you again, you will not survive the next encounter. Whatever you think a Valkyrie is—it's only a fraction of what we truly are. Remember that!"

Maya stood staring into JP's eyes. The bully's emotions betrayed him. He was terrified. She shoved him away. "Go now, and pray we don't meet again!"

JP stumbled away from her. When he was out in the open, he turned back and raised his fist. "This isn't over, freak!"

"*He won't learn. Go get him!*" Grul cawed furiously.

Maya shook her head. "There's no time. If we fail and Odin releases the Midgard Serpent, he'll wish I had ended his life. Come, let's go."

Maya leaped into the air. With the trees offering her cover, she and Grul headed straight up. Finally she changed direction in the sky and sought the entrance to Bifröst.

* * *

"Heimdall," Maya called softly. She was standing within the brilliant glow of the Rainbow Bridge.

"Maya?" the Watchman called back. He left his post and approached the entrance of the bridge.

"Are we alone? Is it safe for me to come off Bifröst?"

When Heimdall nodded, Maya exited the bridge. It was still dark out in Asgard, but she could feel it wouldn't be long until dawn.

"Where is Freya?" Heimdall asked, looking past her.

Maya sighed. "There's been a bit of a delay."

"What? There can be no delays. Freya must come back right now before we are all found out!"

"It's not as simple as that," Maya said. She stepped up to Heimdall and started to tell him about Freya's life on Earth, the friends she had made, and the deal she had struck with the Angel of Death.

"She is risking her life for this human boy?"

Maya nodded. "I have never seen my sister so devoted. It's a friendship so deep, it's unbreakable. Freya has risked everything to give Archie one more week of life." She paused and looked away. "But it's doomed. In a few Earth days the Angel of Death will take Archie, and Freya will never see him again."

"And?" Heimdall asked gently.

Maya sighed. "And I want to give Freya those last few

days to share with him. Once they part, I know my sister will mourn for the rest of her life."

Heimdall shook his head. "I don't know, Maya. Dawn is but a short time away. There may not be Earth days left for them. When the Valkyries gather for the reaping and Freya isn't there, all will be lost."

"I know," Maya said. "But I've got an idea to buy her some time."

The Watchman's bushy blond eyebrows knitted together in a deep frown. "What are you planning?"

"When I was a child, I remember the senior Valkyrie, Broomhilde, had too much mead at Valhalla. She thought it would be fun to let the Reaping Mares out of their stalls for a long, late-night flight."

Heimdall started to chuckle. "I remember. It caused pandemonium. It took all night to catch the mares and get them back into their stalls. When Odin found out, he was livid and demoted her. Your mother then became senior Valkyrie."

Maya nodded. "I am going to do the same thing."

"What? Maya, you can't! If Odin discovers it was you . . ."

"It can't be any worse than sending Dark Searchers after us or unleashing the Midgard Serpent on Earth. If I release the Reaping Mares, it might cause enough of a diversion that I can get Freya back here without anyone noticing."

Heimdall shook his head. "Odin is no fool. He'll know what you did and why."

"Perhaps," Maya agreed. "But by then Freya and I will be back and Loki won't have any proof of where we've been."

"But you'll be punished," Heimdall insisted. He dropped his head. "I don't want to see you hurt."

Maya was deeply touched by his concern. "I know," she agreed softly. "But seeing Freya so happy will be worth Odin's punishment."

The Watchman paused and rubbed his chin with a massive hand. Finally he nodded. "Stay here a moment."

Heimdall went back to his guardhouse. He returned carrying an unopened keg of mead. "Take this. When you get to the stables, open it and spill mead around the area, and then leave the opened keg where it will be found. With luck, Odin will suspect it was a reveler from Valhalla who freed the mares."

Maya was struck silent by his generosity. "I—I don't know how to thank you for this."

Heimdall blushed bright red. "I just hope Freya appreciates you."

Maya nodded and lifted the heavy keg. "She does. She'll also know what a true friend she has in you." Opening her wings, Maya leaped into the air and headed for the stables of the Reaping Mares.

The long stable blocks were far enough from Valhalla that there was little chance of being seen from there. Before landing, Maya used her senses to feel for anyone in the area. She, like all Valkyries, could sense all but a few Asgardians. Circling above one more time, she couldn't feel anyone in the area. All was quiet.

Maya landed before the stable doors and put down the heavy keg of mead. She pulled the cork from the top and tipped it over, letting some of the golden drink spill out. It splashed on her clothes and boots and pooled on the ground.

Maya lifted the keg, intending to pour more out, but she heard a voice behind her.

"Careful there, Maya. You're spilling it. . . ."

Maya dropped the keg and groaned inwardly as Thor and his brother Balder staggered up to them. They were both drunk and hanging on to each other for support.

"What a waste . . . ," Balder mumbled as he stumbled forward and righted the keg. Lifting it above his head as though it weighed nothing, he poured a stream of mead into his mouth.

Maya was almost too frightened to think. Both Thor and Balder were part of the few Asgardians she never sensed. She had been caught. Thinking fast, Maya pretended to have had too much to drink and approached Balder and slapped him on his thick arm.

"Hey, save some for me . . . ," she slurred. "I had to fight a dw-dwarf for that keg. . . ."

Balder tipped the keg in her direction, and the powerful

drink splashed into her face. Maya rarely drank mead but was forced to open her mouth and take a large gulp of the bitter liquid.

Thor came forward and took the keg from his brother. He brought the opening to his mouth and started to gulp. A renowned drinker, Thor had never been defeated in drinking games. This was evident by his finishing the keg before Maya's eyes. He threw the empty keg aside and licked his lips noisily.

"That's just made me thirsty. . . ." He put his arm around Balder's shoulders. "Come, Brother, back to Valhalla. There still might be a few kegs left."

Thor's heavy eyes landed on Maya. "Valkyrie, join us for a drink. You can entertain us with a song."

Maya did her best to look as drunk as they were. She giggled coyly and stumbled into Thor's powerful chest. She turned on the charm as she put her arms around his neck and looked up into his piercing blue eyes. "I—I would love to, b-b-but I'd better get . . ." She hiccuped for effect and giggled softly. "I'd better get home. You know how my mother can be. . . . Especi-especially if I'm drink."

Balder laughed and slapped Thor on the back. "I think she means 'drunk.'"

Thor burst out laughing, and his drink-filled breath nearly choked Maya. He hugged her tightly. "Next time you come with us. . . . And I want a dance, too!"

Maya nodded and pulled free of his crushing embrace. She grinned at him. "Next time . . ."

To keep up the act, Maya staggered away from Thor and Balder and opened her wings. When she tried to fly, she stumbled in the air and crashed to the ground. She sat there, wings askew, laughing as Thor tripped over to help her up.

"Did you s-see that?" she slurred, holding on to him. "The g-ground attacked me."

Thor laughed and brushed off her wings roughly. "You're too drunk to fly. You'd better walk home."

Maya grinned at him again. She went up on her toes and kissed his cheek. Then she staggered away. When she was away from their view, she dashed behind the feed shed for the Reaping Mares and watched Thor and Balder start to sing loudly and stumble away from the stables and back toward Valhalla.

When their voices faded away, Maya crept back to the stables. If this worked, Thor would tell Odin that she'd been here, but at least he and Balder could confirm her drunkenness.

The rest was easy. Slipping into the stables, Maya opened all the stall doors and shooed out the mares. In no time at all the Reaping Mares were gathered outside the stables and launching into the air.

Satisfied that it would slow down the reaping and buy Freya precious time with Archie, Maya took to the sky and headed back to Bifröst.

31

THE FOLLOWING WEEK PASSED IN A BLUR. DAYS WERE spent in school, while nights were passed with Freya, Maya, and Archie soaring in the skies above Illinois looking for places to feed Sylt.

Flying late into the night, they soon discovered they had an unexpected problem. All of Freya's heroic escapades in Chicago hadn't gone unnoticed by the authorities. She knew she'd been seen by several people, including the police, but never expected the military to take the reports of the flying girl seriously. She was very wrong. When Freya, Maya, and Archie approached the city limits, they saw soldiers posted at the top of many of the skyscrapers and were pursued by military helicopters that seemed to be expecting them.

One near capture was especially frightening, as the fast-maneuvering military helicopters chased them through the city canyons and nearly blinded them with their blazing searchlights. It took all their skills to escape the vehicles by climbing high enough in the sky that they couldn't be followed.

After that, they kept exclusively to the open farmlands and forests of Illinois and stayed as far away from human development as they could.

On Thursday afternoon the Valkyries, Archie, and the Geek Squad helped Tamika and Alma move into their new home with Curtis and Carol. It was in the same neighborhood as Leo Max. Food was served, and it turned into a large housewarming party.

It was long past dark when the party broke up and the Valkyries and Archie made their way back to Archie's house. Walking up the path, they found the lights on.

"Mom!" Archie cried as he ran up the steps. He put the key in the lock and charged through the door.

"Archie, is that you?" a woman's harsh voice demanded.

"This isn't good," Orus remarked.

"I think we're in trouble," Grul agreed.

Freya and Maya stood back in the entranceway as Archie entered the living room.

"Where have you been?" his mother angrily demanded. "Don't you know what time it is? And who were those boys who came around earlier looking for you? What kind of trouble are you into now?"

Her slurred words reminded Freya of the warriors at Valhalla who had consumed too much mead.

"I'm sorry, Mom," Archie said. "I was out with friends. There was a party—"

"You don't have any friends," the woman spat.

Before Maya could stop her, Freya charged into the living room and faced the woman. Her hair was the same color as Archie's, but greasy and matted. Her eyes were red rimmed, but unmistakably the same as Archie's.

"Archie has plenty of friends!" Freya cried. "What kind of mother leaves her son alone for weeks at a time? You should be ashamed of yourself!"

"Gee, please," Archie begged.

Freya looked into his pleading eyes. All traces of fun and happiness had faded beneath his mother's gaze.

"Who are you?" she demanded. "What are you doing in my house?"

Freya could feel waves of anguish coming from Archie. He gave an almost imperceptible shake of his head, begging her not to say more.

"I'm Greta, a friend of Archie's. He's been tutoring me in math. He's really good at it, not that you're ever sober enough to realize!"

"Why, you foul little cat, how dare you?"

She charged forward, and Freya could smell the drink and filth on her. The woman raised her hand as if to slap Freya's face, but Freya caught hold of her wrist and bent it back.

When his mother cried in pain, Archie ran forward. "Gee, no, please stop. Please, that's my mother!"

Freya's furious eyes landed on Archie. "This is no mother. You deserve so much better."

The woman's knees gave out, and she crumpled to the floor, drunk and unstable. Freya released her wrist. "You have no idea who your son is, or how precious he is to me. All you think about is yourself!"

"Get out," the woman wailed. "Get out and stay out!"

"Freya, we'd better go," Orus said gently. *"You aren't help-ing Archie. Look at him—she's destroying him. Please, leave him what little dignity he has left."*

Freya took a deep breath. "You're right," she said softly to the bird. "We can come back for our things later."

She approached Archie and led him back to the front door. When they stood on the porch, Freya turned to him. "I'm so sorry if I've made things worse. I didn't mean to. But she's so cruel to you. We'll go over to Tamika's for tonight. Why don't you come with us?"

Archie was humiliated and wouldn't meet her eyes. "I—I can't. I know what she is, but she's still my mother. She needs me."

Freya ached to tell him that it should be his mother taking care of him. Instead she smiled. "Of course, I understand. I'm just worried about you."

He shrugged in resignation. "I'm used to it. But did you hear what she said? Some boys came around looking for us. Do you think it could be JP again?"

"No," Maya said knowingly. "I'm sure we've seen the last of him. It's probably nothing."

"Wait," Archie cried. "What about Sylt? She won't be able to go out flying tonight."

"She'll be all right for one night." Freya leaned closer. "Just try to keep your mother out of the garage. I don't know what Sylt will do if your mother goes in and starts screaming."

"She never goes in there," he said. "I'll just make her some food, and then she'll probably crash for the rest of the night."

Freya reached out and caught Archie by the hand. "We'll be at Tamika's. If you need anything at all, just call and I'll fly right over here."

He nodded but said nothing as he turned back to the door. "'Night, Gee and Orus. 'Night, Mia."

"Good night, Archie," Maya said gently.

The two Valkyries started the long walk back to Tamika's new neighborhood. Maya tried to comfort her sister. "Maybe it's not such a bad thing the angel is coming for him. After we leave, there's no life for him anyway."

Freya looked back at the house where she had shared so much with Archie. "I guess so," she agreed softly.

Before they reached the new house, Freya stopped and turned around. "I've got to go back. I won't let that woman ruin what little time he's got left."

"Freya, stop," Maya said. "I understand how you feel, but this isn't our realm. We are only visitors here and can't get involved."

"I know, but—I am involved." Her imploring eyes looked at her sister. "Maya, what's wrong with me?"

"You know what's wrong. The dance is almost here. On Saturday you will lose Archie forever, and it's hurting you." Maya paused and looked at her sister as though seeing her for the first time. "I never imagined you could feel things so deeply. Archie has really changed you."

"It's not just Archie. It's everyone. I adore Uniik and want to see how Tamika grows up. Look how much Leo Max has changed. He's become brave and strong and looks out for the others. They are all my friends. I don't want to leave them."

Maya gave her sister a powerful hug. "And that is the tragedy for all of you. Freya, I know you are lonely and searching for something that's missing in your life. In time you will grow older and it will ease. But you can't stay here. They are human. You are Valkyrie. The two aren't meant to mix except in Asgard."

Freya dropped her head. "I know that. And I know I shouldn't have let myself care for them. But I do. And now that I've got to go, it is tearing me apart."

Maya kissed her on the forehead. "We still have a couple of days. Find joy in the time we have left. Let the others know that you care. Even if you can't tell them you're leaving, let them know how you feel, so that when you are gone, they will remember."

Freya nodded. "You're right. I'll try."

32

FREYA AND MAYA STOOD OUTSIDE THE SCHOOL, WAITING.
Archie was late, and the morning bell was about to
sound.

"Where is he?" Freya demanded. "He's late."

"He'll be here," Maya offered. "Just calm down."

"If she's done anything to him," Freya threatened, "I
don't care what Odin does to me, I swear I will take off my
glove and reap her!"

Orus leaped off her shoulder and rose into the air. *"Wait
here. I'll see if I can find him."*

Several minutes later, Archie appeared down the street
with Orus sitting on his shoulder. He was walking slowly
with his head down. When he arrived at the school steps,
they could see that his eyes were red from lack of sleep.

Freya leaped down the stairs. "Are you all right?"

Archie nodded. "Just tired. Mom won't tell me where she's been or what's happened to her. This morning she locked herself in her room and started drinking again."

Freya balled her hands into fists. Maya came up beside her and placed a calming hand on her shoulder.

"I'm sure she'll tell you when she's ready," Maya said. "It's late. You'd better get inside. I'll meet you both right here after school."

Freya remained close to Archie all day. Some of the sparkle was slowly returning to his eyes as Tamika and the members of the Geek Squad crowded around him, offering their support.

Orus too was keeping close. The raven spent most of his time on Archie's shoulder instead of Freya's.

By lunch, Archie was more himself and talking about the dance later that night. "My mom says I can't go. But I'm going anyway. Right after school I'll sneak back home and grab my clothes." He looked at Tamika. "Can I come over to your house to get dressed?"

"Sure," Tamika said. "Greta and Mia are staying with us, so you can too."

Leo Max put his arm around Archie. "And we'll all come home with you just to make sure your mother doesn't try to stop you."

"Then it's settled," Freya said. "Tonight we'll all have the time of our lives and dance like there's no tomorrow!"

As the clocked ticked away the final hours, Freya looked around the school with heavy sadness. This was her last day. Tomorrow she would return to Asgard. The only time she would be able to return to Earth—if she was allowed to return at all—would be to reap soldiers on the battlefield.

Each moment became a treasured memory—all the noise, the crowds of kids jamming the halls, and the smell of the school cafeteria. Memories would be all she could take away with her.

"*Are you okay?*" Orus asked. He was back on her shoulder.

"I guess so," Freya said as they walked to her locker. "But I'm going to miss this place so much."

"*Perhaps Odin will let us return,*" he offered. "*If we do a good job, he may let us take a break.*"

Freya shrugged and sighed sadly. "It won't be the same. Time moves so quickly here. If we go home for a short while, most of these kids will have grown up and forgotten all about us."

Orus moved closer to her neck and rubbed against her. "*Yes, they will have grown up, but believe me, they will never forget you.*"

As the final bell rang, Freya closed her locker for the last time. She would leave everything behind. She and Maya waited outside as Archie, Tamika, and Leo Max arrived, their faces flushed with wide grins.

"Well, this is it!" Tamika said. "Let's go get Archie's clothes and head over to my house. This is going to be so much fun. I can't wait for the dance!"

Freya watched her young human friends. Not too long ago, Leo Max had found the courage to ask Tamika to go to the dance with him as his date. She had agreed and was now bouncing with excitement.

"Then what are we waiting for?" Maya said as she put a comforting arm around Freya. "Tonight will be a night we'll all remember forever."

Back at Tamika's house, Freya and Maya put on the dresses Alma had made for them. Freya was wearing a stunning midnight-blue, full-length satin gown with a full, long blue cape of the same fabric mounted to the back of it. The dark color complemented her red hair. Her sister was wearing a delicate pink silk gown that brought out her fair complexion. She also had a full long cape mounted to the shoulders. Both Valkyries had matching satin opera gloves.

Orus and Grul had been scrubbed and had preened their black feathers until they shone like new. Orus strutted around, admiring his reflection in the mirror.

"*By far the handsomest of all,*" he said.

"*Says who?*" Grul complained.

"*Me!*" Orus cawed.

"You're both very handsome," Freya said as she gave Orus a kiss on the beak. Then she whispered into his ear, "But you are the best!"

Alma was wearing her kitchen gloves as she fussed with the dresses. "They fit perfectly. No one would ever suspect what you two have hidden under those capes."

Freya turned to the old woman. "I don't know how to thank you, Alma. These dresses are stunning."

"Stuff and nonsense!" the old woman said, though her fading eyes sparkled. "You girls just have fun."

Carol and Curtis watched them each appear, dressed to the nines. "I wish your mothers could see you all," Carol said. "They would be so proud."

Freya looked down at herself and thought about her mother. What would she say if she knew what Freya had been doing? Her mother had had many adventures when she was growing up. Freya was sure she'd understand . . . eventually.

Moments later Archie appeared from the spare room. His hair was neatly styled, and he was wearing a dark suit. He was struggling with the tie at his neck. Curtis offered to tie it for him. "It takes a bit of practice," he said.

Leo Max arrived wearing a tailored suit and a new, embroidered yarmulke. Curtis went crazy taking loads of photographs of them from every possible angle. He was behaving like an excited new father.

Standing back and watching him, Freya felt the depths of his emotions and knew that was exactly what Curtis was: a new father with a ready-made family. His joy was unmistakable.

She looked over and caught her sister smiling at her. "You did well," Maya softly whispered.

When they arrived at the school, they could hear loud, pounding music and could see colorful lights flashing from the school's gymnasium windows.

Half the school seemed to be filing into the gym. Freya's eyes were bright as she took in the sights of all her classmates dressed up in their best party clothes. The excitement was so high that for a brief moment, she was able to forget the coming dawn and Archie's impending death.

Maya leaned closer. "This is almost as good as Valhalla."

Freya shook her head in wonder. "No, it's much better. Look at them. Aren't they all so beautiful!"

"Yes, you are," Archie said, looking at her. He offered his gloved hand. "Let's go in."

Wearing her own blue gloves, Freya accepted Archie's outstretched hand and allowed him to escort her in.

Inside the gym the music was pounding. Tables of drinks and snacks lined the walls, while the roof of the gymnasium had been decorated with paper streamers and balloons. A single mirror ball had been hung from the center and was spinning slowly, casting diamond sparkles along the walls and down onto the partygoers.

Having lived among humans for several weeks, Freya had come to enjoy a lot of their music. It had seemed strange at first, but now she realized it would be added to the list of things she would miss.

Leo Max was the first to speak as he smiled at Tamika. "Wanna dance?"

Tamika grinned and followed him, and soon they were swallowed into the thick of the moving crowd.

"Go on," Maya said to Freya. "This is your night. Why don't you and Archie dance?"

Freya looked over to him. "Want to?"

"Sure."

They walked together into the crowd and started to dance. Freya watched her friends. It wasn't like any of the dancing she'd seen at Valhalla, but soon she was moving to the beat of the music.

"It's great to see you finally out of your coat!" called Kevin as he danced with Elizabeth. Their eyes were sparkling with the thrill of actually being there.

Soon the whole Geek Squad had found their way to the center of the floor. Song after song, they continued to laugh and dance together. Even Orus joined in, hopping from shoulder to shoulder as he bobbed up and down to the rhythm of the music.

Eventually Maya made her way onto the dance floor, and the two Valkyries danced with Archie, surrounded by their friends. Freya felt an overwhelming sense of belonging. For this one night she was one of them.

When the next song ended, the lights in the gym were turned up. There were cries of protest from the dancers as their principal took the stage.

"Good evening, everyone," Dr. Klobucher called as she raised her hands in the air to get their attention. "I hope you are all having a wonderful time."

All the students cheered and shouted. Up on the DJ's stage, Dr. Klobucher's eyes sought Freya in the crowd. When they found her, she smiled. "Greta, I hope you will forgive me, but I would like to ask a favor." She looked over the crowd. "I'm not sure if she's told you or not, but Greta will be leaving us soon. I hope before you go, you will let us hear you sing."

Gasps came from the Geek Squad. "You're leaving?" Leo Max asked.

Freya felt a lump in her throat and nodded. "It's time I went home."

"Please, Greta," Dr. Klobucher pressed. "We've all heard what a beautiful voice you have. Just this once . . ."

Freya shook her head. "I can't," she said.

"Sure you can," Archie said as his face glowed with pride. "Go on—I've never heard you sing either. Please do it for me, just this once."

That comment cut right through to her heart like a

dagger. Archie was making a final request. How could she say no?

Freya looked over to Maya. "Will you join me?"

"But this is your school and your night," Maya protested.

Freya held out her hand. "Please—just like we do at Valhalla."

"*Come on,*" Orus cawed. "*Let them hear you sing together.*"

Even Grul joined in and prodded Maya to sing with her sister.

Finally she surrendered and took Freya's hand. Together they walked up to the stage and joined Dr. Klobucher. The principal bowed to them both.

"I'm sorry to put you on the spot, but I couldn't let you go back to Asgard without hearing you sing just the once. I've read all about Valkyrie voices, and I know I'll never have this opportunity again. . . ." She stood back and indicated the microphone on the stand. "Please."

With Freya clutching Maya's hand, the two sisters approached the microphone. Without musical accompaniment they both started to sing at the exact same moment. Freya was melody while Maya automatically took harmony. The song poured over the crowd.

Not a sound was heard from the students as the two Valkyries raised their voices, high and clear, and sang as they did at Valhalla. Finally, when the last notes were sung, a long silence filled the gym. Archie and the Geek Squad were the first to break it by clapping their hands wildly and screaming. Soon the entire gym burst into roaring applause.

Maya squeezed Freya's hand and leaned closer. "And you were afraid they'd forget you? Now they'll remember this moment for the rest of their lives!"

Freya's heart was beating fast as she felt the love surrounding her from everyone.

Everyone, but one.

JP stood at the entrance of the large gym. At first no one noticed, but when JP and his gang shoved their way into the room, word spread of his arrival, and the crowd parted in fear.

The moment the principal caught sight of him, she shouted to another teacher, "Call the police!"

JP stalked closer to the stage and shouted, "Valkyries!"

He was wearing Freya's silver breastplate over his shirt. In his hand he was clutching her sword. He pulled it from its sheath, and the lights in the room glinted off the polished steel blade. He pointed it at Freya. "She's a black-winged demon! A Valkyrie sent here to kill all of you!"

Freya and Maya both looked at JP. Suddenly they realized what he and another member of his gang held in their hands. It was the Valkyries' winged helmets.

"No!" Freya howled as JP lifted her helmet and pulled it onto his head.

33

THERE WAS NO REACTION FROM THE HUMANS IN THE room—their ears were not sensitive enough to hear the high-pitched squealing from the two distressed helmets. But the Valkyries could.

Freya put her hands to her ears and tried to block out the terrible sounds. Her sister was bent over in agony. Both ravens cawed and shrieked in pain.

"We've got to go!" Maya screamed, reaching for Freya. "Odin will hear that! He'll come for us!"

"Odin?" Dr. Klobucher demanded. "What will he hear?"

Freya pointed a shaking finger at JP and shouted over the sounds, "It's forbidden for living humans to wear our helmets! Odin will hear the helmets' cries and come for them."

Both Freya and Maya were being deafened by the sounds

from the helmets, but for everyone else in the hall, there was only silence. Because Freya was still standing before the microphone, everyone in the gym heard her response to the principal.

"See what I mean!" JP cried. "They're both monsters!"

Confused expressions turned to fear as the students moved away from the podium.

"He's lying!"

Freya heard Archie's voice rising above the sound of the helmets. She looked into the crowd and saw him, with the Geek Squad, charging forward. "They're just causing trouble."

JP turned the sword on him.

"What are you going to do?" Archie demanded, facing the bully. "Kill all of us? Go on; try it, in front of all these witnesses! Use the sword. But I swear you won't get out of here alive."

"Archie, stop!" Freya shouted desperately. Was this it? Was this how Archie was going to die? Murdered by JP, using her sword?

Archie looked up to her. "No, Gee. For too long we've all been terrified of JP and his gang—but not anymore. I won't be bullied by him or anyone else!" Archie advanced on the bully. "Take off the helmets. Right now!"

"No, Archie!" Freya howled.

"Whose gonna make me?" JP spat as he advanced on Archie. "*You?*"

Archie nodded.

"And me!" Leo Max added. "C'mon, everyone. Let's get him!"

JP took a frightened step backward. "Stay back!" He raised the sword in the air and swished it back and forth. "I swear I'll kill anyone who comes near me! Just stay back."

Suddenly a powerful and commanding voice shouted, "Stop!"

Thor was standing at the entrance doors. His face was contorted in pain from the shrill sounds of the distressed helmets. He raised his hammer in the air and brought it down onto the gymnasium floor with an explosive force.

The impact was enough to shatter all the windows in the building, crack the linoleum floor, and knock everyone flat. Thor charged forward and wrenched Freya's helmet off JP's head. Then he removed Maya's helmet from the other boy. "Those are not yours!"

Thor cast the helmets aside and charged up to the stage. "Valkyries, down here, now!"

Freya and Maya jumped down from the stage and knelt before Thor.

"What in Odin's name are you two doing here?" he harshly demanded. "Do you have any idea the trouble you are in?"

"It's my fault," Freya said quickly. "Please don't punish my sister. She's been trying to get me to go home, but I needed to do something here first."

"You needed to disobey Odin's laws and neglect your duties to Asgard?"

"No, it's not like that," Freya cried, not daring to lift her head to face Thor's wrath. "I came to help the family of the first soldier I reaped. You saw me with him on the bridge. I was trying to make him see the wonder of Asgard, but he wasn't happy knowing his family was in trouble. You've always said it was our duty to make the warriors happy. When he begged me to help them, I had to come. I would have failed in my duty if I didn't!"

"You did this because a warrior asked you to?"

Freya nodded and pointed at Tamika. "That's his daughter. People were threatening her family. I had to help them. This was to be my last night in Midgard. I was coming home right after the dance."

"And you?" he demanded of Maya.

"I'm here to make sure she came back."

"And that incident at the stables?" he asked. "I knew that was a ploy. You don't drink. Did you really think you could fool me? That I wouldn't go back and watch you release the mares and then cross Bifröst? Just how stupid do you think I am?"

"No, Thor," Maya cried. "I don't think you're stupid at all. I just wanted to protect my sister."

"And you," he said to Freya. "Did it ever occur to you to ask me or my father for permission to come here if you wanted to fulfill your duties? Was that so difficult to do?"

"I—I—" Freya started.

Before she could say more, the screaming started again. Driven back to her knees by the sounds, Freya looked up and saw that JP had donned her helmet again. He lifted her sword and was advancing on Thor.

"Are you seriously challenging me, boy?" Thor called over the screaming. "Do you have any idea who I am?"

"JP, stop!" the principal cried from the stage. "You don't know what you're doing!"

JP only made it two more steps before ferocious howling came from the entrance doors. Everyone turned and started screaming in terror at the sight.

Two Dark Searchers stood at the doors. They were dressed in their long, flowing, hooded cloaks and full battle armor. Their huge black wings were open in threat as each carried their deadly black twin swords.

Both Dark Searchers threw back their heads and howled again.

"What are they?" cried Dr. Klobucher.

"Dark Searchers," Thor responded. "Odin sent them after the Valkyries. I tried to get here before them, but they heard the helmets' cries." He turned back to the principal. "If you care for your students, you will get them away from here. The Dark Searchers will kill anyone who gets in their way. Not even I can stop a Dark Searcher from fulfilling their duty."

The two Dark Searchers stormed into the room. Their heads were panning back and forth over the crowds, until they saw JP and his friend wearing the Valkyrie helmets. The Searchers raised their swords and charged forward.

"Stop!" Thor commanded the Dark Searchers.

"Take off the helmets!" Freya cried frantically. "They are calling the Searchers!"

JP and his friend shrieked in terror as the two monstrous creatures ran at them.

"The helmets!" Maya shouted. "Take them off!"

JP's friend was the first to understand and removed the helmet and cast it aside. One of the Dark Searchers followed it as it rolled away. But for JP, it was too late. The Searcher caught hold of him before he could remove it.

The Dark Searcher held JP by the neck and hoisted him easily off the ground. The bully screamed and tried to break free, but the Searcher's grip was too tight.

"Release him!" Thor shouted.

Freya pulled the blue cape free of her dress and exposed her wings. Opening them wide, she leaped at the Dark Searcher holding JP. She struck him hard, and they all tumbled to the ground.

Freya was the first on her feet. She turned to the stunned students in the gym, and with her wings still open wide, she let out a loud Valkyrie howl. "Go!" she roared to the crowd. "Get out of here! Go now!"

"You heard her," Maya called. "Go!" She released her own wings and did a flying tackle on the second Dark Searcher.

Everyone in the gym panicked and ran for the door, clambering over each other in their desperation to get out.

Freya was struggling to get JP free of the Dark Searcher, but the Searcher's grip wouldn't loosen. "Let him go. It's me you want, not him!"

Hearing her words, the Dark Searcher released JP and tossed him aside. His hand flashed out for Freya, but she was faster. She moved just before he caught hold of her arm.

Freya dashed for the weapon in JP's limp hand. She couldn't tell if he was alive or dead. But before she could reach her sword, the Dark Searcher blocked her. The monstrous creature raised his two black swords and advanced on her.

"I said stop!" Thor shouted.

Despite his rank as Odin's son, Thor could not halt the advancing Dark Searcher. Thor charged forward and tackled the large creature to the floor.

"Valkyries, get out of here," he commanded. "Get back to Asgard, now!"

Freya only had seconds. She glanced over her shoulder and saw that the other creature was focusing on Maya. Freya opened her wings and cried, "Fly, Sister, fly!"

There was no time to say good-bye to Archie, but Freya was confident that Thor wouldn't let the Dark Searchers harm him. She flapped her wings and lifted off the ground and flew straight at the gymnasium's shattered windows. Pulling her wings in tight, she slipped through an opening that was too small for the Dark Searchers to follow through.

Moments later Maya was behind her in the sky. Orus and Grul quickly caught up to them as they left Thor and the two Dark Searchers in the gym. Climbing higher, they headed away from Lincolnwood.

But just as they rose higher over the bright Chicago skyline, Orus cried, *"Faster, Freya. They're right behind us!"*

Freya stole a look back and saw the two Dark Searchers gaining on them. Despite Thor's strength, he hadn't stopped them. Flapping her wings hard, Freya tried to out-fly them. But despite being the fastest flier in Asgard, her wings were only half the size of a Dark Searcher's. There was no way she or Maya could ever hope to reach Bifröst before them. Their only hope was to lose them.

"They're too close," Freya called to her sister. "Follow me. We'll try to lose them in Chicago!"

Taking the lead, with her sister close at her side, Freya reached over and caught Orus in her hands and pulled him in tight. "Hold on. This is going to be rough."

She dove lower in the sky and flew only a few feet above the ground. They darted in and out of traffic, and car horns blared as drivers caught sight of the two Valkyries and the winged monsters chasing them.

No matter what they tried, Freya and Maya could not shake their pursuers. But being smaller meant they were more agile in the sky. They quickly darted around a building and heard the howls of the Dark Searchers as their larger, heavier wings clipped the corner of the building and knocked out chunks of concrete.

It was said in Asgard that once a Dark Searcher was after you, there was no escape. The only thing to do was to give up and hope that, if they'd been ordered to kill, death came swiftly.

Freya was not ready to die yet, but she was quickly running out of ideas. No amount of dipping or dodging could get the Dark Searchers off their tails. Suddenly she heard a sound that on previous nights would have been a warning to flee. But tonight she welcomed it.

High above them in the sky, three military helicopters arrived. The beams of their intense searchlights panned the sky.

"Here!" Freya called as she climbed to meet them. She looked over to Maya. "Follow me!"

Freya flew into the beam of a light. At once the other helicopters focused their searchlights on her and Maya. Freya squinted her eyes and tried to see the pilots. But all she saw was blinding white light.

She pointed behind her to the Dark Searchers, who were also caught and blinded in the beams of light. The monstrous creatures howled in pain and dropped their swords as they shielded their unseen eyes from the light. Their wings faltered, and they began to fall from the sky.

But the blinding light was burning the Valkyries' eyes too.

Freya tilted her wings to try to fly out of the beams, but there were too many of them. Trapped and unable to see, both Freya and Maya flew headlong into the side of a building.

Stunned from the impact, they both started to fall.

34

FREYA CRASHED TO THE GROUND WITH A DEAFENING impact. She landed on her wings and felt many of the fine bones snap. The pain drove the wind from her lungs and left her unable to move.

"Freya, are you all right?" Orus cried as he landed beside her.

Freya shook her head. "I've broken my wings."

"You can't fly?"

"I—can't even move. . . ."

"Freya . . . ," Maya moaned. She was lying crumpled on the ground not far from her. Her left leg was at an odd angle, and bone could be seen sticking out of it. Her wings were obviously broken, as blazing red spread across the fine white feathers.

"Orus, where—where are they?" Freya weakly asked.

"Several streets away. They crashed just as hard as you did. I hope they're both dead."

"Don't count on it," Grul cried. *"Nothing can kill a Dark Searcher. Maya, Freya, please, you must get up. They will come for you."*

Above them, the military helicopters continued to shine their lights down. But with the closeness of the buildings, they couldn't land. However, the sounds of sirens and heavy vehicles could be heard getting closer.

"Please get up!" Orus howled. *"The Searchers will get you."*

"I can't," Freya moaned.

"Gee!"

"Archie?" Orus called.

Freya tilted her head to the left and saw Sylt land in the beam of the bright searchlights. Archie, Tamika, and Leo Max were jammed on her back.

"Wha—what are you doing here?"

"We came to give you these."

Archie held up Freya's sword and breastplate. Leo Max and Tamika were holding the two winged helmets.

"How?"

"It was Sylt," Archie explained. "She knew how to find you. Now get up."

"I can't," Freya moaned. "I—I'm broken. I can't move."

"No way," Archie said as he charged forward. "You are not giving up—do you hear me! Now get up!" He caught her gloved hand and hauled her to her feet. "We don't have much time. Put this on."

Freya swayed on her feet and discovered she had broken ribs as well. "What—what happened to JP?"

"He's dead," Archie said. "That Dark Searcher thing killed him. Thor tried to stop them, but they went ballistic and pushed him aside and chased after you."

"Thor couldn't stop them," Freya explained. "No one can. If Odin commanded them to get us, they'll get us. They crashed on another street. But they will be here soon."

"Then you'd better be ready," Archie called.

He was still wearing his gloves as he helped Freya put on her breastplate. She cried in agony as he moved her broken wings aside so he could fasten it around her.

But once the enchanted armor was in place, Freya found its powers reduced the pain she was in and gave her the strength to move again. She stepped over to her sister. Maya was broken and too battered to move.

"Leave me," she moaned. "Take Sylt and go home. Maybe Odin will forgive you."

"I'm not leaving you here for them," Freya said. "Sylt, come."

Leo Max and Tamika climbed unsteadily down from Sylt. Their eyes were huge as they backed away from the winged mare.

Finally Tamika recovered and ran to Freya. "Are you all right?"

"Not really," Freya admitted. "But my sister is worse. Can you help us get her up onto Sylt's back?"

Leo Max was still too stunned to move. His wide eyes went from Freya to Maya, and finally back to Sylt.

"Leo Max!" Freya said. "Snap out of it. It's just me."

Leo Max shook his head. "Wow, Greta . . ."

"I'm sorry I couldn't tell you," she said. "But we're still the same and we're really in trouble and need your help."

"C'mon, Leo Max," Archie said. "Help me get Mia onto Sylt. Just keep your gloves on and don't let any of her blood, feathers, or hair touch you."

Archie, Freya, and Leo Max managed to get Maya onto Sylt. She was fading in and out of consciousness. Her leg was bleeding, she had a deep cut on her head, and both her wings were badly broken.

Archie tore pieces off Maya's dress to bandage her leg. "Gee, you've both got to go," he shouted.

Suddenly the sound of machine-gun fire split the air. They saw flashes coming from the circling military helicopters. Their hearts sank as their eyes followed the line of fire. The Dark Searchers were moving steadily down the street. The bullets from the helicopters did nothing to slow their advance.

"*They're coming!*" Orus cried.

Freya looked back at her friends. "They're only here for us. Stay back. They won't hurt you if you're not a threat to them."

"But they'll kill you!" Archie cried.

Freya reached for her sword. "Not without a fight." She inhaled deeply and spoke through the constriction in her throat. "Thank you, Archie, for everything. You've been the best friend I could ever hope for. I will treasure each memory forever."

"*Freya, don't do this!*" Orus cawed.

Freya handed the raven to Archie. "Stay with Archie, Orus. I can't watch you die."

"*No!*" the raven cawed.

"Don't fight them," Archie begged, clutching the raven. "Just fly away with Mia and stay safe."

"I can't. They're too fast for me. All I can do is try to slow them down so Mia can escape. Please, Archie, get Tamika and Leo Max away from here. I don't want you to see what happens to me. . . ." Unable to say more, Freya turned from her friends and started toward the two Dark Searchers. She heard Orus calling after her, but she ignored his pleas. The pain of leaving them was tearing at her heart. But she turned that pain into rage as she faced the Dark Searchers.

"You want me?" she cried furiously. "You're going to have to fight!"

Raising her sword, Freya charged at the two dark creatures. All her fury rose to the surface as she used the skills she'd been taught since birth to fight them. Swords flashed and sparks flew as Freya's one sword fought against their combined four.

But even as her fury carried her forward, she was wounded and badly outmatched. The tip of a Dark Searcher's sword grazed down her leg. Freya cried out in pain as the blade sliced through her beautiful long dress and into her flesh. A second blade cut deeply into her arm.

Her breastplate offered her protection from human weapons but offered little protection against the Dark Searchers. Moment by moment Freya was losing ground. As she focused on one advancing creature, she could not defend herself against the other.

With each cut and swipe of their blades, Freya could feel herself weakening. She realized they weren't going to kill her quickly. These Dark Searchers wanted to draw it out slowly, to hurt her as much as possible.

As she stumbled backward, the larger Dark Searcher's blade knocked the weapon out of Freya's hand. His fist slammed her through the plate-glass window of a large department store. Without pausing, the creature stormed in after her while the second Searcher returned his attention to Maya.

As Freya struggled to untangle herself from a rack of expensive clothing, the sounds of her sister's weak cries tormented her.

"Fly, Sylt!" Archie was shouting. "Get out of here!"

Gaining her feet, Freya looked for the Dark Searcher. She could hear him pushing over glass counters and sales displays as he searched for her.

With her leg badly damaged, Freya kept low and limped back to the window. As quietly as possible she climbed out. Just before she jumped down from the ledge, a fearsome hand flashed out and caught hold of the edge of her broken wing.

The Dark Searcher screeched in triumph as he squeezed and drew her back to him.

Freya screamed, and her wing exploded in searing pain as the creature crushed the broken bones in his viselike grip. She was powerless to stop him as he came forward—a terrifying, black monster looming above her.

Moments before his other hand went around her neck for the final snap, Archie screamed, "Let her go!"

He was holding Freya's sword and brought it down on the hand clutching Freya's wing. The blade sliced through the creature's black gauntlet and down to the bone of its ghostly white wrist.

The Dark Searcher howled and released her.

Freya fell forward and hit the ground hard.

"Run!" Archie cried as he caught hold of her bleeding arm and pulled her forward. "C'mon, Gee. Get up and run!"

Freya was dragged alongside Archie for several steps, but the wound in her leg slowed them both down. "I can't—my leg is hurt. Archie, go. He'll kill you if he catches you. Just leave me and go."

"Stop whining and run!" Archie screamed. He half dragged and half carried her into the street. "What kind of Valkyrie are you? You're stronger than this. Now run with me!"

She looked up, searching for Maya. "Where's my sister?"

"She's gone," Archie answered. "Sylt took her away, but the Dark Searcher followed her. We tried to slow him down, but he got away from us."

Leo Max and Tamika dashed forward to help, but Freya warned them back. "No, he'll kill you if you help me. I told you to go!"

As they ran further down the street, police vehicles came to a screeching halt before them. "Stop!" an officer shouted as he opened his door and drew his weapon.

From all around, more police and military trucks arrived, pulling right up onto the sidewalk. They were surrounded.

"Run!" Freya warned them. "The Dark Searcher will kill you all. Your weapons are useless against him!"

"Look!" Tamika howled.

Behind them the Dark Searcher was moving again. Ignoring everything else around him, his attention was focused exclusively on Freya.

"Keep moving," Archie called as he released her and lifted her sword. "I'll slow him down."

"Archie, no!" Freya screamed. "Stop!"

Orus cawed, *"Come back!"*

Nothing could stop Archie from holding up her weapon and charging forward. The Dark Searcher held only one sword, as his right hand was all but useless because of Archie's blow. The creature raised his weapon and took Archie on.

Beneath the bright helicopter lights and surrounded by police and military, Freya watched Archie try to block a cut from the skilled Dark Searcher. But at the last moment the creature changed tack. He brought his weapon up and stabbed it deep into Archie's torso.

"No!" Freya howled.

"Archie!" Orus cawed.

Archie stood motionless as the Dark Searcher's sword struck through to his back. When the creature pulled the weapon out, Archie collapsed to the ground.

"Archie!" Tamika screamed.

The police and soldiers opened fire on the Dark Searcher, but their bullets could not stop him. Instead, Orus, Tamika, and Leo Max ran at the creature as he kicked Archie aside and focused on Freya. Orus dove at his head, while the others ran to his rear. Both Leo Max and Tamika jumped onto his massive black wings.

"Get away from him!" Freya howled at them. "He'll kill you. Get down and run!"

"Save Archie!" Orus cawed.

Holding on for their lives, Tamika and Leo Max were madly spun around as the Dark Searcher fought to bat Orus away while trying to shake them off. Black feathers filled the air as Tamika did all she could to pluck them out of the monstrous creature's wings.

While the Dark Searcher was occupied, Freya limped as fast as she could over to Archie. He was still alive, but bleeding heavily from the wound in his stomach.

From somewhere behind them, a distant clock chimed the hour. It was midnight. The start of a new day—the day after the dance. Freya collapsed beside Archie and pulled him into her arms, knowing what was about to happen. There was nothing she could do to save him. She had made the bargain. Soon the angel would come to collect on it.

"I'm so sorry, Archie," Freya said. Tears filled her eyes. "I can't save you."

"It is over, child."

Freya looked up into the face of Archie's Angel of Death as she cradled her best friend.

"Gee?" Archie whispered.

"I'm here."

"I wanted to stay with you," he said softly. "I wanted you to show me Asgard."

"You're going somewhere much better," she struggled to say. "I wish I could go with you. . . ." Finally the loud sobs she fought to contain escaped her.

"Please don't cry. Just go and be safe."

"I'm not leaving you," Freya whispered.

Archie shuddered as pain tore through him. He shivered as he clutched her arms. "I'm so cold."

Freya looked pleadingly into the angel's eyes. "Please," she wept. "I'm begging you, end his pain. Take him now."

The Angel of Death shook his head and smiled gently. "He has fought valiantly to save you, Valkyrie. Archie is a brave warrior who has earned his rightful place at Valhalla. Take him. He is yours."

Freya inhaled sharply, disbelieving.

"But you'd better hurry. His time grows short, if you want to give him your name."

Freya was shaking as she looked down into Archie's fading eyes. "Archie, listen to me. You can stay with me. Just say my name. I'm Freya. I give you my true name. Please, accept it. Say it now."

"Gee?" Archie whispered.

"Not 'Gee,'" she pleaded. "I am Freya. Fre-ya. Please say it!"

With his final, gasping breath, Archie uttered, "Freya . . ." and closed his eyes.

Freya leaned forward and kissed him lightly on the forehead. The moment she touched him, Archie died. Pulling him close, she rocked him in her arms.

35

FREYA PUT ARCHIE'S STILL BODY GENTLY ASIDE AND rose. Her best friend's spirit stood beside her, looking just the same. He had a huge grin on his face. "Wow!" he whispered. "That was intense! Did you just kiss me?"

Freya's emotions were running wild. Archie was still with her, but for how long? "What did you expect me to do, hit you?"

"I don't know. You never said how you did it. Do you do that to all the soldiers you reap?"

Freya actually blushed. "If you must know, no, I don't. I touch them with my bare hand."

"Cool."

"Now will you shut up and focus? In case dying has erased your memory, I still have a Dark Searcher after me,"

Freya said. What was the point of saving Archie if the Dark Searcher killed her now?

"Sorry, Gee. You're right."

"It's Freya," she corrected.

Archie grinned again. "Nah, you'll always be Gee."

Freya lifted her sword and turned toward the Dark Searcher. "Stay here. I'm going to surrender to him before he kills someone else. If I'm lucky, he's been ordered to punish me but take me back to Asgard alive."

"Child, wait," the angel said. He pointed up. "Look."

The Dark Searcher was shrieking in fury as Angels of Death descended from the sky. Holding hands, they formed a tight circle around him, imprisoning him.

Shocked by their sudden appearance, Orus fled as both Leo Max and Tamika fell from the Dark Searcher's wings. They landed on the ground in stunned silence.

"This way, children," urged an angel as she opened the circle a fraction to allow them out.

The searchlights shining from the helicopters above and the flashing of photographs being taken from phones held by the police and soldiers illuminated the brilliant white of the angels' open wings as they surrounded the midnight-black Dark Searcher.

After a moment the police started shouting and ordering everyone to remain where they were while the soldiers moved in and surrounded the circle of angels. Others raised their weapons on Freya but stayed back a safe distance, as if they already knew what she could do.

Trapped within the angels' ring, the Dark Searcher shrieked and charged furiously forward but could not break through.

Freya looked back at the angel in confusion. "I don't understand."

"Just wait a bit and you will."

"Greta!" Leo Max called as he and Tamika ran toward her. Soldiers tried to catch hold of them, but they tore free of their grip. They approached Archie's body.

"Archie!" Tamika shrieked as she knelt down beside their friend.

"He's not there," Freya called. "He's right here, beside me."

"Where?" Leo Max said.

Freya offered her arm. "Touch me, but only where I'm covered."

Both Leo Max and Tamika touched her arm. They gasped in shock when they saw Archie's face.

"Is it really you?" Tamika sniffed.

Archie nodded. "Gee reaped me. That means I can finally see Asgard!"

"*If we survive this!*" Orus cawed as he landed on Freya's shoulder.

"Which isn't likely," Freya said darkly. "Once he breaks free, he'll come after me again. There's no escape from a Dark Searcher."

Gunfire erupted from further down the street. This was followed by an angry shout and the sound of a very heavy hammer hitting something very big.

"Thor's here," the tall angel said softly.

As they watched, a heavy military tank flew through the air. It crashed against a building and hit the ground in a heap. They all saw a deep dent in its thick side.

"And he's angry," Freya added. She looked at Tamika and Leo Max. "Get behind the angel and stay there."

Thor charged through the line of soldiers, knocking aside those who tried to stop him. If a soldier so much as lifted their weapon at him, he hit them with a blow that threw them several yards away. Making it to the ring of angels, Thor tried to break through, but the angels held fast. One nodded in Freya's direction.

"He looks really angry," Archie said.

"Almost as angry as the Dark Searcher," Freya agreed. "I don't think this can get any worse. . . ."

The enraged roars of the Dark Searcher could be heard throughout the city. But then a new and even louder roar could be heard.

"What's that?" Tamika asked, looking up.

"The sound of things getting worse," Freya answered.

Thor paused and looked up. "Father . . ."

"It's Odin," Freya said softly.

* * *

Odin, in full battle armor, was tearing through the night sky, riding Sylt. On his left was the second Dark Searcher, clutching Maya and Grul in his arms. Behind them flew all the Valkyries of Asgard, led by Freya's mother, Eir.

Freya looked over to Archie in regret. "I'm so sorry it's going to end like this. I shouldn't have reaped you. It's not fair."

"Whatever happens," Archie said, "we'll face it together."

Standing at the ring of angels, Thor waved Mjölnir in the air. All the helicopters were driven away as though blown by a thousand winds—making way for his father and the others to land.

Thor stepped away from the angels and walked toward Freya. Stopping midway, he shook his head. "I didn't want this and came here to stop it before it went too far. But I failed. Now I must do as Odin commands."

Thor raised his hammer high in the air and brought it down to the ground with a crushing impact. Beneath the pressure of the hammer, the street cracked and a large pit opened. Ferocious, deafening roars could be heard coming from the newly opened hole.

"No!" Freya cried.

"What is it?" Leo Max asked.

"Thor has freed the Midgard Serpent!" Freya cried. "Odin is going to destroy Chicago because of me!"

36

"VALKYRIE!" ODIN ROARED AS HE CLIMBED DOWN FROM SYLT.

A large eagle alighted beside him. Moments later it changed. Freya's heart sank at the sight of Loki's grinning face.

Freya turned back to Tamika and Leo Max. "Remember what I told you. Stay here with the angel. He'll protect you. Odin does not forgive. It won't matter that you are young and human. He'll punish you, too."

She looked at Archie, pulled off her glove, and offered him her bare hand. "We may not have much time left together. But I don't regret a single thing that's happened."

Archie pulled off his glove as well, and for the first time, they actually held bare hands. "Me neither."

Together they walked to Odin. They both knelt before the leader of Asgard.

"You were warned," Odin boomed. "You know the punishment for running away."

Freya raised her head. "I do, great Odin. But I beg you, please don't punish my sister. She has done nothing wrong. She came here to bring me back to you. Not to stay. She didn't run away. And Orus could not stop me, though he tried. This isn't his fault."

Odin looked back at Maya, lying in the Dark Searcher's arms. "Your sister is far from innocent in this. She released all the Reaping Mares from the stables in a futile attempt to delay the reaping. They have caused havoc in Asgard. Even now, half of them are still flying wild. She tried to disguise her crime, but there was a witness."

Freya shook her head. "She couldn't have done it. She was with me. Who saw her?"

"Me," Loki said. "I knew she would try something to protect you. But she made a terrible mistake."

"Father," Thor said. "Balder and I did see that Valkyrie at the stables, but she was far too drunk to do anything."

"You thick oaf," Loki said. "She tricked you. And she used the same trick on Heimdall to allow her to cross Bifröst."

"He's lying!" Freya shouted.

Odin's face went red with rage. "She has confessed her crime! That she convinced Heimdall to go along with her is further evidence of her deceit."

Freya was left speechless. Maya had endangered herself for her sake.

"As for your raven," continued Odin, "he will be punished with you." His harsh blue eyes blazed as he drew his sword. "Open your wings!"

Freya struggled to open her badly broken wings. She dropped her head and bent forward to offer them up to Odin.

"Please don't!" Archie cried.

"Archie, no!" Freya warned. "I knew the penalty for breaking the rules. Odin must take my wings."

"No!" Archie shouted. "It's not fair. Gee isn't a runaway; she came here to help. She's helped Tamika's family and she helped me!"

"She helped you to your grave, boy!" Odin spat. "If you think I am going to allow you to stay in Asgard, you are sorely mistaken!"

"I gave him my name," Freya said softly.

"What?" Odin shrieked.

"Freya, no!" her mother cried, coming forward. "Tell me you didn't!"

Freya raised her head. "Yes, Mother, I did. And I don't regret it."

"*Freya*," Orus warned.

"Impudent child!" Odin shouted. "If you have given him your true name, so be it. He will join you in your banishment!"

Odin raised his sword higher. Just as it was swinging

down to cut off Freya's wings, the Angel of Death blocked the blow with Freya's sword.

"What is this?" Odin roared. "Azrael, you have no right to halt my justice!"

"In this case, Odin, I believe I do."

"*Azrael?*" Freya was in shock as she gazed at the Angel of Death. "You are Azrael?"

The angel's gentle, warm eyes sparkled. "Fooled you, didn't I?"

"I don't understand," Freya said.

Azrael bent closer to her. "I wanted to meet the Valkyrie that was causing so much trouble and interfering with my angels' work. You were so passionate, so determined to help these people." He rose and faced Odin. "She has done you proud."

"She has betrayed her kind," Odin said. "Broken the rules and left Asgard without permisison. She must be punished."

Azrael shook his head. "You are Odin, leader of Asgard. Freya is a Valkyrie. That is understood. But she is more than that. She came here with good intentions. She has saved lives."

"That does not alter the fact that she broke the law."

"It should," Azrael said. "For too long we have resented each other. We serve the same purpose, and yet there is animosity between us. This Valkyrie has changed that. Look over there. . . ."

Azrael pointed to the others encircling the Dark Searcher. "I did not command them to do that. They wanted to. They have come here to protect her. If you will not allow her back in Asgard, I will gladly claim her for my own."

Odin looked at Azrael in disbelief. "You would claim a banished Valkyrie?"

Azrael smiled at Freya. "I would gladly ask her to join us. You should be proud of her, Odin, not punish her."

From beneath the earth, the roaring increased. The ground trembled and the street cracked further as the Midgard Serpent shot like an erupting volcano to the surface. It loomed several stories high as it pulled itself from its prison deep within the earth. Slithering through the streets like a snake, its long tail grazed a skyscraper. Within moments the building collapsed to the ground in a heap.

The Midgard Serpent roared in delight at its freedom. Its red eyes blazed, and long fangs dripped acid onto the ground. It slid through the streets of Chicago, biting huge chunks out of buildings and devouring the military trucks like they were candy.

"Send him back, Odin," Azrael ordered. "There has been no crime committed here. The world has done nothing to deserve this punishment."

"Only Loki can command his child," Odin said.

Loki stepped forward. "And I won't stop him until this place is in ruins."

Freya pointed an accusing finger at Loki. "But it was Loki who encouraged me to come here. He's just as guilty as I am. He should be punished too."

"What?" Odin demanded. "Explain yourself!"

"Go on, Loki," she challenged. "Tell him, if you dare." She turned to Odin. "I wouldn't have come here if it weren't for him. He suggested I see Midgard for myself. It was Loki who gave Heimdall the sleeping powder that allowed me to cross Bifröst. He said he always does that whenever he wants to come here."

Archie nodded. "And he released a stink bomb at my school. We couldn't go back for a week! He did it to cause trouble."

"*Loki?*" Odin repeated.

"It's true," Azrael confirmed. "Loki is the one who orchestrated all of this. Not Freya or Maya."

Odin's face went red with rage as he faced Loki. "Explain yourself!"

"They're lying to you," Loki cried as he backed away. His eyes were wild and desperate. "You know I would never betray you." After several more steps, Loki transformed into a hawk and flew away.

Odin turned to Thor. "I will see to him later. Go get Jormungand. Without Loki here to command him, it's up to you to drive him back to the pit! And don't be too gentle."

Thor nodded to his father. He raised his hammer and chased after the disappearing serpent.

"They've always hated each other," Freya whispered to Archie. "I just hope there's something left of Chicago when they're finished."

"Silence!" Odin commanded. "Rise, Valkyrie."

Freya climbed painfully to her feet. Archie stood at her side, holding her hand tightly while Orus remained at her shoulder.

"Azrael has pleaded for mercy on your behalf," Odin started. "I will grant that mercy. But you cannot go unpunished."

Freya dropped her head. "I understand."

"I am stripping you of your powers," Odin continued. "They will not be returned until you can prove to me that you are worthy of the title Valkyrie. From this moment forward, you and your human companion will work in the stables of the Reaping Mares. You will be servants to the Valkyries and hold none of their privileges. You are banned from Valhalla and will not be welcome at any of the reapings or celebrations. Until further notice, you are nothing more than a simple citizen of Asgard."

He turned back to the Dark Searcher holding Maya. "You have served me well, Searcher. Release her. Your duty is finished. You may return to Utgard."

The Dark Searcher released Maya and Grul. Her mother and sisters flew instantly to Maya's side to support her.

Odin then faced Azrael. "Your words hold power. Perhaps

it is time we considered working together and not against each other. Will you release my Searcher?"

Azrael bowed. "As you wish, Odin." He called to his angels, "Release him."

The angels encircling the Dark Searcher nodded their heads and separated. Opening their wings, they took to the sky and disappeared.

"You are also excused," Odin called to the Searcher.

The creature growled at Freya and Archie and raised a threatening hand. Then he opened his massive black wings and took off.

"It is time we left this place to the humans and returned to Asgard," Odin continued. He walked back to Sylt, caught her by the reins, and brought her back to Freya. "From the look of you, you're in no condition to fly. I will allow you to keep your Reaping Mare."

Freya's heart was pounding so fiercely, she was sure Odin could hear it. "Thank you," she said respectfully.

Odin came forward and touched Freya on the head. "I remove your powers, Valkyrie. Your touch is no longer lethal and your senses are dulled. You are no better than a human." Odin turned abruptly and approached another Reaping Mare. Climbing up, he ordered the mare into the sky. "To Bifröst!"

Freya's mother gave her a disapproving look as she helped Maya up onto her Reaping Mare. "Do not test his generosity," she warned as she opened her wings and launched into the sky. "Follow us! We have much to discuss."

"Yes, Mother," Freya said softly. When Eir was gone, Freya turned to Azrael. "Thank you so much. You saved my life."

He smiled. "There's no need to thank me. Remember, my invitation is always open. Just call my name, and I will come to you." His smile broadened as he looked from her to Archie. "I have the feeling I'm going to hear more stories about the two of you."

Freya grinned as Azrael opened his wings and vanished.

The streets were in ruin. Shattered glass and rubble surrounded them, and fires blazed while dust settled from the collapsed buildings.

Tamika and Leo Max ran forward. "Are you going to be all right?"

Freya nodded. "Odin has removed my powers. I'm just like you now."

"Except for the wings," Leo Max commented, grinning at her.

"Is Archie still here?" Tamika asked.

Freya offered her arm, but when the others touched it, they couldn't see him. "I guess without my powers, you can't see him anymore. But I promise you, he's right here with me and always will be."

"*Freya, we had better go,*" Orus warned. "*It won't take much to get Odin angry again.*"

Freya nodded. She inhaled deeply and looked at her two friends. "We must go. I fear I won't be able to visit you again." Once again, pain clutched her heart at the painful good-bye. "I will miss you both so much. Will you be all right getting home?"

Tamika nodded. "I've called Curtis. He'll be here soon."

"Just stay hidden until he comes," Freya warned.

Tamika nodded again. "We will." Forgetting the danger, Tamika threw her arms around Freya and hugged her tightly.

Terrified at first, Freya realized she could now touch her friends. She pulled Tamika closer. "You take good care of your little sister and give Alma a big kiss from me. Please let her know I will treasure every moment we shared. And say my farewells to Curtis and Carol."

Tamika sniffed. "I will."

Leo Max's face went bright red as he faced her. "Bye, Greta. I'm sure going to miss you."

Freya pulled him close and held him tight. "I'll miss you, too. Remember, the Geek Squad is looking to you. I'm counting on you to keep up our good work. Look out for the younger students and please tell Dr. Klobucher what happened here and that I'm okay."

Leo Max nodded. "I will."

Freya smiled and gave him a kiss on the cheek.

"Wow!" He sighed as he staggered back, then grinned at Tamika. "I just got kissed by a Valkyrie. How cool is that!"

"*Freya, please,*" Orus prodded.

Freya nodded and reached for Sylt. Archie was the first to climb up. It took Freya much longer, and she only managed to get onto Sylt's back with the help of Tamika and Leo Max. Every part of her hurt as she took her place behind Archie. "I will remember you both, always."

Tamika and Leo Max waved and chased after Sylt as the Reaping Mare opened her wings and started to run.

Rising above Chicago, Freya could see that Thor had managed to trap the Midgard Serpent on the edge of Lake Michigan and was driving the monstrous beast back underground.

More police and military vehicles surrounded him, while black helicopters watched from the sky.

"Will Thor be okay?" Archie asked.

Freya slipped her arms around his waist and rested her weary head against his back. "He'll be fine. It's the humans we should worry about."

Archie burst into laughter as he whooped happily. Before too long his eyes went wide at the sight of the shimmering Rainbow Bridge.

"Is that Bifröst?"

Freya peered over his shoulder and nodded. "Welcome to Asgard, Archie," she said gratefully. "Welcome home."

A GUIDE TO THIS WORLD

Norse mythology is old. It's not just old; it's really, really old! It's also known as Scandinavian mythology and was created, retold, and loved by the Vikings. The Vikings, or Norsemen, settled most of Northern Europe and came mainly from Denmark, Norway, Sweden, Iceland, the Faroe Islands, and Greenland.

As you get to know the Norse myths, you might notice there are some similarities to the ancient Greek myths (including flying horses—but not my sweet Pegasus). Here's a simple comparison.

In Greek mythology, you have the Olympians and the Titans. The "younger" Olympians, in fact, came from the "older" Titans, and yet, there was a war between them and the Olympians won.

In Norse mythology, you have the Aesir and the Vanir. The "younger" Aesir came from the "older" Vanir, and yes, there was a war! But the difference is, in Norse mythology, neither side won—they called a truce.

Here's a big difference. In Greek myths, you have the place called Olympus. But in Norse myths, there are in fact nine worlds, or "realms" as they are sometimes called. In each of these realms, you have some really weird and wonderful creatures. And you know what? We are part of those nine realms. We're in the middle bit. And instead of Earth, our world is called Midgard.

Now, some of you may think you don't know Norse mythology at all. You do, but what you have learned may not be correct.

What's the biggest mistake I hear all the time? Okay, here is a really big one. I mean *big*. He's huge. He's green and has a bad temper. Yes, I'm talking about the Hulk. He is *not* part of Norse mythology. Neither are Iron Man, Hawkeye, Black Widow, nor many of the other characters from the Avengers movies. But no matter how many schools I visit, the moment I mention Thor or Loki, the students immediately think that the Hulk and the other characters are part of Norse mythology.

Trust me, they're not.

Don't get me wrong: I love the Avengers and Thor movies as much as anyone. But they are the creation of Marvel, Paramount, and Disney. The real Norse myths are much older and have a much richer history.

So, as you enter the world of Valkyrie and Norse mythology, I would like to introduce you to some of the characters you may meet along the way.

Some will appear in this book; others will appear in the

later books in this series. But I also encourage you to go to your local library or bookstore and check out more books on Norse myths. Believe me, with all the heroes and monsters you'll meet, you will soon love them as much as I do!

—Kate

NAMES AND PLACES IN NORSE MYTHOLOGY

YGGDRASIL—Also known as the Cosmic World Tree, Yggdrasil sits in the very heart of the universe. It is within the branches of this tree that the nine realms exist. Yggdrasil is supported by three massive roots that pass through the realms. It is said that the fierce dragon Nidhogg regularly gnaws on one of the roots (when he's not eating corpses— don't ask). The Well of Urd, where Odin traded his eye for wisdom, sits on another root. Water from that well is taken by the Norns, mixed with earth, and put on the tree as a means of preventing Yggdrasil's bark from rotting. They also water the tree. It is said that a great eagle sits perched atop the tree and is harassed by a squirrel, Ratatosk, who delivers insults and unpleasant comments from the dragon Nidhogg, who resides at the base. Yggdrasil gives the nine realms life. Without it, they and we would cease to exist.

AESIR—This is the name of the group of younger gods, like Odin, Thor, Loki, Frigg, and the Valkyries. These are warrior gods who use weapons more than magic.

VANIR—This is the name of the older gods. Not much is known about them, but there are some familiar names. Freya and her twin brother, Freyr, are two well-known Vanir who were traded to Asgard in a peace exchange after the war. The Vanir are more earthen/forest-type gods who deal with land fertility and use a lot of magic.

ODIN—He is the leader of Asgard, the realm of the Aesir. A brave, strong, and imposing warrior, he presided over the war with the Vanir. He has many sons, most notably Thor and Balder. Odin carries a powerful spear, Gungnir, and wears an eye patch. It is said that Odin journeyed to the Well of Urd, where he exchanged his eye for wisdom. Each night Odin can be found in Valhalla, where he celebrates with the fallen heroes of Earth's battlefields. His two wolves sit loyally at his side.

FRIGG—The devoted and very beautiful wife of Odin, she is the mother of Balder and is known for her wisdom. Sadly not a lot more is known about her, other than that she knows everyone's destiny. In later mythology, she is often confused with Freya and their deeds are mixed.

THOR—The son of Odin, he is known as the thunder god and is often compared with Zeus from the Greek myths. Thor is impossibly strong, with flaming red hair and a raging temper. He is known for being a fierce but honorable warrior. Thor is a sworn enemy to the frost giants, but calls Loki (who is part frost giant) a friend. They had many adventures together. Thor is also known for his mighty hammer, Mjölnir, which was created by the dwarf brothers Sindri and Brokkr on a mischievous bet with Loki. After its creation, they gave it to Thor, as he was one of the few strong enough to wield it. (By the way, Loki lost the bet and the two dwarfs sewed his mouth shut.) Thor is actually a married man—his wife is Sif, and they have three children. Note: We use the name Thor every week, as Thursday was named after him. Just think: Thor's day.

BALDER—Son of Odin and Frigg, he is known as the kindest of Odin's sons. Balder is a devoted brother to Thor and can calm his brother's fearsome temper. Sadly, within the mythology, Balder died, and it is widely believed that Loki caused his death and was responsible for keeping him dead.

LOKI—He is the trickster of Asgard. His origins are a little unclear, but it's said that both of his parents were frost giants. He is by turns playful, malicious, and helpful, but he's always irreverent and self-involved. Loki likes to have fun! He enjoys getting Thor into trouble, but then he helps Thor out of the same trouble. Loki is a shape-changer and appears in many disguises. For all his troublemaking ways, it is written that Loki is tolerated in Asgard because he is blood brother to Odin.

HEIMDALL—Ever vigilant watchman of Bifröst, Heimdall has nine mothers but no father. He is a giant of a man and amazingly strong. Heimdall requires less sleep than a bird, and his vision is so powerful he can see for hundreds of miles, day or night. His hearing is so acute that he can hear grass or wool grow. It is written that he carries a special horn, Gjallarhorn, that he will sound at the start of Ragnarök when the giants storm Bifröst.

VALKYRIES—Choosers of the slain, the winged Valkyries are an elite group of Battle-Maidens who serve Odin by bringing only the most valiant of fallen warriors from Earth's battlefields to Valhalla. There, the warriors fight all day and feast all night, being served food and mead by the Valkyries. In early mythology, the Valkyries could decide who would live or die on the battlefield, but later this was changed to only collecting them for Odin. The Valkyries arrived on the battle-fields riding blazing, winged horses, and their howls could be heard long before their arrival. It is written that the Vanir goddess Freya, who was traded after the war, was in fact the very first Valkyrie. Again, within the mythology, she gets to keep half the warriors she reaps—but it's not written what she does with them. The other half go to Odin.

FROST & FIRE GIANTS—Throughout the mythology, the frost and fire giants often appear, and there are many stories about Thor's encounters with them. Fearsome, immense, and violent, they each live in their own realms. Frost giants are from Utgard in Jotunheim, and the fire giants come from Muspelheim. Though there are some peaceful giants, most seek to conquer Asgard. To offer an idea of size, there is one story in which Loki, Thor, and two humans venture to Utgard to meet the frost giant king, but get lost in a maze of tunnels. It is later discovered that these tunnels were, in fact, the fingers of a frost giant's glove.

DWARFS—Both good and bad, dwarfs play a large part and fill an important role in Norse mythology. They are the master craftsmen and architects of the building of Asgard. It was dwarfs who created Thor's mighty hammer, Mjölnir, and Odin's spear, Gungnir. There are many stories of the dwarfs and their amazing creations.

LIGHT & DARK ELVES—These are the two contrasting types of elves. Dark Elves use dark magic, cause a lot of trouble, and can be very dangerous; they are hard to look upon and seek to do harm. Whereas the Light Elves are fairer to look at than the sun, use their magic for good, and help many people.

MIDGARD SERPENT—Also known as Jormungand, the Midgard Serpent is the son of Loki and his giantess wife, Angrboda. The Midgard Serpent is brother to the giant wolf Fenrir and Hel, Loki's daughter and ruler of the underworld. It is written that Odin had Jormungand cast into the ocean, where he grew so large he could encircle the Earth. There is a ongoing feud between Thor and the Midgard Serpent. It is written that Jormungand is big and powerful enough to eat worlds.

RAVENS—Ravens play a large part in Norse mythology, and Odin himself has two very special ravens, Huginn and Muninn, who travel through all the realms and return to Odin at night. They sit on his shoulder and tell him everything that is happening in the other realms. They are known for their wisdom and guidance.

VALHALLA—Odin's great heavenly hall for the heroic dead has a curious problem. In the mythology, there is a question of where Valhalla actually is. Most say it was part of Asgard, but others suggest it is in Helheim, the land of the dead. One thing is clear: Valhalla is a wondrous building where the valiant dead from Earth's battlefields are taken. Here they are served and entertained by the Valkyries who delivered them there. They drink and feast with Odin and continue their training until the day comes when they are called back into service to fight for Asgard during Ragnarök.

BIFRÖST—Also known as the Rainbow Bridge, this is a magnificent, multicolored bridge that links Asgard to Midgard and some of the other realms. It is said to have been created by the gods using the red of fire, the green of water, and the blue of air. Bifröst is guarded by Heimdall the watchman.

THE NORNS—There are three Norn sisters who dwell at the Well of Urd at the base of Yggdrasil. The oldest is Urd, the middle sister is Verdandi, and the youngest is Skuld. These are the goddesses of destiny, similar to the Greek Fates. Urd is able to see the past, while Verdandi deals with current events. Skuld is able to see everyone's future. It is said that they are weavers, weaving people's destiny. If a thread is broken, the life ends.

RAGNARÖK—Also known as the apocalypse of the Norse gods and the end of everything, Ragnarök (in the mythology) is said to have been started by a very insane Loki and his wolf son, Fenrir, along with the frost and fire giants. They took on Asgard, and during the war all the gods were killed. Odin was killed by Fenrir, who was then killed by another of Odin's sons. Thor and the Midgard Serpent fought a battle to the death in which they managed to kill each other. Heimdall was the last to fall at the hand of Loki. It is during Ragnarök that Odin called on the warriors of Valhalla to fight for Asgard—but there were no winners. And it was from the ashes of Ragnarök that a new world was formed from the survivors—the world that we inhabit today.

DARK SEARCHERS—The Dark Searchers did not actually exist in Norse mythology. They are my creation because, in all my research, I couldn't find a mention of Odin's police force. So I created them for that purpose.

AZRAEL & THE ANGELS OF DEATH—Now, some of you may already know that Azrael and the Angels of Death don't come directly from Norse mythology. That's very true. But as they are known all over the world in almost every culture, and since they do similar jobs to the Valkyries and have wings just like the Valkyries, I thought it would be fun to mix things up a bit. To avoid confusion, I set it up so that the Valkyries only deal with the most valiant warriors reaped from Earth's battlefields, who are then taken to Valhalla— thus staying true to Norse mythology. Azrael and his Angels of Death deal with everyone else—thus staying true to many other cultures.

ACKNOWLEDGMENTS

Time is strange—never forget that.

For you, this book might be brand new, as it's just coming out in the United States. But I originally wrote it back in 2013 for my English publisher between Pegasus books. Actually, I lied. . . . (Yes, we authors do that on occasion.) I have now written two versions of this very same book—one was the 2013 edition for the United Kingdom market, and then *this* one that you are reading right now, with a lot more adventure and mischief. (And if I am honest, this is my favorite version.) It was completed last year.

So at the time that I wrote *Valkyrie–Mark I* in 2013, my father became ill and things went a little . . . well . . . funky!

You see, normally I love to visit the places I write about. For the Pegasus series, I enjoyed going back to New York, then to Las Vegas, then to Greece, and even to Hawaii!

When I started *Valkyrie*, I planned to go back to Chicago for research—I had lived there as a kid, but I couldn't remember it enough to write about it. But with my father so sick, I couldn't go.

Were it not for the skills and care of my father's amazing surgeon, Professor Peter Taylor, and the staff at St. Thomas Hospital in London who pulled him through, neither version of this book would have been written.

'Prof,' I am still eternally grateful to you! (And I hope you enjoy your appearance in this book.)

ACKNOWLEDGMENTS

As I couldn't leave my recovering father, I reached out for help. I needed someone who could be my eyes over there and see the things I couldn't see for myself. So I called the schoolboard in the Chicago area where I set the book, and through them, I met a very special woman, Dr. Linda Klobucher, who at the time of writing *Valkyrie—Mark I* was the principal in a Chicago–area school before being promoted. Linda became my long-distance tour guide and a good friend. While I stayed in the United Kingdom, she was always available to talk with me and guide me through the school system and answer any questions I had about what a principal would and wouldn't allow—especially if a winged Valkyrie, dressed in Steampunk clothing with a large raven on her shoulder, showed up on her doorstep!

You were invaluable, Linda. Thank you so much! And look, you're back in a school and this time, you get to meet Loki, too!

I would also like to thank **Fiona Simpson** at Simon & Schuster for letting me write *Valkyrie—Mark II*. She made writing this version so much fun as we have both fallen head over heels in love with Tom Hiddleston, who plays Loki in the Thor films. Yes, those of you who read this, please imagine Tom's Loki when you read about my Loki.

Finally, I would like to give extra-special thanks to my dad for surviving the operations that would have killed a lesser man. He's still with me and still my biggest supporter and best friend.

I love you, Dad. . . .

FREYA'S ADVENTURE CONTINUES IN

THE RUNAWAY

VALKYRIE

THE RUNAWAY

KATE O'HEARN

AUTHOR OF THE PEGASUS SERIES

ADVENTURE TAKES FLIGHT!

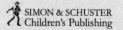